A Spot of Trouble

A SPOT OF TROUBLE

TERI WILSON

THORNDIKE PRESS
A part of Gale, a Cengage Company

Copyright © 2021 by Teri Wilson.
Turtle Beach #1.
Thorndike Press, a part of Gale, a Cengage Company.

ALL RIGHTS RESERVED

Thorndike Press® Large Print Softcover Romance and Women's Fiction.
The text of this Large Print edition is unabridged.
Other aspects of the book may vary from the original edition.
Set in 16 pt. Plantin.

LIBRARY OF CONGRESS CIP DATA ON FILE.
CATALOGUING IN PUBLICATION FOR THIS BOOK
IS AVAILABLE FROM THE LIBRARY OF CONGRESS.

ISBN-13: 978-1-4328-9493-1 (softcover alk. paper)

Published in 2022 by arrangement with Sourcebooks, LLC.

Printed in the United States of America
1 2 3 4 5   26 25 24 23 22

For all the dogs I've known and loved

CHAPTER 1

For as long as Violet March could remember, Turtle Beach, North Carolina, had been a one-Dalmatian town.

Not entirely true, because until the day Violet found Sprinkles at a pet rescue fair in nearby Wilmington and adopted her on the spot — pun intended — there had been zero Dalmatians in her hometown. None whatsoever. A Dalmatian drought, so to speak.

But now Violet had Sprinkles, Turtle Beach's total Dalmatian population. Everyone in the seaside town knew the spirited black-and-white dog belonged to her. Violet and Sprinkles were inseparable. If Sprinkles had been a person, they might have been soul mates. But alas, Sprinkles was a dog. An adorable, spotted sweetheart of a dog with an unfortunate penchant for getting into trouble, which made it all the more baffling that someone would have the nerve to try and dognap her in broad daylight.

"Hey! Hey, you, stop it right now!" Violet flailed her arms and screamed. Sea foam swirled around her ankles as she jogged from the shallows onto the warm, dry sand.

Bringing Sprinkles to the dog beach, the island's small dedicated stretch of shoreline for dogs to romp and play, had become something of a ritual on the mornings Violet taught yoga. After an hour or so of chasing a tennis ball and barking and jumping at the waves, Sprinkles could almost sit still until final relaxation pose. Of course, Violet never imagined the dog beach could be a hotbed of canine crime.

Violet called out again, but the dognapper didn't even flinch. He just kept walking in the opposite direction with Sprinkles tethered to his wrist by a long red leash. She glanced around, half-expecting her dad or one of her brothers to jump out from behind a clump of seagrass and come to her rescue. They had a tendency to hover. A lot.

But for once in her life, her personal protection squad was nowhere to be seen. She was on her own, not a blue police uniform in sight. On any ordinary day, this would have thrilled Violet to pieces. Now, not so much.

"Let go of my dog!" she yelled, sprinting

and kicking up sand in her yoga clothes.

A few heads turned her way, but the early morning crowd at the dog beach skewed older. Geriatric, mostly. The senior citizens of Turtle Beach were well-acquainted with Violet and therefore accustomed to the chaos that surrounded her on any given day. Naturally, they seemed more amused than alarmed when she darted past.

Their dogs, on the other hand, sprang into action, quickly giving chase. Within seconds, there were half a dozen dogs nipping at Violet's heels. By the time she made it to the far end of the dog beach, someone had taken a bite out of the hem of her lululemons. Mrs. Banks's corgi, most likely.

Perfect. Just perfect.

"Hey," she yelled again. "What do you think you're doing?"

This time, the criminal stopped. He turned around and arched an amused brow as he took in the sight of her bent over, breathing hard, with a random collection of dogs milling about her feet.

So he thought dognapping was funny, did he?

She glared at him, and that's when she noticed the letters stitched onto the pocket of his charcoal gray T-shirt — TBFD. Turtle Beach Fire Department. Violet felt her eyes widen in horror.

The dognapper was a fireman, because of course he was.

Not that Violet had anything against firefighters and their kitten-saving skill set *per se.* It was complicated, that's all.

The fireman's brow furrowed. "I'm, ah, walking my dog. This is the dog beach, is it not?"

"Walking your dog? Very funny." Sprinkles was the only Dalmatian in town. Again, *everyone* knew that.

She punched three numbers into her phone.

"Did you just dial 911?" The fireman cocked his head, and Sprinkles instantly mirrored his movement. They looked rather adorable together — the dognapper and the traitor.

"Of course I did."

"You really don't need to do that." He pointed at the silver badge sitting right below the letters stitched onto his shirt pocket. "I'm one of the guys who comes when you make that call. Is there something you need help with?"

Violet ignored him — manly wide shoulders and all — and gave the details of her whereabouts to the 911 dispatcher. The operator, Patty Jenkins, knew Violet by name. It was a small town, and Mrs. Jenkins sat at a desk approximately ten feet away from her father's office.

"Send my dad . . . or Joe, or Josh. Send anyone, but please tell them to get here quickly. Someone is trying to kidnap Sprinkles." Violet's gaze flitted from the top of the fireman's head to the tips of his polished black boots. "A *firefighter.*"

"Oh, dear," the operator said.

"Exactly." Violet would have identified which fireman in particular was trying to abscond with her four-legged best friend, but she didn't recognize him. So she ended the call, crossed her arms, and pinned the offending man with a glare. "The police are on the way. Don't even think about running."

"I wouldn't dare," he said drolly.

His utter shamelessness after being caught red-handed was really beginning to get on her nerves. As was Sprinkles's nonchalance. Didn't she realize she was in danger?

The dog let out a squeaky yawn and plopped into a down position at the fireman's feet. Violet sighed as Sprinkles closed her eyes and rested her chin on the toe of his boot.

Seriously?

Sprinkles had developed Stockholm syndrome in a matter of minutes. Maybe it was a Dalmatian–fireman thing. Or maybe it had something to do with her kidnapper's charmingly mussed dark hair and his startling green eyes. Bottle-green, like corked glass floating in the ocean with a secret love note hidden inside.

Not that Violet had noticed those things. Much.

The dogs that had joined her on the chase down the shore definitely seemed to notice. They sniffed at the fireman's feet, wagged their tails, and in general fawned all over him. When he crouched down to pet the corgi, the collective tail-wagging went into overdrive.

Honestly, the whole tableau was beginning to look like a page from one of those sexy firefighter calendars. Violet was aggressively annoyed.

"Just give me my dog, okay?" She sighed, hating the tiny hint of desperation in her voice. Clearly this man had no idea how much she loved her pup. "If you do the right thing now, maybe you won't get arrested."

"Arrested?" He stood, much to his canine fan club's disappointment. Tails drooped. A poodle mix sporting pink bows on its ears let out a mournful whine. "Yeah, that's not going to happen."

Good grief, he was smug. She couldn't wait for her dad or one of her brothers to show up and slap a pair of handcuffs on him. His perp walk was going to be a thing of beauty. Maybe she'd video it and put it on YouTube. Or TikTok, or Instagram stories, or whatever social media site the kids were using these days.

Violet herself wasn't ancient. At twenty-eight, she was technically a millennial. But she taught gentle yoga at the senior center, which meant most of her closest friends used walkers. Naturally, she'd developed something of an old soul herself.

She glared at the firefighter, who looked light years from needing a walker. He could probably downward dog all day long without tipping over once. They held each other's gazes for a beat or two — just long enough for Violet's cheeks to go warm. Her insides were suddenly full of butterflies, which she attributed to the fact that she was currently the victim of a crime. Then the wail of a police siren pierced the loaded silence.

Violet shot the fireman a triumphant smile. "Not going to happen, huh? Keep telling yourself that, Cruella."

Never in his life had Sam Nash been likened

to a Disney villain.

On the contrary, people typically slotted him nicely into the Prince Charming camp. Sam wasn't particularly fond of that label either, but he had to admit that it was preferable to being compared to a sinister diva with a fondness for Dalmatian fur and an unfortunate two-tone wig.

"Look," he said to the obstinate woman who seemed intent on having him thrown in jail, "this is all nothing but a misunderstanding."

But she didn't appear to hear him because she was too busy waving wildly at the two uniformed police officers who'd just crested the dune and were headed in his direction.

Common sense told Sam he should be relieved at their presence. Maybe now he'd have an opportunity to explain himself. Between the three of them, maybe they could talk some sense into his accuser. But some strange instinct made him feel like his trouble was just getting started.

Sure enough, as the officers drew closer, Sam could see the scowls aimed squarely in his direction. The two cops had apparently already chosen a side in the Dalmatian war and it wasn't his. His only supporters appeared to be the lingering dogs. A Lab mix nudged its head beneath his hand, angling for a scratch behind the ears.

With a sigh, Sam acquiesced.

He'd thought long and hard before picking up his life and moving to Turtle Beach. Everyone at his station back in Chicago thought he'd lost his mind. *You'll die of boredom,* they had said. *The only actual fires you'll see are sparklers on the Fourth of July.*

Sam hoped they were correct. He could use more boredom in his life. He craved it, actually. All he wanted was a quiet little existence in a quiet little seaside town. How had things managed to go so wrong so quickly?

He shifted his focus back to the flailing woman. *She* was the reason. No doubt about it.

His temples throbbed with irritation, and somehow the fact that he found the troublesome woman attractive irritated him even more. Not that he was remotely tempted to do anything about that attraction. Ever. It was just kind of hard not to notice the way the waves lapped at her feet as if she were some kind of furious moon goddess.

"Joe! Josh!" She let out a high-pitched squeal and threw her arms around the nearest cop. Sam had a sudden vision of himself behind bars. "Thank goodness you're here."

The officer who wasn't currently being

bear-hugged narrowed his gaze at Sam. "What seems to be the problem here?"

The retirees at the other end of the beach were now watching the scene with rapt interest.

"He's got Sprinkles." The woman pointed toward the spotted dog at the end of Sam's leash. "He stole her when I wasn't looking, and now he won't give her back."

"This isn't your dog," Sam said. It seemed important to get that little nugget of information out in the open before the discussion went any further, especially in light of all the police PDA.

The two cops glanced at the Dalmatian, whose name was Cinder, not Sprinkles. She'd been Cinder since the day Sam adopted her from the city pound.

"She definitely looks like Sprinkles," one of the policemen said.

The other officer nodded. "And Sprinkles *is* the only Dalmatian in Turtle Beach."

"Exactly." The woman glared at Sam and held out her hand. "Give me the leash."

"No," Sam said.

"No?" Officers Joe and Josh echoed simultaneously.

"No," Sam repeated, more firmly this time.

The nearby corgi snorted his displeasure

at hearing one of dogdom's least favorite words repeated in such rapid succession. The retirees were now headed their way, a few of them leaving winding trails in the sand from the wheels of their aluminum walkers.

"Sprinkles, wherever she is, isn't the only Dalmatian in town. Not anymore." Sam nodded toward his dog, still maintaining a perfect down position beside him despite the epic level of the surrounding chaos. "This is Cinder. She belongs to me, and my name is Sam Nash. We're new to Turtle Beach."

"And you're a . . ." Officer Joe looked him up and down. "A fireman?"

One of the senior citizens — an old man wearing suspenders and a newsboy cap — shook his head in apparent disgust.

Sam had no clue why *fireman* seemed to be a dirty word all of a sudden, but he had no intention of sticking around to chat about it. He didn't want to be late for his first day on the job, plus he had a beach house full of moving boxes that needed unpacking.

He nodded. "I'm the new fire marshal. Cinder is my partner. Check the name on her tag."

The policemen peered at Cinder and then

17

back toward Sam's nemesis, which was somewhat of a foreign concept for Sam since he'd never had a nemesis before. Not even close. But if he had to have one, at least his nemesis was nice to look at, with waves of tumbling strawberry-blonde mermaid hair and eyes the color of sea glass.

She was a mess, though. *Clearly.* A brazen, beautiful mess.

"Please." She rolled those lovely blue-green eyes so hard they practically rolled right out of her head. "Are you saying I can't recognize my own dog?"

Sam shrugged one shoulder. "That's exactly what I'm saying."

"Impossible." She tucked a lock of her mermaid waves behind her ear.

One of the cops cleared his throat. The other one's lips pressed together in a slight grimace. The retirees glanced back and forth between them. Officers Joe and Josh seemed conflicted, which made Sam feel like he might just walk away from the dog beach a free man.

"Violet," Officer Joe said in a measured tone, "do you think maybe . . ."

Before he could finish his thought, a blur of black-and-white spots leapt into their midst and shook itself, spraying all those assembled — human and dog alike — with seawater.

Correction: not just seawater, but some horrible combination of seawater and whatever fishy substance the spotted troublemaker had recently rolled in.

Senior citizens fled as quickly as they could in all directions while dogs barked at the ensuing panic.

"Oh my God." Officer Joe covered his mouth and nose with the crook of his elbow.

Officer Josh choked out a gagging sound.

Violet's cheeks went as red as a fire hydrant. She shot a sheepish glance at Sam and then quickly looked away.

"Sprinkles, I presume?" Sam arched a brow while the newest Dalmatian on the scene writhed around on its back in the sand, pleased as punch to be the center of attention.

"Yep." Officer Josh nodded and stepped out of range of the flying sand. "That's definitely her."

The dog was an even bigger mess than her owner. Why was Sam not surprised?

"Sprinkles, stop. Stop it right now," Violet said.

Sam had zero faith that the dog would obey, but miraculously, he was wrong. At the sound of Violet's voice, Sprinkles hopped into a sit position and stared up at

19

her, wild-eyed, pink tongue lolling out of the side of her doggy mouth.

It might have been cute if the animal hadn't smelled like she'd just crawled out of a whale carcass.

The stench was beyond horrendous. Sam's eyes watered. "I take it I'm free to go now?"

The officers nodded, again in unison. "Yes."

Now that Sam was no longer bracing himself for life in prison, he took a closer look at the silver bars pinned to their uniforms. The same last name — *March* — was engraved on both of them.

Interesting.

He wondered if Violet's last name was March as well. That would explain the bear hugs. But Sam didn't have time to stick around and ask questions. Besides, he wanted to get as far away from Sprinkles as he possibly could.

Violet too, for that matter. She wasn't as stinky as her dog — far from it, actually. At some point during their confrontation, he'd caught a hint of sugared vanilla from her wind-tossed hair. The woman was trouble, though. And she seemed to have no intention of apologizing for making a spectacle out of him. Or for calling the police. Or for her dog's vile smell.

"Cinder," he said, and his dog hopped to her feet, the perfect picture of canine obedience.

Sprinkles's head swiveled in their direction. She wagged her tail and came closer as Cinder's nose twitched. Sam remembered reading an article in *National Geographic* a while back that said a dog's sense of smell was approximately one hundred thousand times stronger than a human's. Poor Cinder.

"They really do look a lot alike." Violet's bow-shaped lips curved into a contrite smile.

She was right. Nose-to-nose, the two dogs looked like mirror images of one another. With their glossy black-and-white coats, they matched each other spot for spot, from the tips of their tails to their identical black heart-shaped noses.

But it still wasn't an apology, and Sam was in no mood for niceties.

He gave Cinder's leash a gentle tug and brushed past Violet without a word. She huffed out a breath, and just before Sam got out of earshot, he heard one of the elderly bystanders mutter an undeniable truth.

"This town might not be big enough for two Dalmatians."

CHAPTER 2

What have I done?

Sam stood on the sidewalk at the intersection of Seashell Drive and Pelican Street, studying the modest downtown area of Turtle Beach. For starters, "sidewalk" was a bit of a stretch. It was more of a gravelly path, surrounded by overgrown seagrass on either side. Downtown itself appeared to take up no more than six square blocks of the narrow barrier island, stretching from the Salty Dog Pier at one end to the Turtle Beach Senior Living Center at the other. From where his feet were planted, Sam could see the foamy ocean waves of the town's beachfront in one direction and just a glimpse of the smooth glassy surface of the intracoastal waterway in the other. The island, his new home, was *that* narrow.

"Maybe this town *isn't* big enough for two Dalmatians," he muttered.

Cinder's ears swiveled to and fro.

"Just kidding," Sam said, resting a reassuring hand on the spotted dog's smooth head.

Still, picturing an idyllic beach town in your head and seeing it in person were two entirely different things. Sam had never been much of a beach person. Or a small-town person. He was very much a Dalmatian person, though. That point was non-negotiable.

As for the rest, he'd adapt. Turtle Beach was clearly the complete and total opposite of Chicago, but that was the whole point, wasn't it? Sam had upended his entire life, based on nothing but a fifteen-minute Zoom interview and a perfunctory Google search of the North Carolina coastline. Now here he was, living the dream.

Thus far, though, his new life hadn't been nearly as serene and peaceful as the Turtle Beach brochure promised. He wondered when the idyllic part was supposed to kick in. With any luck, soon.

As in immediately.

"Let's do this," he said to Cinder, more out of habit than anything else, as he headed toward the firehouse.

As usual, Cinder walked alongside him in perfect heel position. Sam didn't need to prompt her to stick by his side. Unlike her carbon copy disaster of a Dalmatian — the memorable Sprinkles — Cinder knew how to behave. In fact, before they'd left Illinois, Cinder had been awarded the Chicago Fire Department's esteemed Medal of Honor in recognition of her long and faithful service.

Emphasis on *faithful.* Every black spot on Cinder's body would fall off before she'd embarrass him the way Sprinkles had just humiliated Violet. It just wouldn't happen. Then again, Sam had invested countless hours into training his dog and bonding with her because he was a responsible pet owner. Somehow he doubted Violet fit that particular bill.

But that wasn't Sam's problem — not unless her disorderly Dalmatian had a habit of violating the fire code. From what he'd witnessed thus far, he wouldn't put it past her.

Sam frowned as the firehouse came into view, not because of the matchbox size of it, but because sand had somehow made its way into his shoes already. He was going to have to learn to deal with that oddly specific problem, just as he was going to have to remember to slather sunscreen onto his face every morning and to avoid even the remote possibility of another Dalmatian confrontation at dog beach.

Weirdly, he was also going to have to grow accustomed to the town's apparent animosity toward firefighters. Two police officers caught sight of him as he approached the firehouse, and they openly scowled at him from the paved driveway of the police station, situated directly across the street. Even Cinder noticed. She let out a low rumbling noise and moved closer to Sam until he could feel the growl vibrating through her black-and-white body.

"It's fine, Cinder," he murmured.

It was *not* fine. It was, in fact, the very opposite of fine. Sam smiled and waved at the police officers like any normal person would do, but was met with nothing but confused, albeit slightly less hostile, glances.

"Did you just wave at those cops?"

Sam turned to find a Turtle Beach firefighter, one of his own, polishing the shiny red exterior of the pumper truck sitting just outside the apparatus bay.

"I did," he said.

"Yeah, we don't do that." The other firefighter shook his head. "Especially now."

Sam didn't even know where to start. There was so much to unpack here, he was at a loss. "We don't do what, exactly? Interact with fellow first responders?"

The fireman let out a snort of laughter.

"Not when they're cops. Come winter and fall, maybe, but not now."

Sam glanced up and down the quaint street where eager beachcombers loaded down with collapsible chairs, sun umbrellas, and colorful towels were already making the trek from the narrow rows of beach cottages over the dunes toward the sea. "Tourist season?"

"What? No. *Softball* season." The fireman shook his head. "You really *are* new here, aren't you?"

"Sam Nash." Sam held out his hand.

"Griff Martin. Welcome to TBFD." Griff shook Sam's hand and then glanced down at Cinder, sitting in a polite stay position at Sam's feet. Apparently, the sight of a firefighter waving at a pair of police officers had been so much of a novelty that Griff had yet to notice the spotted dog. "Whoa. First day on the job, and you've somehow managed to dognap Violet March's Dalmatian. Maybe you know more about softball season than I realized."

Sam's gut clenched. *Not again.* "This dog doesn't belong to Violet March. She belongs to me."

Griff shot him an exaggerated wink. "Sure she does."

"I'm dead serious."

Griff's face split into a wide grin. "I like you, man. You're funny, but everyone knows Sprinkles is the only Dalmatian in town."

Sam's first day in Turtle Beach was beginning to feel like the movie *Groundhog Day.* And not in a good way. He glanced across the street toward the police headquarters, preparing himself to try and talk his way out of another arrest for canine-related crimes.

Griff shoved his hands in the pockets of his TBFD-issued cargo pants and leaned a little closer — close enough for Sam to catch a whiff of coffee on his breath. "Stealing the police department's unofficial mascot is a baller move, but just so you know, the police chief's daughter is off-limits. You should return Sprinkles to wherever you found her. Chief Murray's orders: we can't mess with Violet — particularly not after what happened last year. Things went a bit too far."

Again, so much to unpack. But against all odds, Sam was suddenly less concerned about Cinder's mistaken identity than he was about Violet March and whatever misfortune she'd encountered last year, seemingly at the hands of a firefighter.

He thought about her tousled mermaid hair and the foamy ocean waves swirling at her feet and, for the first time, wondered if he'd mistaken the look in her luminous blue-green eyes for fury when in fact it had been something else — vulnerability.

Nope, she'd been livid. Just maybe not as unhinged as he'd previously thought.

Don't ask. Do. Not. It's none of your concern.

"What happened to her?" he said.

Damn it, he'd asked.

But before Griff could clue him in, the man who'd conducted Sam's Zoom interview last month came striding toward them. His welcoming smile faded as his gaze trailed from Sam's face all the way down Cinder's leash to the Dalmatian's tail, sweeping the pavement in a happy wag.

Sam knew what was coming, but frustration seethed from his every pore nonetheless.

"What are you doing with Violet March's dog?" Chief Murray crossed his big, beefy arms as he stared down at Cinder.

"This isn't Sprinkles," Sam said wearily. Was it possible to scrub the spots off a Dalmatian? Or maybe connect them like a giant dot-to-dot puzzle? Anything to make Cinder look less like Sprinkles and put an end to the Dalmatian speculation.

"This is Cinder." The dog's ears perked up at the mention of her name. "She's a fire

28

safety dog. She's trained to accompany me on inspections and to demonstrate fire safety techniques during presentations."

A long, awkward pause followed. The only sounds Sam heard were Cinder's soft pants and the ocean roaring in the distance. He missed the rattle of the L train, the moaning stops and starts of city buses, and the grind of morning traffic. The constant hum of Chicago's street noises were in his blood, and he felt adrift without it — yet another thing about his move he hadn't anticipated. After all, people paid good money to hear waves crashing against the shore on apps for their phones or sound systems. Not Sam, per se, but people.

Normal people . . . people who didn't wake up in the middle of the night in a cold sweat, followed by three torturous hours of staring at the ceiling, immune to the calming effects of the nearby sea.

"Huh," both Griff and Chief Murray said after a beat, as if Sam's description of Cinder's duties had been spoken in some kind of foreign language.

Sam's head pounded. He had a sudden craving for deep dish Chicago-style pizza, the world's best migraine cure.

"So this dog is like your partner?" Chief Murray bent to take a closer look at Cinder.

"Yes." They'd covered this already in Sam's interview. He was sure of it. He wouldn't have packed up and moved to North Carolina without telling his new chief about his dog. Cinder was half the reason Sam had been able to make the change from fighting fires to seeking a job as a fire marshal.

The job offer from TBFD had been a godsend. After Chief Murray's email had arrived, Sam had been too busy counting his lucky stars to wonder why such a small department needed to add a full-time fire marshal to its roster. As crazy as things seemed, they were beginning to make sense.

"Just so we're clear, I'm not really interested in playing softball," Sam said.

He was here to do a job, not to become involved with the community. Besides, it had been a long time since Sam had held a bat in his hands. Nearly a year.

Chief Murray straightened, regarding Sam through narrowed eyes.

"Dude." Griff shook his head. "Participation in the summer softball tournament against the police force is mandatory."

Sam sighed. This place was beyond nuts. He should have turned tail and run back when he'd almost been arrested. "Mandatory? Doesn't that contradict the very nature of extracurricular activities?"

"Griff's right," the chief said. "Not only is it mandatory, but it's also the whole reason you were hired. Guns and Hoses starts Saturday."

Guns and Hoses. Sam's mouth quirked into a half grin, despite himself. The name of the tournament was cute, like everything else in this whimsical beach town.

Except maybe the oddly competitive nature of said softball tournament. And whatever unfortunate thing had happened to Violet March.

He knew he shouldn't worry about it. In fact, all signs thus far had pointed to the obvious conclusion that if he was going to survive here, he needed to stay as far away from Violet and Sprinkles as possible. Had the ongoing Dalmatian situation taught him nothing?

Chief Murray slapped him hard on the back — hard enough to rattle all thoughts of the police chief's daughter and her troublesome spotted sidekick right out of his head. "Welcome to Turtle Beach, slugger."

In retrospect, Violet realized she'd been a tad hasty at the dog beach this morning. The firefighter had tried to explain what

31

was going on, and she hadn't let him. As her brothers Josh and Joe had oh-so-helpfully pointed out after the chaos died down and her yoga friends aimed their walkers back toward the Turtle Beach Senior Living Center, she'd treated *a* fireman like he was *the* fireman. The result had been nothing short of a complete and utter Dalmatian humiliation.

The poor man had apparently been a resident of Turtle Beach for a grand total of twelve hours — information which Josh had managed to discern with a single call to the town's one and only Realtor, who'd conveniently been his prom date back in his days at Turtle Beach High. As much as Violet hated to give the new-in-town fireman the benefit of the doubt, she realized he'd probably never heard of Guns and Hoses.

Yet.

That would change, obviously. In the meantime, she might owe him a *teensy* apology for trying to get him arrested. Softball season hadn't even officially started yet. If she was going to get through the annual tournament with a modicum of dignity intact, she needed to try to defuse the situation.

Besides, his dog was awfully cute. Despite the uniform, he clearly possessed one of her favorite qualities in a man — an appreciation for Dalmatians. How terrible could he possibly be?

Careful, there. Remember what happened the last time you let your guard down around a pretty face in a fire helmet.

As if she could forget.

But she didn't want to date the man. Been there, done that, got the T-shirt. Never again. Violet was over romantic relationships. From here on out, all she cared about was Sprinkles and her shiny new cupcake truck.

And her family, obviously. And her friends. And the police department completely annihilating the fire department this Saturday in the opening game.

Okay, fine, she cared about a lot of things, but dating occupied the last spot on the list. Absolute rock bottom. The fact that she was currently standing in front of the fire station with a pink bakery box in her hands and Sprinkles at her feet was a simple matter of self-respect. She hated the weird combination of guilt and sadness she always saw in Chief Murray's eyes when he looked at her, and she knew good and well that every cupcake the TBFD bought and consumed was a pity purchase. Not that her cupcakes weren't good — they were *amaz-*

ing, thank you very much. She just wanted to move on and return to despising firemen in a normal, healthy, *sports-related* way.

Violet squared her shoulders and glanced down at Sprinkles. "We can do this. Five quick minutes inside the belly of the beast, and then we're out of here."

But when she took a step toward the bright red door of the firehouse, the Dalmatian didn't budge. Violet gave the leash a gentle tug, and still . . . nothing.

Across the street, one of her brothers' fellow officers exited the police station and came to an abrupt halt when he caught sight of her. The donut in his hand fell to the ground.

Super. This was already turning into another embarrassing episode.

"We're fine!" She waved at the policeman. "Just dropping off some cupcakes. No cause for concern."

Translation: *please don't run and tell my dad and brothers.*

The last thing she needed was for her family to come marching over here as if she were a hostage.

"Sprinkles, please. Just listen for once. There's a vanilla bacon maple cupcake with your name on it if you'll just follow me into the firehouse and stick by my side for moral

34

support," Violet whispered.

The promise/bribe worked, thank goodness. Sprinkles sprang forward and bobbed happily at the end of her leash as Violet pushed through the red door. She didn't normally feed her dog cupcakes, for the record. Desperate times and all that.

"Violet." Griff Martin blinked hard from his seat in the dispatch area when he caught sight of her. "Um . . . what are you doing here?"

He looked past her, no doubt expecting her to be accompanied by Joe, Josh, or other various members of the TBPD.

She raised her chin. She was a grown woman, and she could take care of herself and get her life back on track all on her own. "I'm here to see the new fireman. We had a little misunderstanding earlier this morning."

"Look." Griff held up his hands. "I told him to give the dog back and he insisted it wasn't yours."

"Oh, I know." Violet tipped her head toward Sprinkles. "Sprinkles is fine, see?"

Griff's gaze narrowed. "They really do look an awful lot alike, don't they?"

Thank you! She shot him a victorious grin. "Yes, they do."

Sprinkles was cuter, though. Obviously.

"Can you just tell him I'm here?" She glanced down at the pink bakery box in her hands and then back up at Griff's bewildered face. "I have a little peace offering for him. It was the least I could do after his near-arrest. I'll just give it to him, and then we'll be on our way."

"Hoo boy. Near-arrest?" Griff winced. "I'm not even going to ask. Sam's getting set up in his new office. Follow me."

He rose from his creaky office chair and led Violet toward the common area of the firehouse, where her appearance in enemy territory brought everything to an immediate standstill. No one moved. Or breathed. Or uttered a word. A firefighter who Violet recognized as the Hoses' first baseman spilled coffee down the front of his shirt from a ceramic mug that read *WTF Where's the Fire* as he gaped at her. A pair of firemen on opposite sides of a Ping-Pong table froze comically in place while their tiny white ball bounced across the room.

Sprinkles's toenails click-clacked against the tile floor as she scrambled after it, nearly jerking Violet's arm out of the socket in the process. The bakery box came perilously close to slipping from her grasp. She managed to keep hold of it long enough for Sprinkles to trot back to her side with the

Ping-Pong ball in her doggy mouth.

"Here you go," Griff said, stopping at a closed door situated behind two neat rows of leather recliners facing an enormous flat-screen television. "This is the new guy."

"Thanks." She pasted on a smile. "I'll take it from here."

"My pleasure." Griff gave Sprinkles a scratch behind her ears and headed back toward the dispatch desk.

Violet pretended not to notice the warning glares he shot at the other firemen as he passed through the common area, but a ribbon of relief wound its way through her as they stopped openly staring at her.

Okay. She took a deep breath and knocked. *Here goes nothing.*

"Come in," someone growled from the other side of the door. She would've recognized that cranky tone anywhere.

Violet wondered why he had an office. From what she knew about firemen — which was more than she cared to admit — they didn't sit at desks all day. In fact, the last time she'd darkened the door of the firehouse, Chief Murray had been the only member of the department who'd had an actual office. His was located just off the galley-style kitchen, and a quick glance confirmed it was still there.

Whatever. She just needed to make nice and hand over the cupcakes so she could go back to the dog beach with her head held high.

She opened the door and stepped inside, where the aforementioned grumpy fireman sat bent over the most meticulously organized desk Violet had ever set eyes on. A desk plate with the words *Sam Nash, Fire Marshal* on it was placed near the edge of the smooth wooden surface. Oh right, he was a fire marshal, not a regular fireman. That explained the office. Four fountain pens were lined up neatly beside his name plate, spaced apart at perfectly equal distances. The file in front of Sam contained a stack of paper so pristine that it looked like he'd just taken it off the printer. Not a crease in sight.

Sprinkles's identical twin rested on a fire engine–red dog bed in the corner of the room, regarding Violet with soft brown eyes.

"Hi," Violet said.

Sam finally looked up.

"Oh. Hi." He pushed back his chair and stood. Why did it suddenly feel like there wasn't nearly enough air in his tiny office? "It's you."

Sprinkles scurried toward him and spat the Ping-Pong ball out of her mouth, where it bounced at Sam's feet. Miraculously, the other Dalmatian completely ignored it.

Sam's gaze shifted toward Sprinkles. "And you too."

Sprinkles wagged her tail and nudged Sam's hand until he patted her. Violet's heart gave a rebellious little tug. Did he have to look so good petting her dog? There was a gentleness in the way his fingertips ran over her smooth, black-and-white coat — a tender reverence that put a wholly inappropriate lump in Violet's throat.

"Don't worry. She's had a bath since you last saw her," Violet said, trying her best to focus on something less dangerous, like Sam's insanely organized office supplies.

"Yeah, I can smell that." Sam wiggled his nose. "Am I imagining things, or does she smell like cake now?"

"Oh, that's not her. I brought you cupcakes." She thrust the pink box toward him.

His gaze remained impassive. "You did?"

"As a peace offering." Her face went hot. "It's what I do — I'm a baker."

She added that last bit because it seemed crucial to point out that she hadn't gone to any extraordinary lengths to cook something for him. She was a career woman, not Betty Draper.

Granted, she was a career woman who

spent most of her time in a frilly pink polka dot apron and still lived in the rambling March family beach house with her father and two older brothers. Plus she'd owned her cupcake truck for less than a week, but those things didn't make her any less of a professional.

"I see." Sam glanced down at her whimsical logo: a Dalmatian behind the wheel of a food truck topped with a giant spinning cupcake. "Sweetness on Wheels, that's you?"

"Sure is. Like I said, I just wanted to come by and apologize. Things are kind of nuts here when it comes to softball, and for a minute, I thought you were trying to steal Sprinkles as some sort of prank. But I realize now that you're new in town. Cinder clearly belongs to you, and you obviously don't know a thing about our nutty little feud."

Sam's gaze met hers, and then that stern mouth of his curved into a lopsided smile that made her go all gooey inside, like one of her molten hot chocolate cupcakes. Ugh, what was wrong with her?

She plunked the bakery box down on his desk with shaky hands, and when she looked back up at him, her gaze snagged on something over his left shoulder — something that snapped her immediately back to reality.

Sam raked a hand through his perfect hair. "Actually, I —"

Violet cut him off before he could continue. "What is that?"

Her tone went razor sharp, prompting Sam's smile to vanish as quickly as it had appeared.

His gaze narrowed. "What's what?"

Violet wasn't about to spell things out for him. She didn't have to. The damning evidence was hanging right there on the back wall of his office in the form of a framed newspaper article with a huge headline that read *Local College Hall of Famer Sam Nash Turns Down MLB Contract to Join Chicago Fire Department.*

Sam was practically a Major League Baseball player? This could only mean one thing. He was a ringer!

The fire department had brought him to Turtle Beach and installed him in a fancy office for the sole purpose of snagging the Guns and Hoses championship trophy this season. What's more, he didn't even have the common decency to try and hide it.

How low could a person get? How dare he come marching into town with his athletic build, his Hall of Fame muscles, and his despicably handsome face and think he could just hand the TBFD a victory. It was basically stealing. He deserved to rot in her father's single-cell jail across the street. Maybe she should call 911 again.

"Violet?" Sam's brow furrowed, as if he hadn't a clue what she was suddenly so upset about.

Sprinkles and Cinder touched noses, tails wagging, and the adorable sight of the two dogs together nearly broke Violet's heart. Somehow the fact that Sam had a Dalmatian made his betrayal so much worse. He didn't deserve such a spotted sweetheart of a dog. Violet couldn't *believe* she'd wasted a single second feeling bad about falsely accusing him of dognapping. She'd swallowed her pride and baked him cupcakes, and the man was nothing but a Dalmatian abomination.

Sam held up his hands. "I'm not sure what's going on here, but —"

Finally, he followed her gaze and turned to glance over his shoulder. He muttered an expletive and ground his teeth so hard that an ultra-manly knot flexed to life in his jawline. Violet averted her gaze before she accidentally went all swoony again.

"Look, I can explain," he said.

Why did that seem to be the one thing

men always said when they'd done something atrocious?

"Don't bother. I've heard that line before." Most recently, from another fireman who'd worked at this exact station — a fireman who hadn't been able to explain a thing, except that he'd used her.

Everything always came down to softball in Turtle Beach. When was she going to learn to steer completely clear of anyone with a badge?

She snatched the pink bakery box off of Sam's desk. "Come on, Sprinkles. We're leaving."

"Seriously, you're taking my cupcakes back?" Sam planted his hands on his hips and actually had the nerve to look incredulous.

"I certainly am," Violet said.

No more playing nice. She was finished with giving him the benefit of the doubt. Her initial instincts about Sam had been right all along. She should never have let herself be swayed by his charming doggy dad routine or his devoted Dalmatian.

From now on, when it came to firemen, Violet March had finally learned to see things in black-and-white.

CHAPTER 3

Sam's office still smelled like frosting the following morning. The warm scents of sugary buttercream and whipped vanilla hung in the air, as tempting as the fiery Miss Violet March herself.

Not for Sam, of course. He could resist. He *would* resist. He'd rather run straight into another burning building than get tangled up with her again.

There was no reasoning with Violet. He'd tried to explain that the newspaper clipping on the wall hadn't been his doing. Chief Murray had apparently discovered the article on the internet when he'd been checking up on Sam's qualifications and had been so slaphappy to have found a fireman with a .333 college batting average that he'd printed the damn thing out and stuck it in a frame. But of course Violet was too impetuous to stick around and listen to Sam's perfectly logical explanation.

Color Sam shocked. He'd known Violet was trouble when she accused him of dognapping. For some silly reason, though, when she'd turned up in his office the day before with that pretty pink box in her arms and her boisterous Dalmatian tethered to her slender wrist by a leash decorated with tiny cartoon cupcakes, he'd let down his guard. Only for a moment . . . but that tiny sliver of a second had been almost long enough to forget why he'd come to Turtle Beach to begin with. Spoiler alert: it wasn't to let himself get wrapped around the beautiful little finger of the police chief's daughter.

He should feel grateful, really. The fact that she apparently thought he was part of some grand softball conspiracy against the police department guaranteed that she'd give him a wide berth from now on, and that was exactly what Sam needed. Space. It was why he'd given up his brownstone in Chicago and left the city he'd called home for his entire life to start anew on the windswept beaches of the Carolina coast. He could breathe here. He could heal. He could sink his toes in the sand, close his eyes, and forget everything that had gone so terribly wrong three months ago — everything he'd lost. Everything he'd loved.

His new life wasn't about putting out fires. It was about preventing them, both the actual kind and the metaphorical. The rush he used to get when he rode up on a fire in the rig was gone, and it wasn't coming back. He used to live for the burn in the back of his throat and the sooty smell of his hair after he walked away from a call and peeled away his turnout gear. They'd meant he'd done something real, something important.

Something else had fundamentally shifted inside of him, though. He no longer craved the burn at the back of his throat. He loathed it, and he'd set out to do anything and everything in his power to prevent it. That was what the move to the Turtle Beach Fire Department had been about. As a fire marshal, he could stop tragedies before they ever happened — especially in an underserved community like Turtle Beach. His new hometown had never had a full-time fire marshal, but he was here now. He could do his part to make the town as safe as possible. Coming here had never been about softball, no matter what Violet might think.

Sam was content to let her believe whatever she wanted, however. He'd just as soon skip another round of apology cupcakes. The sight of her standing across from his desk had rattled him, and he didn't like being rattled. He didn't need the distraction of her soulful sea-glass eyes or her full cherry-red lips any more than he needed her Dalmatian spitting Ping-Pong balls at his feet.

Even so, when he'd stumbled out of bed this morning, poured himself a mug of steaming black coffee, and carried it out onto the deck of his new beach cottage, his entire body had flooded with heat at the sight of Violet riding a bicycle along the boardwalk on the bay side of the island.

Her bike was a vintage beach cruiser, Tiffany-blue with fat cream-colored tires and a wicker basket attached to the handlebars. Was she wearing a helmet? No, of course not. Her strawberry hair streamed behind her, kissed by glittering gold sunlight, and to make things even more dangerous, Sprinkles ran alongside the bicycle, attached once again to Violet's wrist with the pink cupcake leash. The whole scene was an accident waiting to happen.

Sam's grip tightened on his coffee cup. Beside him, Cinder let out an uncharacteristically mournful whine.

"We're going back inside," Sam said as cool, salty air caused Cinder's ears to flap in the breeze. He had no desire to stick around and watch that crazy dog drag Violet into a wall or the ocean, minus appropriate protective gear.

Yet he'd inexplicably remained rooted to the spot until his coffee had gone cold and Violet had ridden out of sight, just a swirl of golden light and black-and-white spots in the distance.

"Have you got cake in here?" Griff said as he leaned against the doorjamb of Sam's office, a damp towel slung over his shoulder.

Every fire station in America started its morning shift in the same way — inspecting all equipment and apparatus, followed by cleaning the rigs. Washing the fire trucks was as routine and predictable as the rising sun. Sam wondered when he'd get used to starting the day without a soapy sponge in his hand now that he rode a desk instead of a shiny red fire truck.

"Nope," he said without elaborating. "No cake."

"Weird, because it smells like cake in here." Griff crossed his arms. "Also, I personally escorted Violet to your office yesterday, and I distinctly remember the bakery box in her hands."

Sam glowered at him. "There's no cake."

"Geez, I was just asking." Griff shrugged. "Too bad, because her cupcakes are out of this world."

"Well, you won't find any of them in this office," Sam said, aggressively straightening the stack of papers on his desk.

He wasn't sure why the lack of cake in his life bothered him so much all of a sudden. Cake was unhealthy and frivolous. It rotted the teeth. He'd never wanted a bite so badly in his life.

"Okay, then. The new guy doesn't like cake. Duly noted." Griff sank into the chair opposite Sam.

Cinder's tail thump-thumped against the floor until Sam nodded, giving her permission to rise from her dog bed to greet the new visitor. Even so, she was ever polite, gently dropping her chin onto Griff's knee and gazing up at him until he placed his hand on top of her smooth, spotted head.

Griff snorted. "Your dog looks a lot like Sprinkles, but they don't act the same at all."

Sam didn't need to ask why. His tenure in the small beach town had been brief thus far, but he'd seen enough of Sprinkles to know exactly what Griff was referring to. "That's because Cinder is trained and Sprinkles clearly isn't."

"Right, because Cinder is a fire dog and all that."

Sam shook his head. "That doesn't have

anything to do with it. Or it shouldn't, anyway. All dogs should be trained in basic obedience, even pets."

Griff's eyebrows drew together as he seemed to consider Sam's words. "Sprinkles isn't a bad dog. Violet takes her pretty much everywhere, so she's familiar to the whole town."

"So I've noticed," Sam said. Over the course of the past twenty-four hours, no less than fifteen people had asked him what he was doing with Violet March's Dalmatian. It was getting old and, frankly, a little insulting.

Could no one tell the difference between his highly trained partner and Violet's unruly, dotted little monster?

"She wouldn't harm a flea. She's just a little" — Griff scrunched up his face — "excitable."

Sam rolled his eyes. "That's one word for it."

"Sprinkles is a sweetheart, you'll see. Plus she's a rescue. Violet adopted her up in Wilmington. The poor thing had been living on the streets before the city pound picked her up."

"If Violet is 'off-limits,' how do you know so much about her dog?" Sam asked, trying not to think too hard about how he'd become the type of person who used annoying air quotes.

Griff shrugged one shoulder. "Word gets around, plus the paper ran an article about it shortly after Violet adopted her."

Sam stared blankly at him. Two days ago, he couldn't have conceived of a town where a pet adoption would make the local paper, and now he was living in one. Just another small-town quirk that had never crossed his mind.

He pinched the bridge of his nose. "It doesn't matter if Sprinkles is a rescue or not. I adopted Cinder from a shelter in Chicago."

"Really? I never would have guessed." Griff appraised Cinder anew. He offered his hand, and she gently placed her paw into his palm for a shake. "Impressive."

"Every dog can *and should* be trained in basic obedience," Sam said, wincing as Sprinkles sprang to the forefront of his mind, writhing in the sand at the dog beach, reeking of dead fish and all manner of decaying sea life. "A dog that can't follow simple orders causes chaos, and it's just not safe."

Griff arched a brow but said nothing.

"I'm serious," Sam said. Why did he feel compelled to defend himself all of a sud-

51

den? "Sprinkles might be friendly and cute, but she's also impulsive."

"Mmhmm," Griff said, nodding as his mouth twisted into a subtle smirk.

Sam wasn't finished. "She's flighty, easily distracted, and thoroughly undisciplined. Just because everyone in town knows and loves her doesn't mean she isn't without fault."

Griff's smirk grew larger until it seemed to take up his entire face. "I hear you."

Sam leaned forward in his chair, because Griff didn't seem to be getting his point. "Mark my words, sooner or later, someone is going to get hurt."

"I can't argue with that. You might be right." Griff gave Cinder a final scratch beneath her chin, then hauled himself out of the chair. "It's just kind of funny, though."

"What is?" Sam barked. He had another headache, and it wasn't even 9:00 a.m. yet.

"For a minute there, it almost sounded like you weren't talking about a dog at all." Griff flashed him a suggestive grin. "Cute, but flighty? Friendly, but easily distracted? Beloved by everyone she meets, but utterly impulsive?"

Heat crawled up the back of Sam's neck, and he redirected his gaze to the stack of papers on his desk. He knew what was coming next, but he didn't want to see the knowing look in Griff's eyes when he said it. Especially when Sam's thoughts were still lingering on the most important snippet of their conversation. *Mark my words, sooner or later, someone is going to get hurt.*

Griff chuckled under his breath. "If I didn't know better, I would've thought you were talking about Violet March herself."

Violet coasted her bike to a stop as she turned into the wide driveway of one of the oldest and grandest homes in Turtle Beach.

Yes, she still lived with her family in the house where she'd grown up. But living at home wasn't so bad when it meant a sprawling, three-story beach house propped up on tall pilings with sweeping views of the Carolina coast. Especially since her brothers had taken over the third floor apartments for themselves, leaving just Violet and her Dad in the main residence. Plus there was plenty of room in the open air garage beneath the house for her shiny silver Airstream trailer with its spinning cupcake on top.

When her cupcake truck wasn't parked on the boardwalk or the softball field or anyplace else sugar-starved tourists and locals gathered, she kept it right here at home, alongside her dad and brothers' police cruisers, a towering pile of sun chairs, and various other beach paraphernalia. Like Josh's kayak. And the family croquet set. And her dad's fishing poles, which she had just nearly plowed into, thanks to Sprinkles.

"What is it with you and the smell of fish, all of a sudden?" Violet wailed as she gave the handlebars a hard yank to the right.

Her front wheel bumped up against the kayak as she came to a wobbly halt. Sprinkles promptly pounced inside the narrow boat, and it rocked from side to side. With her pink tongue lolling out of the side of her mouth, she looked like a dog enjoying an amusement park ride.

"Get out of there, silly." Violet grabbed the cardboard holder of frosty, whipped coffee drinks she'd just pedaled to the boardwalk to procure from her bicycle's wicker basket. "It's time for coffee."

It was also time to clue her dad and brothers in on Sam Nash's secret identity as a baseball phenom. Oh goody, this should be fun.

Not.

After leaving the firehouse yesterday, Violet had nearly walked directly across the street and straight into her dad's office at the police station. She couldn't do that, though. One look at the pink box in her hands, and her father would have blown a gasket. She knew better than to go waltzing into the firehouse laden with cupcakes and good intentions.

She should have, anyway.

It was fine, though. She could take care of herself, and she definitely wouldn't be making that mistake again. Her dad, however, didn't need to know about said mistake. The last time she'd fled the firehouse with her heart in tatters, he'd ended up in a screaming match with Chief Murray right there in the middle of Seashell Drive. They'd both been so red-faced that Violet had worried one of them might have some sort of cardiac episode. Griff Martin had nearly been forced to turn a fire hose on the two men.

What this situation needed was delicacy, so that the police chief and the fire chief didn't accidentally end up brawling in the street again. Delicacy, plus frozen coffee with a heaping dash of chocolate and caramel should do it. The Milky Way frozen latte from Turtle Books, the island bookshop that doubled as a coffee bar down on the boardwalk, was her dad's favorite thing in the entire world — as evidenced by the wide smile that creased his face when she plopped it down in front of him on the long table on the beach house's second-floor porch.

The March family gathered on the deck every morning for coffee and most evenings for dinner. The house sat on the southern-most tip of the island, known as the crest to locals, separate from Turtle Beach's neat rows of beach cottages. Violet's great-grandfather had built the rambling house by hand back in 1952, when the Marches had been among the first families to move onto the secluded island, seeking their own little slice of Southern paradise.

All these years later, Turtle Beach still felt that way to Violet — serene, idyllic — despite the recent Dalmatian migration and the accompanying arrival of Sam Nash. Out here on the crest, where the water from the bay spilled into the salty depths of the Atlantic and dolphins frolicked just offshore, it was easy to forget about Sam, his annoy-ingly sweet dog, and his major league–wor-thy bod.

Then why can't you?

"What's this?" Violet's dad picked up his frozen coffee drink and took a big sip from its oversized, colorful straw. "Is today a special occasion?"

She shrugged. "I just felt like taking a little bike ride this morning, and while I was over at the north end, I stopped by the board-walk."

It wasn't a *total* lie. Sprinkles needed her morning exercise, and Violet wasn't quite ready to show her face or her Dalmatian at the dog beach again. Not without police backup. Or possibly a bag to wear over her head.

"Don't worry, I got one for each of my favorite police officers." She plucked two more frozen coffees from the cardboard carrier and offered them to Josh and Joe.

"Thanks, sis," Josh said, gulping half of his down in one big swallow, an ice cream headache waiting to happen.

Joe, the more patient brother, narrowed his gaze as he took his cup from Violet. "I'm with Dad. What's going on? You never go for a bike ride this early."

"Can't I do something nice for my family without being interrogated?" Honestly, sometimes it wasn't easy being the only member of the household who wasn't actively involved in law enforcement.

"Don't question it." Josh shook his head. "At least she's not down at the dog beach trying to arrest people."

Joe arched a brow. "Or bringing random mutts home and bathing them for free."

Violet glared at her brother. "That only

happened once."

It had happened a handful of times, actually. But they'd all stemmed from a single misguided, altruistic episode in which Violet thought she was rescuing a stray chocolate Lab mix she'd seen trotting up and down the shore all alone. Violet had a certain fondness for Dalmatians — a Dalmatian infatuation, some might say — but she was also a proper, equal-opportunity dog lover. She wasn't a Dalmatian *snob,* for goodness' sake. So she'd taken the lost dog home to bathe and blow-dry him. She might have also spritzed him with her favorite lavender-and-marshmallow-scented body spray from Bath & Body Works, only to find out that he belonged to the reclusive fisherman who lived right next door.

In true Turtle Beach form, word of Violet's dog-saving efforts had spread like wildfire. Other loose pups started popping up on the beach directly in front of the March house. It only took her three more rounds of sudsing and spritzing for Violet to realize that people were "losing" their dogs on purpose to take advantage of her complimentary grooming services.

Really, though. That had nothing to do with the matter at hand. Why did her brothers insist on bringing it up so often?

Violet sat down with a huff. "If you must know, I have some news."

She was just going to have to rip the Band-Aid off and tell them about Sam before they heard about his baseball prowess from someone else. It wouldn't be pleasant, but she couldn't hold it in any longer. She'd tried — oh, how she'd tried. Much to her irritation, Sam Nash had even popped up in her dreams, which could only be attributed to the giant secret she knew about him. Once the police force knew he was a ringer, she could properly forget about him once and for all.

"News?" Her father glanced down at the newspaper spread in front of him, anchored to the table with a conch shell.

"Not so much news as gossip, really." But once word got out to the general public, Sam's smug face would probably be staring back at her from the front page of the *Turtle Beach Gazette.* "Accurate, *verifiable* gossip."

"Spit it out, Vi," Josh said blithely.

What a joy it was to live with three men. Sometimes Violet really missed her mother. It was possible to miss someone you'd never really known, wasn't it?

"Fine." She cleared her throat. "You know the new fire marshal?"

"You mean the guy with the dog that looks just like Sprinkles?" Joe said. Sprinkles cocked her head and bounded toward him at the mention of her name.

"The one you wanted us to throw in jail?" Josh added.

"Yes, that one," Violet said primly. She was never going to live it down, was she?

"I caught a glimpse of that dog myself, yesterday." Her dad shook his head. "It was an honest mistake, Cupcake. It could have happened to anybody."

But it hadn't happened to just anybody. Like most of the embarrassing things around here, it had happened to Violet. Then she'd tried to shower Sam with apology cupcakes, and the situation had gone from bad to worse.

"Thanks, Dad." She took a deep breath. Her poor father had no idea what was coming. "Anyway, you're about to wish for a real reason to toss the new fire marshal in jail, especially this Saturday."

Her father's smile faded. "Saturday, as in opening game day of Guns and Hoses?"

Both of Violet's brothers grew still, their faces etched with matching expressions of concern.

There was no other way to say it, so she just blurted out the truth. "Sam's a ringer.

He's in the collegiate Hall of Fame and could have played professional baseball but joined the fire department instead."

Now that she thought about it, Sam had made a most unusual choice — a *heroic* choice, as much as she loathed to think about him in such glowing terms. It wasn't every day that someone gave up a lucrative sports career to fight fires.

"You're kidding," Joe said flatly.

Josh shook his head. "No way. I don't believe it."

Violet's father didn't say a word, even as his face turned an alarming shade of red.

"It's true. He's even got a framed newspaper article about it hanging on the wall of his office," Violet said.

Seriously, who did that? There was nothing that could explain that level of egotism. Sam might be a literal hero, but he was also obviously some sort of Dalmatian-loving narcissist.

"This is bad," Josh said.

Joe nodded. "Really bad."

"Surely there's something we can do. Does Turtle Beach even *need* a fire marshal?" Josh's gaze slid to their father.

The older man's brows drew together. "It's Murray's call. Emmett left, and it's up to the chief to replace him with whomever he sees fit."

Oh, so this whole mess is my *fault?* Violet's chest went tight. No one could seem to look directly at her all of a sudden, just like every other time Emmett's name came up in conversation.

Sprinkles abandoned Joe to tiptoe toward Violet and drop her sweet spotted head into Violet's lap. She rubbed one of the Dalmatian's soft, supple ears between her thumb and forefinger and wondered if any of this would be happening if her mother were still alive. Surely not.

Violet had never known her mom. Adeline March had always been something of a legend in Turtle Beach — the hometown girl everyone fell in love with, most notably police chief Ed March and fire chief Murray Jones. After she died giving birth to Violet, it was as if the whole town lost its mind.

At least that's what Violet's friends at the retirement center always said. Adeline's untimely passing cast a long shadow over their quaint little island, and sometimes Violet still felt like a little girl, fumbling her way through the dark.

"Maybe it's time to put an end to the annual tournament," Violet said as calmly as she could manage. "Don't you think twenty-eight years is long enough?"

Nearly three decades, and somehow, the animosity between the two teams grew deeper and deeper every year. Whoever coined the phrase "time heals all wounds" had clearly never sat through nine innings of Turtle Beach's first responders doing their best to annihilate one another on the softball diamond.

Josh snorted. "You can't be serious. We're not going to run scared just because Chief Murray brought in a ringer."

"He's right," Joe said. "It's a matter of honor. We beat them last year, and we can do it again. This just means we have to work harder to crush them."

"No," Dad said tersely. Sprinkles's tail drooped between her legs at the sudden hardness in his tone. "This means *war.*"

Violet sighed. So much for trying to defuse the situation. She'd have a better chance of teaching Sprinkles to make her bed in the morning than she would getting the TBPD to forget about softball.

Her dad grunted, pushed away from the table, and stormed inside the beach house. Josh clomped after him.

Ugh, men.

Joe was the only human who stayed, staring quietly out at the water rushing gently ashore beneath the pink morning sky. Sprinkles stayed by Violet's side too, of course. Until a pelican glided by overhead, and she scrambled after its shadow moving across the deck's worn wooden slats.

Joe shook his head at Sprinkles and then turned his attention back to Violet. "Can I ask you a question?"

"No, I haven't accidentally bathed any random dogs lately. Let it go, already." She was never telling him about the one cat. Ever.

"My question isn't pet-related."

Violet shrugged. "Okay, then. Ask away."

Her brother's gaze narrowed, and all of a sudden, he seemed to be looking at her with his Resting Interrogator Face, which Violet swore he must have learned from binge-watching *Criminal Minds* on Netflix. The only real-life interrogating he ever did on Turtle Beach involved benign things like misappropriated beach chairs and missing towels — most of which had been swept away by the tide rather than legitimately stolen.

The look didn't have anything to do with misplaced terry cloth, though. Not by a long shot.

"How exactly do you know what the

inside of the new fire marshal's office looks like?"

CHAPTER 4

"He didn't ask you that!" Ethel Banks, owner of the corgi who'd recently taken a bite out of Violet's lululemons, gasped, eyes wide behind her purple-framed trifocals. "What did you say?"

Violet had forgiven Max the corgi for chomping on her yoga leggings. In an effort to reclaim her dignity, she'd chosen to forget most of what had gone on yesterday morning at the dog beach — other than the bits involving Sam's smug attitude and the TBFD logo stitched onto his T-shirt. Those things were important to hang onto, lest she become tempted to bake for him again. She had no reason to hold a grudge against an innocent dog, though — especially when the stout little pup belonged to one of her oldest and closest friends.

Ethel was one of a trio of residents at Turtle Beach Senior Living Center who were near and dear to Violet's heart. A volunteer yoga teacher probably wasn't supposed to have class favorites, but Violet couldn't help it. Her affection for the three older ladies was quite *in*voluntary. Violet had been drawn to Ethel Banks, Mavis Hubbard, and Opal Lewinsky from her very first day as their instructor. She loved the neon spandex they always wore to yoga class and the way they frequently tied colorful balloons to the other residents' walkers when they weren't looking.

The three women also remembered Adeline March in perfect detail and often told Violet stories about her mother — stories she'd never heard from her father before. Getting her dad to share anything about her mom was like pulling teeth. Ethel, Mavis, and Opal were convinced his stoic silence was because Violet reminded him of Adeline. According to her friends, Violet and her mother had much in common — the same strawberry-blonde hair, the same delicate features, and, most notably, the same sense of chaotic whimsy. Violet was never sure if the older women were telling her the absolute truth or exaggerating for the sake of sentimentality, but it didn't really matter. She hung on their every word, rapt.

The feeling was quite mutual. Ethel,

Mavis, and Opal were Violet's closest confidantes, and she unburdened herself to them often. Like now, when Ethel, Mavis, and Opal stood in a cluster around Violet's cupcake truck as she prepared for Tuesday night bingo, the busiest night on Turtle Beach's weekly social calendar.

"You didn't tell Joe that you'd actually been inside Sam's office, did you?" Mavis held onto her aluminum walker with one hand and pressed the other hand to her heart. Nibbles, her tiny teacup Chihuahua, sat trembling on a blanket in the walker's wire basket.

"No, are you kidding?" Violet carefully piped icing onto a vanilla cupcake. "I told him I'd heard about the framed article in Sam's office from Griff Martin."

She paused to examine her handiwork. So far, she'd decorated three dozen cupcakes with bingo letter and number combinations. B4, I19, N33 and the like. She'd pretty much covered B, I, and N. Now to start on G and O.

Bingo night was scheduled to begin in less than fifteen minutes. The first half hour was always reserved for early birds. But by seven o'clock, just about everyone on the island would pack into the lobby of the senior center, tourists and locals alike. Tuesday night bingo had been a Turtle Beach summer tradition since Violet was a little girl. She could still remember sitting between Josh and Joe, stamping her bingo cards with her hot-pink sponge-tipped dauber, holding her breath when she only had one square left. Bingo nights meant RC Colas and MoonPies. Breezy dresses and sunburned shoulders. The whole town cheering every time someone yelled *Bingo!* at the top of their lungs.

The only things about bingo night that had changed over the years were the snacks. A few years ago, Violet had volunteered to run the concessions stand for her senior friends. She'd replaced the MoonPies with homemade cupcakes, changing the flavors from week to week and giving them silly names like *Lucky Streak Strawberry Shortcake, Gimme a Bingo Brown Butter Fudge,* and the ever popular *I Never Win this Game Gooey Gumdrop.* And now, two years later, she was running her own cupcake truck business, all thanks to bingo night.

Violet still ran the concession stand every Tuesday, which meant she needed to get started carrying her cupcakes inside. Tonight's featured flavor was *Beach Blanket Bingo Bavarian Cream.* Sure to be a big hit with the over-seventy crowd.

"Did Joe believe you?" Opal shook her head. "His Interrogator Face is so good. I don't know how you didn't crack."

"I managed," Violet said. She'd seen Josh and Joe play police officers enough times as kids not to be intimidated by Joe's most commanding facial expression. All she had to do was think about the time he'd accidentally handcuffed himself to the railing on the outdoor deck when he was nine years old, wearing nothing but his Star Wars underpants.

Note to self: remind Joe of Star Wars underpants episode the next time he pokes fun at me for repetitively falling for faux lost dog scenario.

"I think he bought it, but I'm not totally sure. I told him I couldn't stick around to discuss it because I had cupcakes to bake." She held up G51 and I18. "Can I offer you ladies a freebie before the crowds descend?"

"Oh, we couldn't possibly," Mavis said.

"Speak for yourself." Ethel inched her walker closer to the window of the cupcake truck and held out a hand. "Don't mind Mavis, Vi. The only reason she doesn't want one is because she's watching her figure."

Opal waggled her eyebrows and reached for I18. "You mean *Larry* is watching her figure."

"What?" Violet propped her elbows on the tiny counter of her cupcake truck's window and peered down at Mavis blushing fiercely below. "Mavis! Do you have something going on with Larry Sims?"

She probably should have seen this coming. Mavis's happy baby yoga pose had seemed *extra* happy ever since the quiet older man with the rotating collection of knit cardigans had moved into the senior center three weeks ago.

"Absolutely not. Don't be ridiculous." Mavis squared her narrow shoulders. "We have nothing in common. The man barely leaves his room. He's practically a recluse."

"Have you tried luring him out?" Violet asked. "Maybe invite him to join us in the lobby tonight. Everyone on the island loves bingo."

Opal shook her head. "It's hopeless. He'd have to miss *Jeopardy!*, and he's apparently a big fan. When it's on, everyone in the building can hear him screaming out the answers from behind his closed door."

Violet offered Mavis a hopeful smile. "He sounds really intelligent."

Nibbles sighed dramatically, turned three circles, and collapsed into a minuscule pile on her blanket.

"Maybe so, but as I said, I'm not the least

bit interested in him. He has a *cat.*" Mavis shuddered in feline-induced horror. "A fluffy gray Persian."

"I see." Violet nodded.

No wonder her tiny dog seemed to have a mammoth-sized opinion on Mavis's potential beau. It was the age-old dilemma — could a dog person ever be truly happy with a cat person?

Violet glanced at Sprinkles lounging on the back window seat of the Airstream in the area she always kept cordoned off with a pet gate so her Dalmatian could accompany her to work every day. Sprinkles was a handful . . . even for a true dog person. Violet knew this about her Dalmatian. Tossing a cat into the mix would only end in frustration.

Still, it didn't take Alex Trebek-level genius to see that Mavis might be harboring a secret crush on Larry Sims, fluffy gray Persian or not.

"Speaking of romance . . ." Opal cleared her throat. The three older women all exchanged knowing glances. "We wanted to talk to you about your fire marshal."

A burst of laughter exploded from Violet's mouth. "Ha. Good one."

They *were* joking, weren't they? Opal, Mavis, and Ethel probably knew more about the feud between the police and fire departments than Violet did. They'd been around back when it started, which meant they were fully aware of its seriousness.

They'd also taken turns holding Violet's hand last year after her humiliating breakup with Emmett. Since then, every time a fireman looked her way, her friends threatened him with bodily injury. Her brothers had started referring to the trio of older ladies as "the OG Charlie's Angels."

They didn't seem to be laughing along with her right now, though, which definitely seemed odd. "Wait. You're not seriously suggesting there's anything remotely romantic between me and Sam Nash, are you?"

No one said a word.

"And he's hardly *my* fire marshal." Violet waved her hands and a dollop of frosting flew from the tip of her pastry bag, landing conveniently on Sprinkles's snout. The Dalmatian licked it away with a swipe of her tongue.

Opal frowned. "Actually, he is. Technically speaking."

Okay, fine. Maybe he was, but only insomuch as she was a taxpaying resident of Turtle Beach and she lived in his jurisdiction. He didn't *belong* to her, like Sprinkles did. Although the thought of keeping him on a leash wasn't without merit.

"We couldn't help noticing the sparks between you two yesterday," Ethel said. "Everyone did."

"Well, everyone's wrong." Violet straightened, and her head hit the top of her cupcake truck's window with a bang.

Ouch. She blamed Sam for the goose egg she'd probably have tomorrow. Everything had started going horribly wrong the moment he'd strolled into town with Cinder in tow. He'd disrupted the town's delicate Dalmatian equilibrium, and now things were going haywire. It was the only logical explanation. Even Mavis, Ethel, and Opal had been affected. Clearly.

"Too bad, because your dogs looked absolutely precious together," Mavis said.

Violet thought about the way Sprinkles and Cinder liked to greet each other by touching the tips of their heart-shaped noses together. Mavis was right. They were sweet together — far sweeter than Violet felt comfortable admitting.

"Perhaps we were mistaken." Opal bit into her cupcake.

Ethel regarded Violet over the top of her purple glasses. "He's awfully handsome, though."

Sam's chiseled face flashed in Violet's

consciousness, and warmth filled her chest — obviously a reaction to the head injury she'd just suffered.

"Is he? I hadn't noticed." She untied the bow on the sash of her polka dot apron and re-tied it so she wouldn't have to look at her friends' skeptical expressions.

"Maybe you can notice now." Ethel cleared her throat. "Because he's here."

"What?" Violet's head jerked up. "He's here at the senior center? *Now?*"

She glanced out the cupcake truck's order window, past her three friends and their walkers decorated with quilted hanging pouches to hold their bingo daubers, and sure enough — there was Sam Nash and his trusty spotted sidekick, walking right toward them.

Violet's heart beat hard in her chest at the sight of him. Ethel wasn't wrong. Sam was awfully handsome.

Emphasis on *awful.*

Ugh. What was he doing here?

"You said it yourself, dear." Ethel shrugged. "Everyone on the island loves bingo."

Sam's footsteps slowed as he caught sight of the shiny Airstream trailer topped with its pink rotating cupcake parked in front of the senior center.

He very nearly turned around to reverse course. He wasn't sure if he was ready for another uncomfortable encounter with the island's beloved Dalmatian enthusiast. Perhaps his evening would be better spent unpacking a few of the moving boxes that were stacked around his rented beach house like a cardboard maze.

No, he thought. *This is your job . . . the whole reason you're here.*

Right. He couldn't avoid Violet forever. Turtle Beach was a small island. He was just going to have to power through and act like a trained professional, even though the island seemed to be getting smaller by the minute.

Cinder fell in step beside him as he hastened his pace. Already, the enticing aromas of sweet cream and warm vanilla were wrapping themselves around him, heady and lush.

Enough already. Stop thinking about cake, you idiot.

He stepped off the gravel sidewalk to make way for a pair of barefoot teenagers headed toward him with comically huge surfboards tucked under their skinny arms, but they shifted to block his path.

"Bro," one of them said, frowning at

Cinder. "Isn't that —"

Annoyance spiraled through Sam. *This again.*

"No . . . bro," he said sharply. "This Dalmatian is named Cinder, not Sprinkles. And she belongs to me, not to Violet March. What's more, she's a *highly trained animal!*"

Super, he was screaming at minors now. Cinder looked up at him, utterly disgusted.

Sam knew he was just projecting. If anyone was disgusted by his behavior, it was Sam himself. But if one more person in this wackadoodle beach town accused him of dognapping, he was going to lose it.

The surfers exchanged dubious glances.

"Bro," they said in unison.

"I'm sorry." Sam forced a smile. "This is my dog. Just trust me, okay?"

The teens both glanced at Cinder again.

"Bro," Sam said again. A plea.

"Whatever, bro," one of the teens said, clearly unconvinced.

Fortunately for Sam, the lure of the waves proved more enticing to the surfers than a dognapped Dalmatian. They shrugged and resumed their trek to the nearby beach access with their boards pointed toward the sea.

Sam heaved a sigh of exhausted relief. He could take a hint — it was time to pack it in

77

for the day and retreat back to his quiet beach house where no one else could mistake him for a gender-flipped Cruella de Vil. He'd simply have to check out bingo night at the senior center on the following Tuesday evening.

But then Sam looked up and spied Violet exiting her cupcake-mobile carrying an enormous tray of decorated baked goods. Sprinkles pranced behind her, leaping in the air every now and then to nip at Violet's polka dot apron strings. It was all so thoroughly charming and eccentric, save one thing — the overtly amused expression on Violet's heart-shaped face.

She'd just witnessed the entire exchange between Sam and the surfers, because of course she had. The woman was everywhere.

"Cinder, I hope you're in the mood for bingo," he muttered.

Now he *couldn't* leave. Doing so would be tantamount to admitting defeat. Sam had yet to fully identify the nature of their battle, but he wasn't about to back down.

He plodded on, reaching the doors to the senior center just a few steps behind his beautiful adversary. Her huge tray of cupcakes tipped at a precarious angle as she attempted to hold onto it with one hand and push the handicapped-accessible automatic door button with the other.

"Here. Let me get that for you," Sam said, pressing his palm against the big blue button in an effort to avoid a cupcake avalanche.

"Thank you very much, but I can do it myself." Violet banged the button seconds after Sam did.

The double doors slid halfway open before they stuttered to a halt and then closed again.

Violet shot Sam a frosty look, and they both pressed the button again at the exact same time.

The cupcakes wobbled, Cinder and Sprinkles trotted inside, and then the doors slid shut again, trapping the dogs on one side of the glass and their human counterparts on the other. A Dalmatian separation.

"Oh, no." Violet gasped. "Look what you did."

Sam rolled his eyes. "I'm hardly the one responsible for this predicament."

He reached for the button a third time, but so did Violet. Again the doors slid open and closed as the matching Dalmatians swiveled their spotted heads back and forth in time with the movement.

"Would you *stop*?" Violet groaned.

"I was just trying to help." He held up his

hands. "Be my guest."

The dogs aimed their soft brown gazes at Sam, then at Violet, back at Sam, and finally came to rest on the teetering cupcakes. Sam caught a glimpse of their matching pink tongues as they panted in unison, fogging up the glass.

Violet slammed the button again, and this time, Sam had to reach out and prop up one end of her tray to keep the cupcakes from sliding to the ground. He probably should have let them fall, but good manners plus the strange shot of adrenaline that seized him every time she was in the vicinity prevented him from doing so.

Mostly the adrenaline thing.

Violet flashed him a tight smile. "Thanks, but I've got everything under control."

The doors slid open a fraction of an inch and then froze in place.

Sam arched a brow. "Completely under control. Roger that."

"You're impossible." Every polka dot on Violet's flirty little apron trembled with fury as she pressed the button repeatedly, to no avail.

Three cupcakes hit the pavement — *plop, plop, plop.*

Violet's face crumpled. Sam had never known anyone in his entire life who wore their heart on their sleeve the way she did. It would have been adorable if it wasn't so completely maddening.

She spun to face him head-on. Another cupcake flew off the edge of the tray to meet its doom on the pavement. "What are you doing here, anyway? Do you even *like* bingo?"

Sam frowned. "Does anyone?"

Violet's mouth fell open, her cherry-red lips forming a perfectly horrified O.

"I'm not here to play bingo." He couldn't think of anything he'd rather do less, except maybe argue with the nutty cupcake queen of Turtle Beach while two Dalmatians and the sum total of the town's elderly population watched from behind a pair of malfunctioning glass double doors. "I'm on duty."

"How so, exactly?" she asked.

"Tuesday night bingo is advertised all over town. For reasons I can't begin to contemplate, it seems to be quite popular, so I'm here to make sure it's safe."

"Safe?" She let out a laugh. "It's a bunch of senior citizens hosting a game night. How dangerous could it possibly be?"

Mercifully, the doors chose that moment to finally slide open, so Sam was spared the unpleasant task of providing Violet with examples.

Now he could finally get inside, count the bingo enthusiasts to make sure the size of the crowd didn't exceed capacity, and get back to avoiding any and all Dalmatian altercations.

"Thank goodness." Violet swished past him, carrying the surviving cupcakes as Sprinkles pounced on the dropped ones. Seconds later, the naughty Dalmatian followed hot on Violet's heels, heart-shaped nose twitching at the frosting-scented air.

Cinder let out a tiny whine as the other Dalmatian trotted away. The crowd of retirees who'd gathered by the entrance to watch the ensuing fireworks between Sam and Violet slowly dissipated. Walkers clattered against the tile floor, headed toward the group of long tables stretching from one end of the lobby to the other. The bingo caller — a white-haired man dressed in a loud Hawaiian shirt, shorts, and athletic tube socks paired with Birkenstock sandals — sat at a smaller table at the front of the room. An area just to the right of the entrance had been set up for purchasing bingo sheets and daubers, manned by other residents of the senior center.

Other than the official bingo hosts, the crowd was a much more diverse bunch than Sam had anticipated. Couples, families with small children, teens, and tweens tucked themselves in and among the senior citizens. Sam spotted a few locals he'd come across since moving to the island, but a good number of the bingo enthusiasts were tourists, fresh from the beach with sunburned noses, damp hair, and sand in their flip-flops.

Sam had never seen anything like it, certainly not in Chicago. *Wholesome* was the word that sprang to mind, and Sam's bruised and battered heart gave an undeniable tug as he stood there taking it all in.

What he was about to do wasn't going to go over well.

"We're so happy to have you join us, Marshal Nash." One of the ladies at the sales table waved a newsprint bingo sheet at him. A minuscule Chihuahua sat in the wire basket of her walker and gave Cinder some serious side-eye as Sam approached. "It's only five dollars to play."

He held up a hand. "No, thank you. But please call me Sam."

"Okay, we will." She glanced at the two gray-haired ladies on either side of her, and they all beamed at him.

Another member of the trio cleared her throat and shot a loaded glance at Violet, who was setting up shop at a long counter adjacent to the bingo caller. "So you're here just for the cupcakes, then?"

Sam snorted before he could stop himself. "Hardly."

The Chihuahua growled, either at Cinder or at Sam's apparent disinterest in Violet's sugary offerings. He wasn't sure which.

"Actually, I need to have a quick chat with whoever is in charge here." Sam glanced around the room but couldn't make much sense of the bingo hierarchy. "Could you point me in the direction of a responsible party?"

One of the women peered at him over the top of her purple eyeglasses. "Sure, our activity director is —"

The Chihuahua mom cut her off with a sharp elbow jab. "*Actually,* the person you need to speak with is Violet March."

"Really. Are you certain?" Sam angled his head.

"What? Violet's not —" Her friend with the glasses frowned and gave a start. "Oh right! Violet's the one in charge. You should definitely go talk to her."

Sam regarded the three women, longing for a single ordinary encounter with some-one in this town. Just one. He'd take any-thing.

"All right." He took a deep breath. "I'll go

84

have a word with Violet."

"Excellent," the Chihuahua-mom said, and they all grinned at him again, ear to ear.

Sam snaked his way through the ever-growing crowd with Cinder glued to his side. A few people reached out to pet her as they passed, but she politely ignored them and focused on the task at hand, just as Sam had trained her to do. The set of his shoulders relaxed a little when only two or three people mistook her for Sprinkles.

Progress. He'd take what little he could get.

A line had formed at the cupcake counter by the time Sam got there, so he fell in place at the end to wait his turn. Cinder sat as still as stone, inching forward only when Sam did. The bingo caller began bellowing letter and number combinations just as they reached the front of the line.

"You again," Violet whispered, her generous smile going strained around the edges. Sam was immediately and irrationally bothered by her palpable disappointment at the sight of him. "Would you like a cupcake?"

Sam's mouth watered.

"No, thank you," he said under his breath.

A flicker of hurt passed through her aquamarine eyes. "Fine, then. I'm sure

85

Cinder won't mind a little nibble."

"O seventy-four," the bingo caller said into his microphone. "That's O. Seven. Four."

He pronounced the number four like the word *foe,* which for some reason seemed hilarious to Sam. He stifled a grin while Violet broke a small chunk off a cupcake decorated to look like a B4 bingo ball and bent down to offer it to his Dalmatian.

"Thanks again, but no," he whispered. "Cinder is working."

Violet straightened and narrowed her pretty mermaid eyes. "It's not chocolate, if that's what you're worried about. I know better than to feed dogs chocolate cupcakes. This is just simple Bavarian cream."

Sam's stomach growled, and Cinder cocked her spotted head. Bavarian cream didn't seem simple in any way, but damn if it didn't sound delicious. "I believe you, but it doesn't matter what flavor it is. Cinder can't have treats of any kind while she's working."

"But she's a dog," Violet said, dropping the whisper altogether. "That's just mean."

A nearby bingo player shushed her, and her cheeks went as pink as the cupcake atop her silver Airstream.

"It's not mean," Sam whisper-screamed.

"It's professional. She's a working dog."

"It's *super* mean." Violet popped the bite of cupcake meant for Cinder into her own mouth. Then she licked a dollop of frosting from one of her fingertips, and Sam was momentarily spellbound.

"You, Sam Nash, are a meanie," she hissed.

"B eleven. That's B. One. One," the caller shouted.

Sam let out a laugh. "Did you just seriously call me a meanie?"

This wasn't second grade. They were grown adults.

"Shhhh." A nearby retiree — yet another member of #TeamViolet — glared at Sam.

"I did." Sprinkles's mischievous head popped up from the other side of the counter to snatch a treat from the tray and then disappeared. Violet's cheeks went a shade or two brighter than cupcake pink. "See? Dogs like treats, especially Dalmatians. Even if they're working dogs. I suppose you don't let her have a paycheck either?"

"That's not how it works," Sam said flatly.

Violet looked down at Cinder and then back at him. "So she's basically slave labor."

How was he having this absurd conversation?

"I feel for her." Violet shook her head. "She's obviously deeply unhappy, having to stand beside you and act like a robot all day long."

"A robot?" Sam heard his own voice rise above the tumble of bingo balls in their spinning wire cage. "She's not a machine, she's *trained.* You might want to look into that yourself."

"Ouch," the bingo caller said into his microphone.

"You know what?" Violet's eyes glittered. "Cinder is the perfect name for your Dalmatian."

"Because I'm a fireman." Sam sighed. *Here we go again.* He'd never met anyone who loathed firefighters at all, much less with this particular brand of intensity.

"No." Violet shook her head and smiled sweetly at him. *Too* sweetly. "Because it's short for Cinderella, and the poor little thing is always doing your bidding."

"Bingo!" someone shouted, and Sam had no idea if it was a legitimate win or if he was being mocked.

Either way, he was finished here — one hundred percent done. And so was everybody else. They just didn't realize it yet.

"The number of people in this lobby exceeds the amount permitted by the Turtle

Beach fire code. I'm sorry," Sam said, even though he was suddenly not sorry in the slightest. "I'm shutting you down."

CHAPTER 5

The *nerve.*

Violet trembled with rage as she sped home in her cupcake truck. She was shaking so hard she probably could have given Nibbles the Chihuahua a serious run for his money.

How could Sam have done such a thing? Granted, things had gotten a little heated between them. She'd probably crossed the line by calling Cinder slave labor. But come on, he wouldn't let her have a teeny tiny bite of a cupcake? That seemed like cruel and unusual punishment for a perfectly lovely Dalmatian who never put a paw wrong. And as the police chief's daughter, Violet knew a prisoner when she saw one.

Did he really need to punish the entire island, though? Clearly the man had no clue how seriously the residents of Turtle Beach took their bingo.

Violet wasn't about to let him get away

with it. Her father had been right.

This means war.

"You have to win the softball game this Saturday," she blurted to Joe after she'd parked her cupcake truck at a furious angle, stomped up the three flights of stairs to his apartment at the March family beach house, and pounded on the door until he answered.

His eyes lit up at the sight of the loaded baking tray in her arms, and he held the door open wide. "Cool, you brought cupcakes."

"I'm serious, Joe." She walked past him and dumped the tray on his butcher block kitchen island while Sprinkles made herself at home in Joe's favorite recliner. "The police need to crush those lowlife firefighters."

"Aren't you the one who suggested just this morning that we end the feud?" He picked up a cupcake, jammed it into his mouth, and reached into the refrigerator for two bottles of beer. "Want one?"

Seriously? *Read the room, Joe.* "Thanks, but I'm not really in the mood for beer."

He shrugged and perused the remaining cupcakes. "Since when do you care so passionately about softball?"

"Since this." She reached into the pocket of her swing dress, pulled out a folded slip of pink paper, and slapped it down on the kitchen island with sufficient force to cause the cupcakes to jump in place.

Joe looked at it and then back toward Violet. "Given your current state of agitation, I'm almost afraid to ask."

Violet crossed her arms. "Go ahead. Read it."

He tipped his beer bottle back for a generous swallow before picking up the paper. Violet paced the length of the small kitchen while he unfolded it.

"This is a ticket," he said. And then a vein popped out in his neck. "For a fire code violation!"

The tension in his voice roused Sprinkles from the recliner. She leapt over the back of it and bounded into the kitchen to paw gently at Joe's knee.

"Now do you see why I'm so upset?" Violet threw her hands up.

Joe studied the ticket and absently ran a hand over Sprinkles's head. "This ticket is for a violation involving maximum occupancy rules. What did you do? Throw a party in your cupcake truck during business hours? I didn't think you let customers in there."

Violet fumed. Of course her brother would think she was to blame. "I did nothing of the sort. I didn't do anything wrong at all. Sam Nash just strolled into the senior center and shut down bingo night."

"And he ticketed *you* for the violation?" The vein in Joe's neck was looking angrier by the second. "That doesn't make sense. You don't even work there."

Violet was sort of hoping he wouldn't hone in on that detail. "Someone apparently told him I was in charge."

"Don't tell me." Joe tossed the ticket onto the kitchen counter and reached for his beer. "It was the Charlie's Angels, wasn't it?"

"Yes, but —"

"Violet, I've said this before and I'm going to say it again: you need to find some friends your own age."

Why did everyone keep saying that to her? She was perfectly happy with her social life, thank you very much. And Turtle Beach was a tiny island. Who exactly was she supposed to hang out with? Sam?

She shuddered in horror at the very thought of it. "Ethel, Mavis, and Opal are perfectly harmless. You're totally missing the big picture, here. Sam closed down bingo. He's obviously a monster."

A monster whose slugging percentage was the best in University of Chicago's history.

Yes, Violet had Googled him, and no, she wasn't proud of it.

"I thought I told you to stay away from him," Joe said.

"I *am* staying away from him. I can't help it if he showed up at bingo night with an obviously evil agenda."

"I don't know." Joe shook his head. "Bingo night does get pretty packed. I don't know what the maximum occupancy numbers for the senior center look like, but he may have been right. I'm a little surprised he didn't issue a warning instead of writing up a violation right out of the gate. It makes me wonder if he was somehow antagonized."

He arched a brow. Resting Interrogator Face activated. Violet must have been off her game. She didn't see it coming.

She swallowed hard, and Sprinkles slinked out of the room. So much for loyalty. "I didn't antagonize him. I simply told him I thought he was mean for not letting his Dalmatian have a tiny bite of cupcake."

Joe took a sip of his beer and waited for her to crack and say more.

Dang it. Opal was right. Joe was frighteningly good at this. "I also might have told him that Cinder was obviously short for Cinderella since the only reason he kept her around was to do his bidding."

"And there we have it."

Violet sighed. "Oh, please. I know you agree with me. I've seen you give Sprinkles food right off of your plate. Just because Cinder is a 'working dog' —"

Joe held up a hand. "Wait. Is Cinder Sam's official partner?"

"I suppose so." She shrugged, and then remembered that Joe had been trying to get the TBPD to allow him to get a canine partner for years.

But that was different, wasn't it? Police dogs actually chased criminals, found illegal drugs, and prevented bombings. What did fire dogs do? It wasn't as if they could hold a fire hose with their paws.

"I wonder if he'd be willing to give me some advice." Joe frowned. "Just so you know, working dogs shouldn't be given treats while they're on duty."

Now Violet was the one who probably had an angry little vein throbbing in her neck. "You're completely missing the point. Sam needs to be stopped."

"If you're upset about the ticket, you should have made it clear that you don't actually represent the senior center in any official capacity." Joe drained his beer and reached for another cupcake.

"What was I supposed to do — let him

ticket a bunch of ninety year olds?" No way. Over her dead body. "It's not like it's a real ticket, anyway."

Joe's brow furrowed. "What are you talking about? Yes, it is."

"Hardly." She reached for the ticket and crumpled it into a ball. "If Sam Nash thinks he can scare me with a little slip of pink paper, he doesn't know who he's dealing with."

"Violet." Joe dropped his head and sighed.

"Don't worry about me. I know exactly what I'm doing." But did she, though? Did she really? "All I need is for you and the rest of the force to bring your A game this Saturday."

Until then, Violet would simply have to take care of things herself.

Sam wasn't exactly sure when he'd started letting Cinder make his bed in the mornings. It had sort of just happened, and now it was simply part of their daily routine. When Sam's alarm went off at 5 a.m., he stumbled out of his king-size bed and headed to the bathroom while Cinder grabbed hold of the sheet with her teeth and pulled it back in place. Next, she dragged the duvet over the sheet, and *voilà,* the bed was made.

He'd never set out to teach the dog to do household chores, but Cinder was exceptionally smart. And observant. Like most Dalmatians, she was also extremely energetic.

That was the thing most people failed to understand about the breed. Sure, their spots were striking. And those Disney movies? Cute as pie. But Dalmatians were sensitive and highly spirited animals. Their sharp intellect made them quite trainable, but it also meant that Dalmatians were smart enough to get into all sorts of creative trouble if they didn't have a suitable outlet for all that boundless energy. Case in point: Sprinkles.

When Sam first brought Cinder home from the shelter where she'd been living for nearly three months, she'd been a nervous wreck. Whatever had happened to her before being rescued by the good Samaritans at the shelter had left its mark. The Dalmatian had been afraid of house flies, ceiling fans, doorways, and the television. It didn't matter what sort of programming Sam landed on — even the Hallmark Channel sent her scurrying for cover beneath the coffee table.

In the beginning, Cinder's training had nothing to do with fire safety. The idea of having her as a partner hadn't even crossed his mind. He just wanted to help her to be a happy, well-adjusted pup. He'd started out by offering her a cookie every time she happened to poke her cute little heart-shaped nose out from beneath the table when the television was turned on. By the end of the day, she felt comfortable venturing out from her hiding place if he kept the volume on the flat-screen turned down low. Come Saturday night, Cinder was ready to sprawl on the sofa with a bucket of movie butter popcorn for Netflix and chill.

So of course Sam had been keen on teaching her new things. Within a month, it became clear she had the makings for an excellent fire safety dog, plus he loved the idea of taking her to work with him every day. She was his best friend in the whole world. Eventually, she'd become his work partner too. Sam trusted his Dalmatian with his life. He'd sacrifice himself for her in a heartbeat, and he knew she would do the same.

Still, Sam couldn't seem to shake Violet's words from his consciousness as he leaned against the doorframe of his bedroom, toothbrush dangling from his mouth while Cinder made his bed.

She's obviously deeply unhappy, having to

stand beside you and act like a robot all day long.

It was nonsense. There wasn't an ounce of truth to it, but Sam couldn't help but wince as Cinder pulled the duvet over his bedsheets and then trotted toward the kitchen to turn on his coffee maker.

He'd had nothing to do with the bedmaking. The Dalmatian had simply seen Sam do it himself enough times to make an impression on her. But he was guilty with respect to the coffee trick. It had only taken him three mornings to train Cinder to rise up on her hind legs and press the power button with one of her front paws. Sam loaded up the coffee maker with fresh grounds and a filter before he went to bed every night, and by the time he finished brushing his teeth in the morning, he had a fresh pot of French roast waiting for him. It honestly wasn't that big a deal. Heck, most women thought it was cute.

Somehow, Sam sensed that Violet March would disagree.

He wasn't sure why her opinion should matter. It *didn't* matter.

Sam frowned into his coffee, swirling with fresh cream and guilt. Cinder glanced up at him from her spot by the sliding glass door where she'd settled down to gnaw on a thick rawhide bone with a big knot on either end.

"You're happy, aren't you, girl?"

Cinder lifted her head and looked at Sam with her usual expectant expression. There wasn't a trace of Dalmatian indignation on her precious face, just pure devotion . . .

Which somehow made Sam feel even worse.

"From now on, I make my own coffee, okay?" he said, feeling both resolute and ridiculous all at once.

Cinder liked learning new things — at least it seemed like she did. Sam wasn't sure of much of anything anymore, thanks to his beautiful adversary in the ongoing Dalmatian war.

"And no more making the bed. That's got to stop. Try to just relax when you're at home." He took a shameful swig of coffee and then set the mug down with a plunk. "Come here, and I'll show you."

Sam strode back to the bedroom. Cinder scrambled to her feet and followed, identification tags jangling.

"See?" Sam pulled back the duvet.

Cinder's gaze swiveled toward the bed and then back at Sam. She let out a baffled whimper, followed by a soft woof.

"I'm serious," Sam said.

He fell onto the bed and flopped around,

mussing the sheets as best he could. Then he stood and stared down at the catastrophe of a bed. Maybe he'd gone a little overboard, but surely this would get his point across.

He planted his hands on his hips and waited. Sure enough, within seconds, Cinder scrambled toward the bed and clamped her mouth over the edge of the sheet.

"Leave it," he said firmly.

The leave it command was one of the most important in Cinder's arsenal of tricks, and she'd perfected it years ago. The thickest, juiciest rib eye steak in the world could be lying on the floor at the scene of a fire, and Cinder wouldn't go anywhere near it if Sam told her to leave it. Of course, they'd never actually been to a burning building teeming with premium beef, but if ever they were, Cinder was prepared.

As soon as he gave the command, she loosened her jaws, dropped the sheet, and backed away from the bed. No sweat. Dog training really wasn't that difficult. Violet should really give it a try sometime.

"Good girl." Sam stroked Cinder's smooth, spotted neck. "That's right. We're slobs now."

He laughed to himself as he headed back toward the kitchen to finish his coffee. Sam and Cinder would never be slobs, but perhaps they could afford to be a tad less regimented at home. At least enough to convince Sam that there was no truth whatsoever to Violet's ludicrous accusations.

Cinder was nothing like a robot, and Sam certainly didn't think of her as slave labor. He could make his own coffee and tuck in his own sheets. And if the bed never got made at all, so what? They lived at the beach now. This was how relaxed islanders lived.

Or so Sam had heard.

But when he strolled back to his bedroom to get dressed, the bed was back in pristine shape, duvet pulled tight and pillows positioned just so. If he didn't know better, he would have sworn the sheets had been fashioned into hospital corners.

Sam jammed a hand through his hair, tugging hard at the ends. Cinder jumped onto the foot of the bed and wagged her tail, thoroughly pleased with herself.

Or was Sam mistaking that gleam in her soft brown eyes for satisfaction when it was really something else? *Deep unhappiness,* perhaps?

No way. Not possible.

Sam sighed. One thing was for sure — untraining his Dalmatian was going to be more challenging than he'd anticipated.

■ ■ ■ ■

After a few more rounds of remaking, unmaking, and re-remaking the bed, Sam gave up and headed to work. He and Cinder walked to Seashell Drive, then turned left and made their way through Turtle Beach's tiny strip of downtown until the firehouse came into view. He knew better than to wave at the police cruiser that crawled past him, but he didn't hesitate to greet the business owners who were opening up their beach shops and the pedestrians on the opposite side of the street.

That's how small towns worked, right? Everyone went out of their way to speak to one another, even if only to accuse the newcomer of dognapping.

Weirdly enough, not one person along the sandy stretch of downtown stopped to ask Sam what he was doing with Violet March's Dalmatian. Sam should have been thrilled, and he would have been, if not for the large number of dirty looks aimed in his direction.

Something weird was going on. In the few days he'd spent thus far as a resident of Turtle Beach, he'd grown accustomed to being glared at by anyone in a blue uniform.

Everyone else in town had been perfectly pleasant — Violet being the one notable exception. Even the locals who'd mistaken Cinder for Sprinkles had been relatively friendly about it. They'd been more curious than anything else.

Not so this morning. He waved to the group of fishermen crowded around the entrance to the pier, and not one of them returned the gesture. They all seemed to look right through him. When he walked past the Turtle Beach post office — which for some reason doubled as an old-fashioned roller skating rink in the evenings — every person inside cast him icy stares.

"Is it my imagination, or are we on the receiving end of some serious side-eye this morning?" Sam muttered.

Cinder kept her head held high, clearly unbothered by the drama. Sam envied her nonchalance.

Why should he care if everyone on the island suddenly seemed to hate him, though? A quiet, solitary life was exactly what he'd been looking for when he'd come to the Carolina coast.

Wasn't it?

"I don't know what you did, but it must have been bad," Griff said, shaking his head as he leaned against the shiny red fire truck parked just outside the apparatus bay when Sam and Cinder arrived at the firehouse.

Sam felt himself frown. He'd been doing a lot of that lately. Frowning. When exactly was the relaxing part of his new stress-free life supposed to kick in? "What are you talking about?"

"Chief Murray is on a tear. He said he wanted to see you the second you got here." Griff gave Sam's right arm a poke.

Sam frowned yet again. "What was that for?"

"Just checking. I thought maybe you injured your swinging arm." Griff shrugged. "It seemed like the only thing that would make Murray so freaking mad."

"My arm is fine." Unfortunately. Sam would have welcomed a torn rotator cuff if it meant he could get out of Guns and Hoses, but he was pretty sure even that wouldn't do the trick. Murray would probably make him bat left-handed. Or with his feet.

Griff jerked his head in the direction of the firehouse. "Well, you'd better get in there. He's waiting for you in his office."

Sam nodded. "Thanks for the warning."

Surely all of this drama wasn't about bingo. He'd only been doing his job. That crowded lobby had been an accident waiting to happen.

That couldn't be it. Why would the general public, and especially the fire chief, care this much about game night at a retirement home? It just wasn't possible.

"Nash." Chief Murray's nostrils flared and his eyes went flinty when Sam walked into his office. "Do you want to tell me what the hell happened last night at bingo?"

Okay, so maybe it *was* possible for the greater population of Turtle Beach to be emotionally invested in bingo. Go figure.

"The crowd was too large for the space." Sam shrugged. "So I followed procedure and shut down the event."

"Tell me you didn't." Chief Murray sighed.

"I did." Sam moved to sit down in one of the chairs facing the chief's desk but decided against it when Murray pounded his fist on the disheveled stack of papers in front of him.

Sam would stand. Standing was good. It would also allow him to make a faster getaway if one was needed, which was starting to seem like a very real possibility.

"Bingo night has been a Turtle Beach tradition for more than twenty-five years, and we've never closed it down. Ever. What *procedure* were you following, exactly?"

Chief Murray narrowed his eyes at Sam.

Was he joking? The answer to his question seemed too obvious for Sam to answer. "Well, sir, I followed fire code procedure."

Murray rolled his eyes.

"Tradition or not, it wasn't safe. People were packed into that lobby, and at least half of them were seniors with mobility issues. If there'd been a fire or a bomb threat, people would have been trampled," Sam said.

"A bomb threat?" Murray let out a bark of laughter. "Son, do I need to remind you that you're not in Chicago anymore? We don't have bomb threats in Turtle Beach. We barely even have fires."

"With all due respect, sir, a tragedy can happen anywhere. Any time. Any place." Sam's gut churned. He shouldn't have to spell things out like this for a fire chief, for crying out loud.

He wondered if Murray had ever been on a call like the one that had ended Sam's career in Chicago. Obviously not, or they'd never be having this conversation.

"You were out of line." Murray threw his hands in the air. "Did you consider giving them a warning, or perhaps asking for a few volunteers to leave and come back next week?"

No, actually. Sam hadn't considered anything of the sort — probably because he'd been too busy exchanging verbal hand grenades with Violet.

"My phone has been ringing off the hook all morning with complaints." Chief Murray pointed a beefy finger at Sam. "About you."

Right on cue, the red rotary telephone on the chief's desk let out a piercing jingle. Murray closed his eyes and pinched the bridge of his nose. Cinder cocked her head at the ringing sound.

Murray picked up the phone. "TBFD, Chief Murray speaking."

Sam shifted his weight from one foot to the other.

"Yes, I'm aware that bingo was shut down," the chief said. "It was a mistake, and I apologize. As you know, Marshal Nash is new in town, and he just got a little overeager. We'll make it up to you."

The chief paused, then glanced up at Sam. "Actually, Nash himself will make it up to you. You have my word."

Sam's chest felt weighted down all of a sudden, as if he was being crushed by an elephant . . . or perhaps the antiquated expectations of a tiny beach town.

"Tomorrow at ten o'clock. He'll be there.

I promise." Chief Murray slammed the phone back down on the receiver.

"Who was that?" Sam asked.

Anyone but her. *Please.*

If Sam's boss was going to make him grovel to every bingo-loving elderly resident of Turtle Beach, he would. But he drew the line at apologizing to Violet.

Not that she would let him, anyway. He'd tried to help her get inside the senior center with her giant tray of cupcakes and look how that had turned out. They'd practically short-circuited the automatic doors.

"That was the director of the Turtle Beach Senior Living Center. She wanted to remind me that the proceeds from bingo night go toward the Turtle Beach Preservation Society. The residents are very upset. They've been saving up to donate more park benches up and down the dog beach." Murray cast a pointed glance at Cinder. "I would think that would be a project you could get on board with."

"It is." Sam nodded, even though he still couldn't quite work out how the lack of seating at the dog beach was his fault when he'd only been doing his job.

"Good. It's all settled — you're to go over there tomorrow morning and make things right." Murray waved toward the door.

"Now get out of my office and try not to cause any more trouble, would you?"

"Um." Sam frowned. "How exactly am I supposed to make things right?"

"How should I know? You created this mess, and now you're going to fix it. Is that clear?"

Sam nodded.

Clear as mud.

He turned to go, but Murray stopped him as Cinder scrambled to her feet.

"If I were you, I'd take that Dalmatian with you when you go. All the residents over there are dog crazy. Didn't you say Cinder could do special tricks?"

"I said she's trained to do fire safety demonstrations," Sam countered.

"Good. Do that. They'll love it. Just make it cute, okay? You need to charm the socks off of those retirees. Understood?" Chief Murray said. The red phone on his desk started ringing again, and the chief groaned.

Make it cute. Somehow Sam had missed that part of the fire code.

"Understood."

CHAPTER 6

Thank goodness for small-town gossip, Violet thought as she heaved a heavy plastic tub out of her cupcake truck the following morning and carried it toward the entrance to the senior center.

In the past, she hadn't been much of a fan of the rumor mill — particularly after the big humiliating breakup with Emmett. Trying to hold her head up high when everyone in town knew that she'd been duped had *not* been fun. But today she was singing a different tune.

Yesterday evening, she'd taken Sprinkles to the dog beach, where she'd crossed paths with Hoyt Hooper, Jr. and his aging Golden Retriever. Hoyt's father — the original Hoyt Hooper, resident and current bingo caller at the senior center — heard via the senior center's head chef that everyone in town had bombarded Chief Murray with complaints about bingo night being called off.

Hoyt Jr. insisted that Sam had been ordered to apologize to the residents *in person* at ten in the morning . . .

Which just so happened to overlap nicely with Violet's 9:30 a.m. yoga class.

She couldn't wait to see Sam grovel. Just the thought of him being disgraced like that was altogether intoxicating — so much so that she'd invented a new cupcake for the occasion. Her special today was a warm cinnamon vanilla cake, stuffed with crushed blueberries and creamy custard center. She'd christened it the humble pie cupcake and fashioned the icing to look like criss-crossed pie crust.

Genius as it was, the cupcake was for her, not for Sam. It was simply Violet's way of venting via whipped butter, eggs, and sugar. She had something entirely different planned for Sam himself. She'd had to make a forty-five minute drive across the bridge to nearby Wilmington last night to get it done, but the result had definitely been worth it. If he thought she was going to just roll over and ignore the ridiculous slip of pink paper he'd given her, he was delusional.

"Good morning, everyone," she called in a singsong voice as she strolled inside the senior center's lobby with Sprinkles prancing alongside her.

The bingo setup had been cleared away and replaced with yoga mats in soothing sea-glass hues. Class didn't start for another twenty minutes or so, but most of her students were ready and waiting, just like always.

Sprinkles paused to sniff at Nibbles, curled into an itsy-bitsy ball on the corner of Mavis's mat on the front row. Once the Dalmatian had confirmed that the tiny lump was, in fact, a dog and not a wayward snack, she moved on.

"You seem awfully happy this morning, Violet," Opal said, exchanging puzzled glances with Ethel and Mavis.

Violet beamed as she unrolled her favorite yoga mat, decorated with row upon row of yummy donuts on a hot pink background. "I am. It's a gorgeous day, don't you think?"

The retirees all gawked at her.

Violet shrugged. "What?"

"Well, dear, we expected you to still be upset about what happened at bingo night," Ethel said.

"She must not know," Opal whispered in a voice loud enough for a room full of elderly yogis to hear her, which subsequently wasn't much of a whisper at all.

"Obviously not," Mavis whisper-screamed back.

Violet planted her hands on her hips. "You guys, I'm well aware that Sam Nash is coming here at ten o'clock, and I'm completely fine with it."

"You're not mad at him about the other night?" Ethel's eyes narrowed. "At *all*?"

"Nope. I'm fine." Violet's smile stiffened. "Totally."

Okay, maybe she wasn't altogether fine, but she would be in about forty-five minutes when Sam showed up.

She pulled the lid off the plastic tub and began removing fresh new T-shirts from inside. "Actually, I have a surprise for you all today."

"What did she say?" Hoyt Hooper said from the back row. "She brought us pies?"

"No!" the man beside him bellowed. "She's got a *surprise.*"

Hoyt frowned. "So no pie, then?"

"No pie," Violet said, trying her best not to sigh. "But here, put this on."

She tossed him one of the T-shirts and wove her way through the maze of yoga mats, giving each of her students a shirt of their own while Sprinkles stretched into a literal downward dog pose on the donut yoga mat at the front of the room.

"What does this say?" Ethel held up her shirt and squinted at it over the top of her purple glasses. "Is that a tic-tac-toe sign?"

Mavis rolled her eyes. "Get with the times. It's a hashtag."

"Hashtag free Cinder." Opal's mouth fell open as she stared at the lettering on the front of her T-shirt. "Oh my goodness."

Ethel blinked. "Isn't Cinder the name of Sam's sweet Dalmatian?"

"Yes, and she's being treated like a prisoner. These T-shirts are a statement. We're standing up for Cinder's rights." Violet pulled one of the T-shirts on and struck a superhero pose.

Once again, Ethel, Mavis, and Opal exchanged glances.

"Stop looking at each other like that. You know I'm right. I tried to give Cinder a treat the other night, and he wouldn't let her eat it." Violet crossed her arms and waited for them to react with the appropriate level of horror.

And waited.

And waited some more.

Finally, she threw her hands in the air. "Would you *please* just put the shirts on? Surely I don't have to remind you that the man shut down bingo night."

"Don't get upset, dear. If it will make you

115

happy, we'll wear the tic-tac-toe shirts." Ethel shimmied into her shirt.

The rest of the seniors followed, and even though it had taken a teensy bit of arm-twisting, the end result was fabulous. At least thirty silver-haired yogis smiled back at her from their mats with #FreeCinder emblazoned across their chests.

Take that, Bingo-Hater.

Violet wasn't usually quite so confrontational, but this was a matter of simple Dalmatian vindication. She was looking out for Sprinkles's spotted sister. Girl power and all that . . . but canine.

That was her story, anyway, and she was sticking to it.

If Sprinkles was overly concerned with the plight of her black-and-white body double, she didn't let it show. Once class started, she gleefully participated, just like she always did. She planted her chin on top of Violet's crisscrossed legs during the opening meditation — a quiet, serene moment when Violet encouraged her students to set their intention for the day's yoga practice. Setting an intention typically involved focusing on some noble quality a yogi wanted to nurture in their life, like gratitude, kindness, or grace. Since *sweet, sweet revenge* didn't exactly qualify as noble, Violet chose to focus on letting go. Which she would totally do . . .

Right after she had the pleasure of seeing Sam walk into the senior center to find an army of zen octogenarians advocating for his Dalmatian's rights to treats. *Namaste!*

"Okay, everyone, let's transition slowly into downward facing dog. If this pose is difficult for you, don't forget you can do it on all fours instead." Violet stretched into a gentle down dog, and Sprinkles did a commando crawl onto the yoga mat until she was positioned directly beneath Violet. Then the Dalmatian flipped onto her back and gazed up at her with her doggy mouth split into a wide grin.

Yoga came naturally to most dogs, because unlike people, they reveled in being present and living in the moment. Violet loved this about her dog, even if living in the moment sometimes involved a tiny amount of chaotic disobedience. That was okay, though, wasn't it? No dog was perfect. Sprinkles might be a little extra on occasion, but Violet loved her. Everyone in Turtle Beach did.

Besides, it wasn't as if Sam's Dalmatian could actually fight fires. That just wasn't possible. Come to think of it, Violet wasn't sure what a fire dog's job actually entailed. Cinder certainly hadn't written out Violet's citation with her sweet, dainty paws. When it came down to it, what could Cinder do that Sprinkles couldn't?

Not much, probably.

Violet glanced at the clock over the entrance to the senior center. Its oversized numbers indicated that Sam would be walking through the door in approximately fifteen minutes. Time to start winding down.

She led the group through a few gentle stretches, finishing in the final relaxation pose, with her students lying flat on their backs and remaining perfectly still for three to five minutes. In recent weeks, the seniors had taken to calling final relaxation "murder victim pose." Like Joe, they really needed to stop watching so much *Criminal Minds.*

Sprinkles sat down beside Violet's shoulder, and Violet kept her eyes closed. She took three deep breaths and then ended the class the way she always did — with a feel-good inspirational quote.

"May all beings be happy, may all beings be healthy, and may all beings be free from suffering. *Namaste.*"

When she opened her eyes, she found two Dalmatian faces staring down at her instead of one. She glanced back and forth between them, and for the life of her, she couldn't tell the two dogs apart. It was as if someone had cloned Sprinkles during murder victim pose. But then a throat cleared somewhere above her and she looked up to find Sam towering over her.

He stared pointedly at her chest, arched a brow, and the stern, ultra-manly knot in his jaw made another angry appearance. *"Namaste."*

#FreeCinder.

Sam's entire body clenched as he glared at the lettering printed across Violet's T-shirt. He'd been dreading this awkward visit to the senior center since the minute he'd woken up this morning and engaged in another back-and-forth with Cinder over the making, unmaking, and remaking of the bed. As unenthused as he'd been about begging forgiveness for simply trying to ensure the safety of Turtle Beach's elderly population, he hadn't anticipated having to do so in front of Violet March.

He *definitely* hadn't foreseen the offensive hashtag. Or the T-shirts. Or the forbidden zing that Violet's saucy little grin sent coursing through him when she opened her eyes and found him glaring down at her. He felt electrified all of a sudden — jittery, as if he'd just downed two or three of her sugary, delectable cupcakes in rapid succession.

Were his hands actually shaking?

Wait a minute.

Sam stiffened. He was supposed to be angry. He *was* angry — thoroughly annoyed, as a matter of fact. The woman was even more of a menace than her unruly Dalmatian, which was really saying something.

But there was something about her that captivated him. He couldn't deny it and, weirdly enough, the more adversarial their exchanges became, the more he wanted to kiss the obstinate smirk right off of her face.

What the hell was happening to him? Sam had never understood couples who thrived on drama and constant arguing. That sort of relationship had always seemed more like misery than anything remotely resembling love or romance.

Being around Violet made him feel alive, though — more alive than he'd felt in a long, long time. After months of numbness, the shock of adrenaline flowing through his veins was so potent that it made his head spin. As messed up as it seemed, he delighted in the sudden delirium.

It's simple chemistry, that's all. He swallowed hard. *It doesn't* mean *anything.*

"Oh, look," Violet said to the matching Dalmatians. "It's Cinder's dad."

Sam chose not to point out that Cinder's "dad" was, in fact, a dog with black-and-white spots, not a human being. He was Cinder's partner and best friend, but somehow he didn't think Violet would appreciate the difference.

#FreeCinder.

Sam forced himself to avert his gaze from Violet's chest. Wordlessly, he offered her his hand to help her up off the floor.

She bit her lip and eyed his outstretched palm as if it were full of expired dog treats, while Sam meditated briefly on the sublime pleasure of her perfect pink mouth.

Finally, she placed her fingertips in his hand and let him lift her to her feet. Fireworks skittered across every inch of Sam's skin at the contact. He couldn't help wondering if she felt it too, but then he reminded himself of the unflattering hashtag. A Dalmatian provocation if he'd ever witnessed one.

"Thank you," Violet said. Her hand felt warm and impossibly soft in his palm, especially contrasted with his rough calluses from years of working in a firehouse.

They stood touching for a prolonged moment until her cheeks flushed and she jerked her hand back.

"Nice shirt." Sam gave her a tight smile and then spun on his heel and walked away. Thankfully, Cinder followed without having to be asked.

"Oh, good. He likes the T-shirts," one of the seniors in Sam's rearview gushed.

He didn't have the heart to correct her. In fact, it made him smile a little bit. They wanted cute? Sam was about to bombard them with it. Those bingo-loving elderly people wouldn't know what hit them. Violet and Sprinkles were about to be toppled right off their favored pedestal.

"Good morning, Marshal Nash." A woman strode into the lobby from one of the offices behind the front desk. "I'm Barbara Nichols, the activity director here at Turtle Beach Senior Living Center. We're glad you could come by today."

"Call me Sam. Please." He shook her hand and then tipped his head toward Cinder. "This is my partner, Cinder."

Barbara's dark eyes lit up. "Isn't she just beautiful? How funny. For a second there, I thought she was Violet's Dalmatian, Sprinkles."

"Right. We get that a lot." Sam forced a smile and glanced toward the lobby where Sprinkles was playing keep-away with Violet's yoga mat. The effort it took not to roll his eyes was monumental.

Barbara shifted her gaze from Cinder back toward Sam. If the pursing of her lips was any indication, she seemed far less impressed with him than she was with his dog.

"You have my sincerest apologies about the other night," he said, trying his best to sound sorrier than he actually felt. "I know how important bingo night is to the community. I'm happy to work with you and the residents to come up with a plan to reduce the number of people in the lobby and ensure the safety of everyone involved."

Sam glanced down at Cinder and gave her a nearly imperceptible silent command, and she bobbed her spotted head up and down as if in agreement with what he'd just said.

Barbara's lips twitched, as if she were trying her best not to smile at him. "And how exactly do you plan on doing that without having to turn away tourists? The rental beach houses tend to attract repeat customers year after year. Families are accustomed to all of our Turtle Beach traditions. It's not only the locals who love bingo night, but our guests too. Plus it's become one of the most vital ways for our senior residents to remain an active, important part of our little beach town."

"I understand." Sam nodded. He couldn't agree more with the idea of keeping the town's population of retirees involved in community events. So far, it was one of the things he liked best about Turtle Beach, even if most of the retirees in question were wearing #FreeCinder shirts at the moment.

"I was thinking that my colleague Griff and I could help set up an outdoor overflow area for bingo nights. You have plenty of space out front. We could set up picnic tables and a flat-screen television to broadcast the bingo caller's announcements. That way, no one would be left out, but it would be a safe environment for everyone involved."

Barbara's eyebrows rose. "You'd volunteer to help us get an outdoor overflow area up and running?"

Sam glanced down at Cinder again and she nodded her head, throwing in a bat of one of her paws for good measure.

"It's a deal," Sam said.

"Indeed it is." Barbara beamed at him.

Over her shoulder, Sam noticed Violet watching them as she finally liberated her yoga mat from Sprinkles. Her smug little grin stiffened in place and another zing of electricity skittered through Sam.

He felt himself smile. If he was being

forced on a cutesy apology tour, he may as well enjoy himself a bit.

You haven't seen anything yet.

Sam flashed Violet a wink.

Game on.

Did he just wink at me?

Violet's face burned with the heat of a thousand suns. What did Sam think he was doing? He was supposed to be groveling right now. He was also supposed to be completely flustered by the #FreeCinder movement. Although, could she really call it a movement when she'd practically had to beg the seniors to wear the T-shirts?

In any case, Sam was playing things way too cool for her comfort. And from where Violet stood, it seemed to be working. Barbara had been livid when she'd heard about Sam shutting down bingo night, and now it looked as though she were batting her eyelashes at him all of a sudden.

Violet's vision went hazy and an uncomfortable knot formed low in her belly. If she didn't know better, she'd think she might be jealous.

Ha. The very idea was laughable. *Ha ha ha ha ha.*

Sam could turn on the charm all he wanted, and it might be effective with Barbara, but it would never work on her. Never ever. It wouldn't work on the residents either, particularly Mavis, Ethel, and Opal. Why did people always underestimate senior citizens? They'd been around the block a few times, and were far too perceptive to fall for the charms of a *firefighter,* of all people.

"Gather 'round, everyone," Barbara called as she sashayed past Violet toward the sitting area dotted with plush recliners and an overstuffed sofa. "Marshal Sam is here for a visit, and he's got a fire safety demonstration for all of us to enjoy."

It was all Violet could do not to snort. What could possibly be enjoyable about a fire safety demonstration? This was going to be the lamest apology she'd ever witnessed. She almost felt sorry him.

"Are you staying, Violet?" Opal asked.

Mavis nodded. "You really should. It sounds like it might be fun."

Ethel tucked her yoga mat into the basket on her walker and pointed the aluminum legs in the direction of the sitting area where Sam was standing with Cinder leaning calmly against his leg.

Violet glanced down at Sprinkles, who'd just begun chasing her tail. Violet's face burned even hotter.

"Maybe I should," she heard herself say. Not that she wanted to stick around for a fire safety demo, of all things.

She couldn't leave before Sam's big *mea culpa,* though. She'd thought of little else for the past sixteen hours or so. And even though an alarm bell had suddenly started sounding way in the back of her head, she couldn't leave. She wouldn't.

It was an apology, followed by a boring lecture about the fire code. What could possibly go wrong?

Sprinkles collapsed in a wiggling heap at Violet's feet, spent from her tail-chasing efforts. Her ears flopped back like spotty little airplane wings and she opened her mouth wide and let out a squeaky dog yawn. And for a brief, shameful sliver of a moment, Violet wished that just this once her dog would act dignified. Not robot-dignified, just a tad less like a topsy-turvy swirl of black-and-white spots.

Violet immediately felt terrible for wishing such a thing. She loved her dog — completely, wholly, unconditionally. Sam was to blame for the sudden disruption of her equilibrium. Ever since he'd strolled into Turtle Beach with his perfect dog, his perfect face, and his near-perfect batting average, she'd been thrown off balance. Up

127

was down, down was up. She'd willingly gone inside the firehouse . . . with cupcakes, no less.

No more. She straightened her #Free Cinder shirt, clipped Sprinkles's leash onto her collar, and joined the group in the sitting area. There was no reason to be nervous. Sam's dog wasn't actually perfect, and neither was his face. In fact, when she looked at him hard enough, she could see a tiny scar near the corner of his left eyebrow. See? Not so perfect after all.

Except he probably got that scar rescuing someone from a burning building. Perfectly imperfect in every way.

Sam's eyes narrowed as he watched Violet watching him. Her face went even hotter, burning with the heat of a thousand and one suns. Possibly one thousand and two.

"Let's get started, shall we?" Barbara clapped her hands and then gestured at Sam with a Vanna White-style flourish.

"Hello, everyone. I'm Sam." He shifted from one foot to the other in an endearing *aw shucks* kind of way.

Violet glanced at Sprinkles. *Can you believe him?* But the Dalmatian wasn't paying her the slightest bit of attention. She was too busy gazing at Sam with hearts in her soft brown eyes, the canine embodiment of Violet's favorite emoji.

Violet seethed while Sam continued.

"First off, I want to apologize for closing your bingo game the other night. I did so purely out of concern for the safety of everyone in the building, but if I could go back in time, I would have handled the matter differently. I'm truly sorry." He pressed a hand to his heart, and Violet wanted to vomit. Surely no one here besides Sprinkles was going to fall for his humble act.

But then Sam arched a brow at Cinder and she covered her face with one of her paws, as if she too was completely embarrassed by the bingo night fiasco. The seniors let out a collective *awwwwwww.*

Wow. Just . . . wow.

This apology was *not* going the way Violet thought it would. The residents were falling like dominoes. Even Mavis, Ethel, and Opal were grinning at Sam from ear to ear.

She took a deep breath. Okay, fine. That move by Cinder had been super cute, but one dog trick could only go so far.

Except it wasn't just one trick. Sam and Cinder had clearly come prepared. Once he assured the assembled retirees that he and the TBFD had come up with a workable plan for the following bingo night, Sam launched into his fire safety spiel. Immediately, Violet realized she'd underestimated her nemesis. Big time.

"Cinder." Sam looked down at his Dalmatian, who gazed up at him with adoration. "What phone number should people dial when they smell smoke?"

Cinder let out nine sharp barks in rapid succession, paused, barked once, paused again, and then woofed one last time.

"That's right, girl. 911." Sam gave the dog a tender scratch behind her ears.

Violet's mouth fell open in astonishment. The seniors burst into applause, and the sudden commotion prompted Sprinkles to hop to her feet and howl like a coyote.

Not now, Sprinkles. Please.

"Cinder, what should people do if their clothing catches fire?" Sam crossed his arms and angled his head toward his dog.

The smarty pants Dalmatian dropped to her belly and rolled over — once, twice, three times.

"Good girl," Sam gushed. "That's exactly right. Stop, drop, and roll."

Another chorus of cheers followed, and Sprinkles's entire back end wagged. Even Violet gave a reluctant clap.

"Cinder, can you show the folks the best way to exit a burning building?" Sam tapped his pointer finger against his temple like he might be struggling to think of something.

Cinder immediately dropped to her belly again and did a commando crawl across the floor.

Sam nodded. "Good dog. Stay low and go. Smoke rises, so it's best to stay as close to the ground as possible and make a quick exit."

The seniors whooped and hollered. To Violet's horror, she spotted Mavis banging the legs of her walker against the floor — the elderly version of a stomp cheer, apparently. Others followed along, and soon the entire senior center was practically quaking with love for Marshal Sam and his insanely talented canine sidekick.

In the midst of the commotion, Sam's gaze fixed with Violet's and his lips twisted into a cocky grin. A boyishly charming set of dimples flashed in his sculpted face, mocking her. Ugh, he was even more handsome without the scowl he wore all the time like it was part of his uniform.

Violet longed for the rumbling floor to split open and swallow her whole, much like Sprinkles had done to one or more cupcakes on bingo night. Now she knew what all the flirting and winking had been about, even after Sam had seen her #FreeCinder shirt. She'd been hoodwinked. The demise of bingo night was rapidly becoming a distant memory. He hadn't just come here to apologize. He'd come with a well-formed agenda.

And part of that agenda had clearly been to give Violet a full-blown Dalmatian education.

CHAPTER 7

"You've gone from being the bingo villain of Turtle Beach to dethroning Violet March as the unofficial town sweetheart." Griff shook his head as he sat on the bench beside Sam on the first official day of Guns and Hoses. "I never thought I'd see the day."

Sam frowned into the emerald-green distance of the softball diamond. They were in the top of the third inning, and the TBFD was up to bat. Cinder sat right alongside the firefighters waiting for their turn on deck.

"Please don't say that. I'm hardly a sweetheart," Sam said.

He'd readily admit that he'd enjoyed the fire safety demo at the senior center a bit too much. When Cinder barked out 911, the look on Violet's face had been priceless. The way her mouth dropped open had bordered on comical, although there'd been nothing funny about the exaggerated *thump-*

thump of his heart as he'd delighted in the fact that he'd managed to surprise her.

Why had one-upping her felt so good? He was above the petty feud that they'd somehow created. And he had a sneaking suspicion that Violet was too. Anyone who volunteered five days a week at a retirement home couldn't be a terrible person, no matter how much chaos her Dalmatian could cause. Before Sam left the senior center, he'd caught a glimpse of the activity calendar posted on the door to Barbara Nichols's office. Violet's gentle yoga class was a *daily* event, Monday through Friday. And that didn't even include her weekly support of bingo night. From what Sam heard around the firehouse, she'd been running the concessions stand for years. Now that her cupcake business had taken off, she donated half of all the proceeds on bingo night to whatever pet cause the seniors supported. This summer, they'd chosen improvements at the dog beach in honor of Violet's happy-go-lucky Dalmatian.

"Sweetheart or not, you're the new town favorite, especially after today." Griff pulled his TBFD baseball cap down low over his face.

"We haven't won yet," Sam countered. "In fact, we're down by a run."

134

It had only taken half an inning for Sam to understand why Chief Murray had been so desperate to recruit Sam from Chicago and get him on the team. The TBFD was *terrible* at softball. No wonder the police department had beaten them the previous year. The pitcher threw more homers than Sam could count. Granted, they were playing slow pitch and the pitching was all done underhand, but still. Had they ever heard of spin? Or a knuckleball?

The hits wouldn't matter if the firefighters in the outfield could catch, but that wasn't happening with any regularity either. A couple of times, Chief Murray and the TBFD driver engineer had smacked into each other going after the same fly ball. Sam himself had hit a homer every time he went up to bat, but he was only one person. He couldn't single-handedly win the game.

"I have to ask." Sam turned toward Griff and lowered his voice so the other firefighters waiting for their turn at bat wouldn't overhear. "Have we always been this bad?"

Griff grimaced. "You noticed, huh?"

"Kind of hard not to," Sam said as the latest firefighter up to bat swung and missed.

Cinder sighed.

"Strike two." The umpire — an EMT

135

named Sue who worked in Wilmington and was therefore neutral in the longtime rivalry between the Turtle Beach fire and police departments — held up two fingers.

Griff shrugged one of his massive shoulders. "To answer your question, no. The playing field has typically been somewhat even. In fact, the trophy seems to go back and forth from year to year. But after the controversy last year, we lost two of our best players. That's why Murray brought you in. I guess he figured you were good enough to replace them both."

Sam lowered his head. Always intuitive to his moods, Cinder rested her chin on his knee. "Are you ever going to tell me what exactly happened last year, or am I going to have to ask Violet to fill me in?"

"What?" Griff shook his head. "No way. You can't do that. Absolutely not."

Sam squinted past left field, to where Violet's cupcake truck sat shining in the Saturday morning sun like silver Christmas tinsel. The line that snaked from her order window stretched all the way to the parking lot.

Turtle Beach's softball field was situated near the boardwalk on the bay side of the island, affording a stunning view of the pink morning sky and sunlight dappling the calm waters of the bay. No one was paying much attention to the beautiful surroundings, either from the bleachers or on the field. Sam had never seen a community so invested in softball. It was strange . . . in a sweet, wholesome sort of way — especially the manner in which the group of residents from the senior center had planted themselves squarely between the groups of spectators cheering for the two opposing sides. Neutral territory. The three older women who seemed to be close friends with Violet sat smack on the front row, wearing a mismatched combination of clothing showing their support for both teams. #Free Cinder T-shirts with TBFD hats. Gigantic red foam fingers on their left hands and blue ones on their right.

Maybe Griff was right. Maybe Cinder's newfound popularity had truly catapulted Sam straight to favored status. Yesterday as he'd been walking to work, three different people had stopped him on Seashell Drive's sand-swept sidewalk to greet Cinder. It had been two days since he'd most recently been accused of dognapping.

"Well, if she can't tell me, you're going to have to spill the proverbial beans." Sam stared hard at Griff. "Tell me."

Griff glanced to the players on either side

of them, neither of whom seemed to be paying them the slightest bit of attention. All eyes were on the softball diamond.

"Fine." Griff's voice shifted to a low murmur. "About a year ago, Violet started dating a firefighter from our department."

"Seriously?" Violet March with a fireman? Sam couldn't see it . . . didn't *want* to see it, unless of course the fireman in question was himself.

Sam shook his head. Where on earth had that thought come from?

"You okay?" Griff frowned at him.

"Peachy." He ground his teeth. "Go on."

"Where was I?" Griff removed his cap, ran his hands through his hair, and replaced the cap.

Don't make me say it, Sam thought. *We were at the part where Violet was dating a firefighter.*

Griff nodded as if he could read Sam's mind. "Oh, yeah. So Violet started going out with Emmett."

Sam breathed a tiny sigh of relief. No one at the firehouse went by that name. Whoever she'd dated must have transferred to another station, although why that seemed like such an important distinction was a mystery he couldn't begin to fathom.

"Wait." Sam's eyes narrowed as he studied

his new friend. Somewhere in the periphery, he was vaguely aware of one of his teammates making it to first base. Finally. "So the big rivalry between the departments must not have been a thing back then?"

Griff let out a laugh. "It definitely was. It's been a thing for as long as I can remember. Come to think of it, I'm not really sure when it started. Or why."

Interesting.

Still, Griff's observation didn't have anything to do with Violet. "Looping back to my original question . . ."

"Sure, sure, sure." Griff lowered his voice another degree and Sam strained to hear him over the commotion of the game. "It was kind of a scandal when Violet and Emmett started dating, given the fact that he was a firefighter. From what I hear, her dad wasn't happy about it at all. Her brothers were more supportive. I think they were kind of hoping for some kind of truce. We all were, to be honest. Everyone but Chief March and Chief Murray, anyway."

Griff sighed and continued. "And Emmett pursued her really hard. From what I hear, she resisted at first, but he really pulled out all the stops — flowers, cards, the whole drill. He used to go running with Sprinkles on the dog beach."

Sam's stomach hardened like a rock.

"Violet fell hard for him after that. Everyone in town knows the way to her heart is through that Dalmatian."

Sam shifted his gaze back toward the cupcake truck where Sprinkles was clearly visible through the trailer's back window. All one-hundred-and-one spots of her.

"But then, on the night before Guns and Hoses, Chief March's playbook went missing," Griff said.

Sam turned back toward him, incredulous. He shook his head. "No."

"Yes." Griff gave him a grim nod. "Emmett stole it. The Marches all live in that huge beach mansion at the end of the island, and one night while he was there visiting Violet, he just made off with it."

"Please tell me he saw it lying around and had a severe lapse in judgment." Not that stealing the playbook under those circumstances would have been in any way acceptable, but it wouldn't be as deceitful as taking advantage of Violet's trust in such a premeditated way.

"Nope, I'm afraid not. In fact, he snuck into her dad's bedroom through a sliding glass door on the deck while she was inside making lemonade." Griff pulled a face.

Bile rose up the back of Sam's throat. He

closed his eyes for a prolonged moment, feeling significantly less smug about his overwhelming victory in their latest Dalmatian altercation.

"The only reason he was dating her was to try and get inside information on the police department's softball strategy. He thought it would be a quick way to impress Chief Murray and snag a promotion to Captain," Griff said.

Sam swallowed hard. "I'm assuming it didn't work since he's no longer part of the TBFD?"

"Correct. Chief Murray was really angry when he found out. He fired Emmett on the spot, along with another firefighter who'd known about the plan and had egged Emmett on. Despite the whole police versus firefighter thing, he's always had somewhat of a soft spot for Violet. Everyone around here does. Like I said, she's always been the sweetheart of Turtle Beach." Griff reached out to stroke Cinder's smooth ears and cast a knowing look at Sam. "Until you came along."

Sam's throat went thick as he sat and watched another of his fellow firemen swing and miss.

"You're out!" the umpire yelled.

The players on the bench rose from their

seats and headed to the field for the next inning. Cinder stood, panting while she waited for Sam to follow suit.

He took a deep breath, raised himself from the bench and strode toward left field — the very opposite direction he should have been headed, given that he'd been assigned to first base.

"Dude." Griff threw his arms up in the air. "We're in the middle of a game. Where are you going?"

"Cover first base for me. I'll be back in a minute."

Violet technically should have been too busy to notice Sam marching toward her across the softball diamond. She still had a long line of customers waiting at her window. The cupcakes were selling like crazy, especially the cookies-and-cream flavored ones that she'd decorated with vanilla and chocolate frosting in a Dalmatian-spotted pattern. She called them the Sprinkles Special, because for reasons she didn't want to think about — *at all* — practically everyone in town had seemed to forget that Sprinkles was Turtle Beach's favorite Dalmatian. The other day, a tourist had even stopped Violet on the street and wanted to know if the dog at the end of her pink cupcake leash was

"Cinder the fire dog."

Violet had been speechless with indignation. Sprinkles might not be able to wield a fire extinguisher with her spotty little paws, but she would always be the town's *original* Dalmatian. Everyone just needed reminding, that's all. Violet wasn't about to stand by and let Sam steal Sprinkles's thunder.

Hence the special spotted cupcakes, although she had a feeling their immense popularity had more to do with the sudden explosion in the Dalmatian population than Sprinkles alone. She tried her best not to think about that, though, just as she tried her best to concentrate on her customers and whipped buttercream instead of Sam Nash and the deliciously snug fit of his softball uniform.

But Sam and his perfectly tailored Hoses team jersey proved impossible to ignore. Her gaze kept straying toward the softball diamond while she handed customers their cupcakes, while she took orders, while she made change. When he went up to bat and hit the ball with an earsplitting crack, the sound hummed through her and goosebumps pricked her arms. She forgot what she was doing as she watched him round the bases and ended up wasting an entire pastry bag of frosting on a single cupcake. So . . .

When he pushed away from the bench, it didn't escape Violet's notice one bit, even though she was in the middle of a multi-cupcake transaction at the time. She could *feel* the intensity of his stare, trained on her with the heat of a white-hot poker.

What was he *doing*? The game was far from over. Wasn't he supposed to be on first base?

"I'll have two of the special Dalmatian cupcakes, please." Her next customer in line held up two fingers. "Just like Sprinkles and Cinder."

"Coming right up." Violet forced a smile. Oh, goody. Now people were linking her dog with Sam's, like they were the spotty equivalent of the dynamic duo.

She placed the cupcakes on pink gingham paper napkins and absolutely forbade herself from glancing in Sam's direction. If he had something to say to her, he could wait in line with everyone else presently crowded around her busy cupcake truck.

But of course the second Sam fell in line, the crowd parted like the Red Sea, urging him forward so he could take care of his apparently urgent buttercream business and get back on the field as quickly as possible.

"After all, you're the star player!" someone gushed, followed by a round of *amens* and *yes, sirees.*

Violet glanced at Sprinkles. *Can you believe this?*

The Dalmatian's tail beat against her cozy window seat. When Violet shifted her attention back toward the order window, Sam stood on the opposite side with Cinder sitting nobly at his feet.

"Hello," he said, as if a player leaving the field mid-game to visit a food truck was the most normal thing in the world.

Every single person in line behind him crept forward, all ears. Even sweet Mr. Beverly who worked the grill at the Salty Dawg Pier gawked at them with open curiosity.

"What are you doing, Sam?" Violet said as a trickle of sweat ran down the back of one of her knees. The interior of the Airstream seemed unbearably hot all of a sudden.

He frowned, as per usual. "I'm not sure, actually. I wanted you to know . . ."

A million unspoken words floated between them as he hesitated. Violet's heart started beating very hard, very fast. Sprinkles hopped down from her perch and poked her nose through one of the tiny openings in the pet gate that kept her separated from the food preparation area of the truck. She let out a quiet whine.

Sam glanced over his shoulder and sighed. "I suppose I just want a cupcake."

"You want a cupcake?" Violet crossed her arms over the *thump-thump-thump* of her heart. If Sam had something he wanted to say to her, she wished he would go ahead and get it out regardless of the fact that they had an audience. *"Now?"*

"Right now. Yes." He nodded.

Suit yourself, she thought as she tried to tamp down her irrational sense of disappointment that he hadn't left the game to sweep her off her feet with some grand gesture.

Clearly she'd been watching too many rom-com movies. Sam had less emotional range than his dog. She doubted he was capable of a grand gesture.

Not that she seriously wanted one. Her feet were entirely unsweepable, thank you very much. "What kind?"

He glanced at the four sample cupcakes she'd drawn in swirls of colored chalk on the A-frame sidewalk chalkboard propped beside her truck.

He squinted at her rendering of the Sprinkles Special and the corner of his mouth hitched up in a half grin. Against his will, probably. "Does that one have Dalmatian spots?"

"Yes, it's the Sprinkles Special," Violet said.

Sprinkles woofed and nudged the pet gate with her nose.

"I'll take one of those, please." Sam shook his head. "Actually, I'll take nine — one for each member of my team."

"Your entire team has an urgent need for sugar?" She opened one of her pink bakery boxes and began lining up nine Dalmatian-spotted cupcakes with a tad too much force.

"Look." Sam sighed again. "I think we should call a truce."

Violet let out a laugh. "You'd better not let my dad or Chief Murray hear you say that. Never going to happen."

"I'm not talking about the fire and police departments. I mean you and me," he said quietly.

The cupcake in Violet's hand fell to the floor with a splat. She blinked. "What?"

"I think you and I should be" — Sam's lips twitched — "friends."

Her tummy fluttered with butterflies and her heart did a funny little flip. Her stupid, stupid heart.

How many times would she fall for this?

"I don't think that's a very good idea,"

she said primly.

Sam shrugged. "Why not?"

The list was too long to recite at the moment, especially considering the customers in line behind him had stopped paying attention to the game altogether, opting to follow the drama playing out at the cupcake truck instead.

Violet closed the lid on the bakery box. "We have nothing in common."

Sam's eyes flashed over to the dog sitting at his feet and the corner of his mouth curled again. "Not true."

"Fine, we both have Dalmatians. That's hardly a reason to be friends."

His eyes flickered back to Violet, and her heart rose in her throat. In truth, she loved the fact that Sam had a Dalmatian. She loved the way that he and Cinder seemed to be best friends, just like Sprinkles and her. She even loved Cinder's amazing fire safety demonstration. How could she not?

"I know how you feel about firemen, and yet when you rescued a dog, you chose the breed that's been known as the firefighters' best friend for more than a century." His smile turned tender, and like the crowd standing behind him, Violet started to forget there was a game going on — a game that Sam himself was supposed to be playing.

"Tell me why you have a Dalmatian. There must be a reason."

Indeed there was, but that reason was none of Sam Nash's business.

Even so, Violet answered his question before she could stop herself. "If you'd really like to know, it's because my mom had a Dalmatian."

"Your mom?" Surprise splashed across Sam's face.

"She died when I was a baby, so I never actually knew her. But I know she had a Dalmatian when she was about my age, so when I spotted Sprinkles at an adoption fair in Wilmington, it seemed like fate." Violet shrugged as if to make light of the conversation, but her insides had gone all fluttery. She usually loved talking about her mom, but doing so with Sam made her feel acutely vulnerable.

Probably because she knew he was about to give her a lecture on responsible pet ownership and tell her that adopting a dog was a serious matter that required serious thought — all things she agreed with, actually.

Violet was used to thinking with her heart, though. Not so much with her head. And yes, it tended to get her in trouble from time to time. But nothing he could say would ever convince her that adopting Sprinkles had been a mistake.

The bookshelves in the March family beach house overflowed with leather-bound photo albums filled with snapshots of Violet's mom. When she'd been a little girl, she'd sometimes take one of the thick volumes to bed with her at night and reverently turn the pages like it was a treasured bedtime story. The more recent albums were practically bursting. Pages upon pages showed Adeline March as a doting mother — building sandcastles with Joe and Josh, fishing with them on the pier in a wide-brimmed hat, standing in the shallows at the crest in a red halter-top swimsuit while the boys chased a beach ball across the sand. An album covered in ivory raw silk contained her parents' wedding photos. They'd gotten married under a breezy canopy on the beach. Her mother had worn a delicate white tulle gown and flowers in her hair. Her dad looked happier in those old pictures than Violet had ever seen him in real life.

Her favorite album was the slimmest one of all, dedicated to Adeline's life before she'd married Ed March. Violet liked it best because it showed what her mother had been like before she'd been a wife and mom. She'd just been Adeline — a girl not much different than Violet herself. She'd grown up in Turtle Beach, gone to the same schools as Violet, and spent her Friday nights roller skating above the post office with every other teenager on the island. At some point, though, she'd gotten a Dalmatian. Violet was mesmerized by the photos of her mother with her beloved dog. In one of them, she wrapped her slim arms around the dog's neck while she grinned at the camera. Another picture showed red lipstick kisses on the Dalmatian's head, mixed among the striking black spots. Violet had been positively enamored of the photographs, and her father's reluctance to talk about the canine only increased her fascination with the striking animal. All she knew was the Dalmatian had been named Polkadot, and one day Violet had hoped to have a dog just like her.

Violet had never seen an actual living, breathing Dalmatian until that day she'd come across Sprinkles at the adoption fair in Wilmington's charming historic district. She'd made the short trip to the mainland for baking supplies and had come home with her very own snuggly bundle of black-and-white spots and tiny pink paws. Violet had expected her dad to blow a gasket, but instead he'd gone all soft and wistful on her, eyes shiny with unshed tears.

And that was that. If Sam thought it made her irresponsible, so be it.

Surprisingly enough, he didn't lecture her at all. Instead, his dreamy blue eyes turned tender and he said the one thing in the world Violet least expected. "Sounds like a good reason to me. Lovely, actually."

She waited for him to roll his eyes. Or shake his head. Or give some other indication that he was simply humoring her — or worse, mocking her. But he didn't. He just stood there looking at her with blue eyes that somehow seemed as if they were seeing her, the *real* her, for the very first time.

Warmth flooded Violet from the top of her head to the tips of her toes. Everything in the periphery faded away, and she forgot all about the softball game, the line outside her cupcake truck, and the wide-eyed stares of the nosy bystanders. All of her awareness was centered on Sam's crooked smile and the crinkles near the corners of his startling blue eyes that hinted at a time before he'd come to Turtle Beach — a time when he laughed more than he scowled. And suddenly she wondered if it might not be so bad to be Sam Nash's friend. Maybe it was what she'd really wanted all along.

Maybe, just maybe, she wanted even more.

But then Sam's gaze shifted toward Sprinkles, and he bestowed the full power of his charm on the excited Dalmatian, smiling at her as if she was every bit as perfect as his own brilliant dog. Sprinkles panted her excitement, and Sam responded with a wink and an affectionate clicking sound.

That's all the prompting it took for poor Sprinkles to burst out of her cupcake truck confinement. Violet could see the mischievous spark in her Dalmatian's eye, but it was too late to prevent the mayhem that followed. Just as she screamed a panicked *noooooooo,* Sprinkles jumped over the pet gate in a single bound.

Then she bounded on top of the counter, flattening Sam's box of special spotted cupcakes before leaping to freedom in a streak of boisterous black-and-white.

CHAPTER 8

"Interference. You're a genius, my dude. A *genius.*" The firefighter sitting across the table from Sam at Island Pizza shook his head and shoved a slice of pepperoni in his mouth.

Another of Sam's teammates nodded. "Seriously, who knows if we would have won that game? It was close, but it could have gone either way."

The game had *not* gone either way. Once Sprinkles flew out of the cupcake truck, she kept on going, dashing onto the softball field and throwing the game into disarray. The batter hit a grounder just as she neared the pitcher's mound, and the Dalmatian pounced on the ball before any of the players could get to it. A prolonged game of keep-away followed, with players from both teams chasing Sprinkles around the diamond. The excitable Dalmatian ate it up. Sam wasn't sure he'd ever seen such a happy dog.

Violet, on the other hand, had been decidedly *un*happy — especially when the referee had declared that Sprinkles's maniacal run around the bases constituted interference and called an immediate end to the game. The real kicker had been the moment the referee declared the fire department the official winners of the opening game of Guns & Hoses, given Violet's numerous familial ties to the police department. That's when Violet had broken down and cried. The tears streaming down her pretty face had been a punch to Sam's gut.

They'd shared a moment before all hell had broken loose, hadn't they? Sam had certainly felt it — like tiny fires skittering across his skin. The molten look in Violet's eyes told him she'd sensed it too. For a second there, he'd felt even more alive than the handful of times they'd been at each other's throats. He'd felt like the old Sam, the man he'd lost sight of and didn't think he'd ever be again.

Actually, that wasn't quite right. He'd felt better than his old self. Standing in the shadow of the giant spinning cupcake atop Violet's truck while she opened up to him about why she'd adopted Sprinkles, he'd almost felt like a new man. A better man. A whole man. Hope had stirred deep inside his chest, and for a brief, shining moment, he'd allowed himself to wonder what it might be like to be on Violet March's good side.

They could be great together . . .

If only he and Violet weren't rivals in multiple nonsensical skirmishes — and if Sam had been looking to get into a relationship, which he absolutely wasn't. He'd come to Turtle Beach in search of a quiet, uneventful, safe life. Violet was none of those things, and neither was her canine partner in crime.

"It wasn't intentional. The whole ordeal was nothing but a freak accident," Sam said, glancing around the table of his teammates. This seemed like important information to get out there, since the other firefighters kept congratulating him on goading Sprinkles into interfering with the game.

That hadn't been Sam's intention. At all. After hearing about Violet and Emmett, he'd simply had enough. He wanted to put old feuds and softball aside and get to know her a little bit. *Really* know her.

Because what he found most intriguing about her ill-fated relationship with Emmett was that she'd been willing to cross the silly line that had been drawn in the sand between the Turtle Beach fire and police departments. She'd allowed herself to be vulnerable, knowing all the while that she was venturing into enemy territory. Some might consider that naive, but Sam found it to be brave.

If the past few months had taught Sam anything, it was that there were two types of bravery. The noble type that allowed some people to run toward danger while others fled was the kind everyone always praised. Somewhere in his new beach house, Sam had a cardboard box full of medals he'd yet to unpack that he'd been awarded for such bravery.

He'd never been good at the other type, though — the raw vulnerability of opening yourself up to emotional pain. The adjective his fellow firefighters in Chicago had most often used to describe him was *stoic.* Sam had always taken it as a compliment. But then he'd seen three of those same firefighters perish beneath a collapsed roof, engulfed in flames, and he'd known the truth. He wasn't stoic in the slightest. He'd gone back to the station and cried like a baby, hot tears spilling down his ash-covered face.

Since then, he'd rebuilt his life entirely, specially designing his new existence to avoid such pain and misery. Not just avoid it, but *prevent* it. Catastrophic fires like the last one he'd fought wouldn't happen here on the Carolina coast. He wouldn't let them.

Nor would he let himself be broken like that again. He couldn't handle it. His new life revolved around his work and his dog. That much he could handle.

So maybe on some level he admired Violet's willingness to wear her heart on her pretty sleeve. She was opposite him in every possible way, which Sam found maddening the vast majority of the time. But somewhere beneath the frustration was a magnetic pull he didn't understand, and sometimes it was almost too much to resist. He was duty and rules and neatly made beds. Violet led with her heart, not her head. She was chaos and cupcakes, and right there, at the top of the fourth inning, he'd wanted nothing more than to take a rich, sugary bite.

"Does Violet realize it was an accident?" Griff said, shooting a furtive glance toward a table where Violet sat with three older ladies from the senior living center. "Because she seems to see things differently."

Of course she does. Sam tossed his slice of pizza onto his plate. He didn't have much of an appetite anymore.

"She's staring daggers at you, bro," another of the firefighters said.

"I realize that," Sam said.

He could feel the fury of her gaze on him all the way across the crowded pizza joint.

Lunch at Island Pizza — Turtle Beach's one and only Italian restaurant, complete with red-checkered tablecloths and repurposed Chianti bottles used to hold drippy candles — was apparently a post-game Guns and Hoses tradition. Given the over-the-top competitiveness of the softball league, Sam had been surprised to find out that both teams headed to the same place after every game. Like so much else about the tiny beach town, it made little sense, but he didn't bother questioning it. Traditions were sacred around here, and he figured it would give him a chance to talk to Violet again and dispel the ridiculous notion that he'd somehow orchestrated Sprinkles's latest antics.

Sam stared down at his pepperoni. "I'm going to go talk to her."

"I wouldn't do that if I were you," Griff said. "Just take the win."

And let everyone think he'd cheated? Heck no.

"I'm doing it." Sam stood, ignoring the collective sigh that rose up from his colleagues.

The chatter in the room hushed as he approached Violet's table.

"Hi, Sam," one of Violet's friends said. She smiled and arranged the checked napkin she'd tucked into her shirt collar so it completely covered the #FreeCinder message printed across her chest.

"Would you like to join us?" The woman who never seemed to go anywhere without the Chihuahua in the basket of her walker nodded to the lone empty chair. Even inside the restaurant, the tiny dog trembled atop its blanket.

Being an official working dog meant Cinder had accompanied Sam inside as well. She waited quietly at his side while he greeted Violet's friends. Sprinkles was notably absent, but Sam wasn't about to ask where the little monster might be.

"I don't think we've formally met. I'm Mavis." The older woman gestured toward the other two retirees at the table. "And this is Opal and Ethel. We're friends of Violet's."

"Nice to meet you, ladies. Thanks for the offer. I'd love to join you for a few minutes," Sam said, winking at Violet as he took a seat.

Her stormy eyes, the same shade of blue-green as the deepest, most mysterious part of the ocean, met his. "What could you possibly want now? Your team already won, remember?"

Sam sat back in his chair, making himself at home, despite the fact that he could see both of Violet's brothers rising from their chairs and heading his way. "Don't tell me you actually believe I tried to lure Sprinkles out of the cupcake truck."

"Of course she doesn't," her trio of elder friends said in unison.

"Absolutely," Violet said at the same time.

"No, you don't," Sam countered.

He didn't believe her for a minute. They'd shared a connection in the moments before Sprinkles had busted loose. She might not want to admit it, but they had. And as he narrowed his gaze at her, he could see the memory of it flickering in her mermaid eyes. In the boom of her pulse at the base of her throat. In the way she couldn't seem to figure out what to do with her hands . . .

Her fingertips fluttered around her collarbones like fragile little birds looking for a place to land. "You made a clicking sound. I heard it. Clearly it was some secret Dalmatian code."

"I've made that sound a thousand times before. So have a lot of animal lovers. It was just a greeting, and it was hardly a secret."

Sam thought about telling her the truth, the whole truth, and nothing but the truth

— that he'd simply wanted to bestow a little affection on the sweet dog. Sprinkles could be a mess at times, but she'd clearly filled an important void in Violet's life. He'd spent more nights than he cared to admit lying in bed wondering why on earth she'd adopted a Dalmatian. He'd just never expected her reason to put an ache in his impenetrable heart.

He couldn't tell Violet those things, though. Not now. They were in a pizza parlor, not a court of law. Besides, Joe and Josh had shuffled over in their blue softball jerseys and cleats and were currently regarding him through narrowed eyes.

"Is everything okay over here?" Josh said.

"Everything's wonderful," Mavis said.

Joe and Josh weren't buying it.

"Vi?" Joe peered at his sister.

"I'm *fine,*" Violet said. "Sam here was just mansplaining to me that he didn't cause Sprinkles to interfere with the game."

"Mansplaining?" Sam laughed, good and loud. "We were having a conversation. I'm simply trying to tell you that what happened was nothing but an accident. I don't cheat."

"If you say so." Violet shrugged.

"And I'll let you in on a little secret." Sam leaned forward, and a forbidden thrill skittered through him when her cheeks flared

162

pink. "I don't care who wins this asinine softball tournament."

Mavis, Opal, and Ethel gasped. Joe and Josh both stared at him as if he'd just sprouted an additional head.

Violet looked as though she was doing her best not to roll her eyes. "I don't believe that for a second, and if you truly don't care, maybe I can help you change that."

Sam cocked his head, and Cinder mirrored him, tilting her little doggy head until one of her ears dangled. "What exactly are you suggesting?"

"Nothing." Joe shook his head. "Violet, stay out of this."

"Stop telling me what to do. This is between Sam and me," Violet said. There was that sweet smile of hers again — the one that dripped equal parts sugar and trouble.

Sam's head told him to get up and walk away before he did something he'd regret, but his body stayed put.

He arched a brow. "It sounds like you're proposing a wager."

"Violet," Joe warned again.

She kept her attention focused squarely on Sam. "Indeed, I am."

"Well, now." Ethel clapped her hands. "Things are finally getting interesting around here."

"I'll say." Mavis's eyes danced, and her Chihuahua panted with excitement.

Josh and Joe heaved twin sighs.

"What are the terms?" Sam asked, as if he was actually considering a bet. Which he definitely wasn't.

Probably not, anyway.

"Winner takes all, obviously. If the police department takes home the softball trophy, *I* win. If the firefighters end up as champions, *you* win." She shrugged. "Easy peasy."

Sam chuckled under his breath. Nothing about this woman was easy. "But you're already one game down."

"So?" She shrugged again. "We were winning before Sprinkles ran onto the field. I guess you're not quite the ringer everyone thought you were."

Sam's mouth went dry, and he suppressed the urge to remind her that he'd spent half an inning at her cupcake truck instead of on the diamond. Why was he suddenly feeling all prickly and defensive? He'd been telling the truth when he'd said he didn't care who won the tournament.

Clearly, he was beginning to feel more invested.

He narrowed his gaze at Violet. "What happens if you win?"

"If I win, you and Cinder have to spend four Saturday afternoons during the height of tourist season on Seashell Drive passing out flyers for Sweetness on Wheels . . ."

That was it? Somehow, he'd expected the founder of the #FreeCinder movement to come up with something more humiliating.

Violet fluttered her eyelashes at him, all sweetness and charm. ". . . dressed as cupcakes."

And there it was.

Joe, Josh, Mavis, Ethel, and Opal all turned and looked at Sam. Funny how Violet's brothers seemed to have fewer objections to a wager now that they knew it could end in Sam dressed as a baked good on the busiest street in Turtle Beach. The cupcake suit would be pink, obviously. He didn't even have to ask.

"You would be providing the costumes, I'm assuming." Sam raised his eyebrows at Violet.

She nodded. "Naturally. I'm the cupcake expert, after all."

Definitely pink, then.

"And as you've pointed out on numerous occasions, I'm the dog training expert." Sam paused as Violet's eyes narrowed. Even though every shred of common sense he possessed told him to stay as far away from this wager scenario as possible, he couldn't. "So if the fire department wins the tournament, you're signing up for obedience lessons."

"Obedience lessons," she echoed.

"Those are my terms," Sam said.

Josh laughed under his breath. "For her or the dog?"

Violet aimed a murderous glare at her brother.

"For Sprinkles, obviously," Sam said. "At the obedience school of my choosing. I assure you it will be based on positive reinforcement techniques — treats, mostly. Knowing your position on treats, you can't possibly object."

Violet grew quiet, no doubt weighing the odds of whose pride would take the biggest hit if they lost. As far as Sam was concerned, it seemed like an equitable arrangement. Also, he seriously doubted anyone in Turtle Beach would be walking around in #FreeSprinkles attire if her Dalmatian started obedience training. On the contrary, the good citizens of their fair beach town would probably heave a collective sigh of relief.

"Those are my terms. Take them or leave them." Sam rose from his chair, fully prepared to go back to the table of firefighters and get on with his normal, uneventful life.

But before he could walk away, Violet flew to her feet, eyes blazing with defiance.

"Fine. It's a deal."

They shook on it, and Sam pretended not to notice how soft and right Violet's hand felt in his, a perfect fit. Because the Dalmatian negotiation was complete and now it was official — Sam and Violet were on opposing teams, and there could only be one champion.

He wasn't going to coddle her like everyone else did. If a wager was what she wanted, then a wager was what she was going to get.

From now on, Sam was playing to win.

Violet lingered as long as possible at Island Pizza. Was it fun watching the firefighters celebrate their victory with pitchers of beer and obnoxious chants that centered around cop jokes and donuts? Hardly.

She couldn't go home yet, though. Going home would mean facing her dad, who she'd been carefully avoiding ever since Sprinkles's romp around the softball diamond.

He was going to be furious. The chiefs took Guns and Hoses just as seriously as the players did, if not more so. To Violet's knowledge, her dad and Chief Murray had never shown up for post-game pizza. All the players did, along with their family members, and the community's numerous softball fans. The chiefs? Never. Not once.

Their absence had never made much sense to Violet. The only time she'd asked her father why he and Chief Murray always skipped the summer pizza parties, he'd said just one word — "tradition."

Well, that just makes things clear as mud now, doesn't it, Dad?

Traditions had to start somewhere, didn't they?

In any case, Violet didn't want to unravel that particular mystery at the moment. Her team had lost, and yes, her dog was at least partially to blame, even if she'd been somehow lured into leaping onto the field by Sam's mesmerizing charisma.

Dalmatian antics aside, by the time Violet left Island Pizza, she felt rather victorious herself. The bet with Sam had given her new life. She was tired of the weird and wholly inappropriate push-pull between them. Tired of never knowing if he was her enemy or her friend. Tired of having to try so hard to ignore him when his presence was a like a fire burning in the middle of the pizza parlor, consuming all her oxygen.

Now the battle lines had been definitively drawn. She was on one side, and Sam was very clearly on another. There would be no more placing cupcake orders in the middle of the game, no more unplanned heart-to-hearts, no more lingering glances in Sam's direction when she thought no one was looking. Sam was going down. The next time she'd allow herself to ogle him, he'd be dressed as a cupcake. As soon as that happened, she'd take a good long look, and then she'd document it for the Sweetness on Wheels Facebook and Instagram accounts. Because of course she would.

Meanwhile, she still had to slink back to the family beach house and somehow avoid her father. This was why grown women weren't supposed to live at home anymore, despite the sprawling serenity of the crest and the fact that she liked to make sure her dad took all his prescriptions and ate something other than grilled meat seven nights a week.

"Look at the time." Mavis glanced at the non-existent watch on her arm. "We should probably be getting back to the senior center."

Opal rolled her eyes. "Why don't you just go ahead and admit that you want to be home in time to watch *Jeopardy*! so you and

Larry Sims will have something to chat about if he ever leaves his room?"

"I don't know what you're talking about." Mavis picked a leftover piece of pepperoni from her plate and offered it to Nibbles, who took it with her tiny front teeth as if she were doing Mavis a favor.

Violet felt an immediate, intense longing for her Dalmatian. Sprinkles accompanied her almost everywhere, and the owner of Island Pizza kindly looked the other way when a certain retiree snuck her minuscule dog inside the restaurant in a walker basket, but due to an unfortunate incident involving flying pizza dough, Sprinkles had been deemed *persona non grata* around here.

"Please. We've all heard the *Jeopardy!* theme song blaring from behind your door every evening like clockwork," Ethel said.

Opal nodded. "It's true."

Violet bit back a smile. "Whatever the reason, I'm happy to give you three a ride home. Sprinkles is probably wondering where we are."

Since Sprinkles wasn't welcome at Island Pizza, Violet had left her dog in Mavis's room at the senior center, glued to the vast array of satellite programming options, most notably DOG-TV. Then Violet had driven their foursome to the restaurant in her cupcake truck. *Jeopardy!* wasn't exactly late-night viewing, so she'd need to drag her feet on the way back to the beach house if she wanted to continue avoiding her father, but she definitely didn't want to get in the way of elderly true love in the making.

Sprinkles was still riveted upon their return, sprawled on Mavis's little sofa with her chin propped on a throw pillow — Dalmatian relaxation at its finest. When Mavis changed the channel just in time to catch the opening bars of the Jeopardy theme song, Violet's dog signaled her displeasure by hopping down from the sofa and pawing at the door.

Violet could take a hint, plus she didn't want to interrupt Mavis's new game show ritual — which, judging by the way she planted her recliner mere inches from the television screen — was intense. So once Sprinkles's pink collar was safely clipped to her cupcake leash, they said their goodbyes and headed home.

On the way to the crest, Violet pulled her silver cupcake truck into the narrow strip of sand-covered pavement that served as the parking lot for the dog beach. She stood in the shallows with gentle waves lapping at her feet while Sprinkles chased the incoming tide and couldn't help but wonder what Sam and Cinder were doing. Some sort of military-esque canine obedience drill, probably. Just the thought of it made Violet's eyes roll. Was it really so awful that she wished Sprinkles would listen and behave because she *wanted* to? Because they had a relationship built on mutual love and respect?

Was she wishing for a miracle?

Maybe she was. She'd always thought of Sprinkles as spirited, and yes, her dog occasionally got into a spot of trouble, but nothing dire. She wasn't Cujo dressed up in a Dalmatian costume, for goodness' sake.

But today had been . . . not great. And now that Violet was alone on a quiet stretch of shore instead of in a noisy pizza restaurant planning her complete and total annihilation of Sam Nash, she was beginning to feel slightly terrible that her dog's antics had caused the police department to lose the game. Surely, they'd bounce back and win the tournament. They had to.

As expected, Violet's dad was sitting on the deck, staring out at the moonlit sea when she and Sprinkles slinked back home in shame. Violet was sort of glad he'd waited up for her, actually. Better to just face the music and get it over with.

"Hi, Dad," she said, wishing she'd had the foresight to bring home a boxed pizza as a peace offering.

"Hi, Cupcake," he said, smiling even though his grin didn't quite reach his eyes.

Violet felt a little pang in her chest at his use of her childhood nickname, which Ed March had adorably resurrected once Sweetness on Wheels had been born. "Can I sit with you for a minute?"

"Of course."

Violet lowered herself into a rocking chair facing the water as Sprinkles greeted her dad, leaving a trail of wet paw prints on the deck.

"You two must have gone to the dog beach on the way home," Dad said.

"We did." Violet took a deep breath. "Listen, Dad. I want to talk about what happened at the softball game."

He nodded. "Okay, then. Let's talk."

"I'm sorry." Violet squeezed her eyes closed, and the tide roared in her ears. When she licked her lips, they tasted of salt and ocean spray.

Why did she feel like a kid again all of a sudden?

Dad finally turned to look at her, and his eyes narrowed. "Josh seems to think Sam Nash was involved somehow. You two aren't . . ."

He couldn't even finish the sentence. Violet didn't blame him — not after the embarrassing Emmett episode.

"Absolutely not." She shook her head. "No way. Never. Not in a million years."

She bit down hard on the inside of her cheek to stop herself from saying more. A simple no would have sufficed. Who was she trying to convince? Her father or herself?

Dad sighed. "Violet."

"You don't have to worry about me. I promise. Sam ordered cupcakes, that's all."

"In the middle of the game." He raised his brows. "Yes, I noticed. Everyone did. You two seemed to be having a quite a conversation at your cupcake truck."

"We were just chatting, that's all. There's no secret love affair going on between us. I have no intention of repeating past mistakes."

"Good." He nodded and for a second, he looked far older than his fifty-seven years. "You know I just want you to be happy, right, Cupcake?"

"I know, Dad."

"And the fact of the matter is that I just don't trust the man."

"That makes two of us," Violet said quietly.

She would have added Sprinkles to the equation, but the Dalmatian was clearly enamored of Turtle Beach's newest fireman, just like everybody else in town.

"For what it's worth, though, I'm not *entirely* sure Sam intentionally set out to get Sprinkles to interfere with the game." Violet cleared her throat. She would never have admitted as much to Sam, but she wanted to be honest with her father. "He made a cute little clicking noise, and Sprinkles just threw herself at him like he was the long lost inventor of dog biscuits."

That was what had upset Violet the most — not that the game had been forfeited, but that her dog might actually have a canine crush on her nemesis. The possibility stung more than it should have. She knew without a doubt that she was her dog's favorite person in the world. But if Sprinkles had to have a crush on someone, did it have to be *him*? Clearly, Sprinkles — sweet, innocent soul that she was — had learned nothing from Violet's tumultuous romantic past.

"Anyway, it won't happen again, Dad. I'm going to do everything in my power to make sure the police department wins the tournament." *Obviously.* "We're just one game down, but I know we can bounce back."

"Heck yes. We can. Sam doesn't seem to be quite the softball savior that Murray seemed to think he was, particularly if he keeps walking off the field in the middle of the game." A small smile crept its way to Ed March's face. And just when Violet thought the conversation was over and she was free to hunker down in her wing of the rambling beach house to plot Sam's demise, her father held up a finger. "One more thing, if you don't mind my asking."

"Sure."

"What were you two talking about for so long in the middle of the fourth inning?"

Violet's face suddenly felt as hot as if she'd just spent an entire day baking on a beach towel by the shore. Visions of Sam's charming dimples and his perfectly chiseled jawline danced in her head.

I think you and I should be friends . . .

"Nothing, really." She kept her gaze glued on the horizon, where a row of pelicans swooped low over the sea, letting the tips of their wings skim the surface of the water. "Just chitchat, mostly about our dogs."

Her dad nodded, and that should have been that, but Violet realized if she elaborated just a little bit, she might have an opening to push for an answer to the question she'd been dying to know for as long as

176

she could remember.

She swallowed hard, brushed her wind-swept hair from her face and tried to keep her voice as calm and even as possible. "Actually, Sam asked me how I ended up adopting a Dalmatian."

Dad went still, like he always did any time Violet tiptoed anywhere close to the topic of her mother. She never pushed, though. Ever. The last thing she wanted was to make her father feel like he hadn't been enough for her or that her childhood had been traumatic. Honestly, it hadn't. Of course she'd wondered what it would have been like to have a mother to read her bedtime stories or braid her hair, but Dad had stepped up and done those things himself. And when he'd been busy with work, the OG Charlie's Angels had stepped in to make sure she was always taken care of, always cherished.

But no matter how much the town rallied, Violet was still curious. She wanted to know more about the smiling woman in the pictures who'd sacrificed everything to give birth to her. She'd just never figured out a way to make her father talk. He seemed to want to leave all those yesterdays right where they belonged — in the past.

Violet kept talking in an effort to fill the

loaded silence. "I told him it was because Mom had one a long time ago. But of course you already know that."

Was she imagining things, or did the salty evening air go heavy all of a sudden? Thick with memories, secrets, and family lore that went deeper than old pictures pressed between the pages of leather-bound books. "How did she end up with a Dalmatian, Dad? I don't think you've ever told me."

"It's getting late, Cupcake," he said.

His rocking chair creaked as he stood and raked a hand through his hair and gave her one last smile before heading inside. Sprinkles sprang to her feet as the sliding glass door closed behind him and came to rest her head in Violet's lap. Her dark eyes glittered in the moonlight.

"Good girl," Violet whispered.

Sprinkles *was* good, no matter what Sam thought. She was sweet and loving, and always seemed to know when Violet needed a little extra comfort. Surely that was just as important as sitting on command or rolling over or knowing how to dial 911.

Okay, maybe that last one really was extra-important. Still, in Violet's eyes, Sprinkles was the most perfect dog in Turtle Beach, if not the world.

She ran her fingertips along the Dalmatian's smooth head, pausing to touch each black spot with the pad of her thumb, like tender little kisses. She wondered if her mother had ever done the same with Polkadot or if Adeline's Dalmatian knew how to do fancy tricks like Cinder or if she'd ever gone to obedience classes like the ones Sam wanted her to attend. What sort of dog had Polkadot been, and where had she come from?

Like so much else, Violet suspected she might never know.

CHAPTER 9

On Tuesday morning, Sam was scheduled to give another fire safety demonstration at the Turtle Beach Public Library. Since news of Cinder's impressive skillset had hit the island's rumor mill, he'd received a mountain of requests for presentations. They ran the gamut from scout troops and beach camps to garden clubs and ocean conservationist groups. Apparently, Turtle Beach was home to a special hospital and rehabilitation center for endangered sea turtles, and even the turtles were allegedly interested in fire safety and prevention.

It was pretty much a dream come true scenario for a newly appointed fire marshal. Since Sam's new role involved stopping fires before they started, the more people he and Cinder could educate, the better, so Tuesdays and Thursdays had been designated as community outreach days on his calendar. He'd devote the remaining three days of the week to various inspections and upholding the current fire code, which no one on the island realized was an actual thing.

That was fine, though. It was his job to get the islanders up to speed, and as daunting as the task seemed at times, it provided the perfect distraction from his wager with Violet March. Word had spread about that too, of course. Nothing that happened in Turtle Beach went unnoticed. His Dalmatian could sneeze and it would probably show up in the *Turtle Beach Gazette.*

"Welcome, Marshal Nash, and welcome to you too, Cinder. We're so pleased you could come today!" Hazel Smith, the librarian, grinned as he entered the building located on the boardwalk alongside Turtle Beach's popular stretch of ice cream parlors, surf shops, and art galleries offering watercolor prints of the island's famed sunsets and local landmarks.

With its shaker shingles and crisp white lattice, the Turtle Beach Public Library looked more like a beach vacation rental than a book lover's paradise, but so did everyplace else on the island. Sam still wasn't accustomed to the casual island vibe. He wasn't sure he'd ever be. This morning, he'd ironed his TBFD uniform and shined his silver badge with a soft flannel cloth, as he did every morning, Monday through Friday. Currently, he was the only person in the room wearing closed-toed shoes instead of flip-flops. Most of the children sitting cross-legged on the floor, waiting for him in the story circle, were dressed in swimsuits and cover-ups.

No wonder he couldn't get Cinder to stop making his bed in the morning. He wasn't exactly setting a great example in the chilled out department.

"We're happy to be here. Thanks for having us." Sam glanced down at Cinder, and she woofed a greeting on command.

"Oh, just look at her." Hazel pressed a finely manicured hand to her heart. "The kids are going to love this."

She ushered Sam to the center of the room, and a chorus of oohs and ahhs followed Cinder as she pranced alongside him. Before Hazel could say a word, half a dozen little hands went up in the air.

"Yes, Kyle?" Hazel motioned to a little boy who looked to be about six years old, sitting on the front row.

He bounced in place, eyes glued to Cinder. "Can I pet the dog?"

"I want to pet the dog too!"

"Me too!"

"Pleeeeeeeease, can I pet her?"

Sam slid his gaze toward Hazel. "Something tells me they all have the same question."

"You might be right." She laughed. "Would it be okay if they took turns petting Cinder? Or is she not allowed to do that since she's a working dog?"

Sam's thoughts careened back to Violet's dismay at not being allowed to feed his dog a cupcake. He would have preferred not to think about her ten times an hour, but he couldn't quite help it. Everything reminded Sam of Violet. It was thoroughly inconvenient.

"Sure, they can," Sam said. "But we should probably give our demonstration first, while Cinder is alert and ready to go."

Being mobbed by a dozen or so small children with salt and sand and all manner of beach smells clinging to their tiny bodies was sure to be exhausting, even for an animal as well-trained as Cinder. Sam himself was already feeling a tad claustrophobic. Fire, he was used to. So much interaction with people, not so much.

He liked people, obviously. He'd just assumed his new island life would be more . . . solitary. Nor had he anticipated that so much of his new job would feel like public relations instead of fire prevention. When he'd signed on to be the island's new fire marshal, he'd imagined inspecting sprinkler systems, electrical systems, and fire extinguishers — not this.

Cinder leaned against his leg and placed one of her paws on the toe of his shoe. *Hello, there. Let's get on with this.*

"Good girl," he murmured, and her spotted ears swiveled back and forth.

"Aren't you two just the *cutest*?" Hazel the librarian's eyes twinkled and she sighed in a very non-librarian type of way. Very fanciful. Very breathy.

Sam suddenly wondered if his presence at the library's circle time had anything at all to do with fire safety. He took a backward step.

Not that there was anything wrong with Hazel the librarian. On the contrary, she seemed perfectly lovely — friendly, sweet, and attractive, with glossy blonde hair and a beaming smile that told Sam she would never dream of printing up T-shirts with embarrassing hashtags on them. Dating her would probably be fun. Drama-free. Easy.

The only problem was that Sam wasn't interested in easy. He was apparently too fascinated by a woman who wanted to dress him up like a pink baked good to have even the slightest bit of interest in anyone else.

Lord help him.

"The kids are getting antsy," he said. "Shall we begin?"

"Of course." Hazel tucked a strand of her silky hair behind her ear. Sam was somewhat distraught to notice a bit of eyelash fluttering.

He turned his attention to Cinder while Hazel proceeded to give the children a gushing introduction of Sam and his special canine partner. And then while the librarian sat by, mesmerized, he got on with his Dalmatian presentation.

To the children's delight, Cinder performed all the same crowd-pleasing tricks that she'd done at the senior center. She barked out 911, showed them how to stop, drop, and roll, and taught the kids how to escape smoke inhalation by staying low to the ground. Since the program was aimed at young people this time instead of retirees, Sam added a few new tricks too.

"Okay, boy and girls, who knows what these are?" Sam pulled a book of matches out of the pocket of his uniform cargo pants.

"Matches!" the children yelled.

Next, Sam removed a small plastic lighter from his pocket. "And what about this?"

"My dad uses one of those to start the grill after he catches a fish," the little boy on the front row said proudly.

"That's right." Sam nodded. "It's a lighter."

He held the matches and lighter up high in the air.

"Cinder, is it okay for kids to play with these things?"

The Dalmatian immediately collapsed to the floor, covered her eyes with one of her paws, and let out a mournful whine.

Sam nodded. "That's right. It's not okay at all, because playing with matches and lighters isn't safe."

His audience — Hazel the librarian included — clapped wildly and marveled at Cinder. The Dalmatian's tail thumped gleefully against the carpeted floor.

"Cinder, what should someone do if they find either of these things lying around somewhere?" Sam said, and then he tossed the book of matches about ten feet away, where it fell beside a display of the summer's hottest beach reads.

Cinder sprang to her feet, ran to snatch the matches with her teeth, and promptly trotted over to the rocking chair where Hazel sat and dropped them in her lap.

"Good girl," Sam said. "If you find a lighter or matches while you're playing, you should always take them to an adult."

The kids dissolved into cheers and excited giggles, while Hazel gaped at the book of matches resting on her thighs. "This dog is a genius!"

According to Sam's watch, only five minutes remained of the half-hour presentation, so he let the children pet Cinder, two at a time. Then he gave them each temporary tattoos featuring a Dalmatian in a firefighter hat, along with a coloring book about fire safety. With any luck, most of what he'd tried to teach the kids would sink in, even after they'd gone back to building sand castles and digging holes on the shore.

"Thank you so much for coming. I'd heard so many great things about you and Cinder, but that was beyond my wildest dreams. You two are just fantastic." Hazel rested a delicate hand on Sam's forearm.

Cinder's dark eyes swiveled toward the librarian and she let out a quiet growl of warning. Sam blinked. Hard. Cinder never behaved this way.

"I'm so sorry," he said. "She —"

"Oh, no worries. I don't blame her for being a bit jealous." Hazel laughed and crossed her arms. "Actually, I was wondering if you might like to go to bingo with me tonight? If Cinder doesn't mind, that is."

Bingo night.

The event was already marked in Sam's calendar with a gigantic star beside it. He'd be there, all right, but in his official capacity, not on a date.

Thank goodness, because he wasn't sure how else he would have been able to gracefully decline Hazel's invitation. "I'm sorry, but . . ."

She waved a hand as her cheeks flamed pink. "It's fine. I'm sure you're busy. I just thought it might be nice. Thank you again for coming to do story hour this morning."

And then, before Sam could utter another word, she dashed toward the circulation desk and began checking out books to Sam's young audience. Cinder trotted to the end of her leash and strained toward the door.

Sam felt himself frown. "What has gotten into you?"

The Dalmatian inched closer toward the exit.

Message received. Cinder was ready to go, and honestly, Sam was too. He didn't usually let his dog call the shots, but in this case, he'd make an exception.

Violet pressed the button on her handheld butane culinary torch and ran its slender blue flame deftly over the cupcake in her hand, toasting its Italian meringue topping to a delicate golden-brown.

Perfect.

Happiness filled her like sunshine. She'd never been so ready for bingo night in her whole life.

"Violet, wow!" Ethel stopped in front of the concession booth, clutching a stack of bingo sheets to her chest. "Your cupcakes certainly look extra special this week."

"They are." Violet plucked one from the tray and offered it to her friend. "Would you like one? They're my special this week: Burn the Fire Department Lemon Meringue."

"Oh, dear," Ethel said. The bingo sheets in her arms wilted like a bouquet of day-old flowers.

"What?" Violet tilted her head. Beside her, Sprinkles did the same.

Ethel could judge all she wanted, but any minute, Sam would be here, saving the day with his overflow seating plan. If Violet was going to be forced to watch a roomful of bingo-loving retirees act like he hadn't just closed down their favorite night of the week a mere seven days ago, she was going to do so while also reminding Sam that he was going down. If he'd thought she was joking about their little wager, he was sadly mistaken.

"Nothing." Ethel shook her head. "I'm sure they're delicious."

"Ooh, what are these? They look divine," Mavis said as she and Opal paused their walkers in front of Violet's table.

"They're her special bingo night cupcakes." Ethel cleared her throat. "Burn the Fire Department Lemon Meringue."

Violet ignored the twin looks of horror on Mavis and Opal's faces and torched another towering dollop of meringue. "It's a three-decker cupcake — moist lemon sponge topped with a layer of zesty lemon curd and a heavy dose of whipped Italian meringue."

"That definitely sounds delicious." Mavis and the other two older women exchanged glances. "But . . ."

Violet arched a brow. "But what?"

"But the name, sweetheart. You usually call the cupcakes something fun and creative," Opal chimed in.

"Burn the Fire Department is super creative." Violet held her culinary torch aloft. "Get it? Because they're firemen."

"Sweetheart, I think she meant you usually name the specials at bingo night something more . . . bingo-related." Mavis waved an encompassing hand at their surroundings. The indoor tables were almost full of seniors and tourists, and Hoyt Hooper, the bingo caller, was already sitting beside the cage of bingo balls, dressed in his usual Hawaiian shirt.

"Besides, dear, we've been discussing it and, well" — Mavis cast a pointed look at Opal and Ethel, who nodded their agreement with whatever Mavis was about to say — "we think Sam seems like a really nice man."

Violet was aghast. They couldn't be serious. "But he's a fireman!"

"We know, but he has that sweet dog, and from what everyone says, you two had a nice little chat the other day at your cupcake truck." Ethel cast a worried glance at the cupcakes. "Maybe you should call them something else."

"You mean the chat we had before the softball game turned into total chaos?" Violet still wasn't convinced the resulting chaos hadn't been intentional. Maybe she was being paranoid, but in a million years, she would never have dreamed that a fireman would go through the motions of wooing her in order to steal her dad's playbook. Live and learn. "Anyway, it's not a big deal. Sam and I have a bet. This is just innocent trash talk. It's what athletes do."

Violet shrugged as if completely unaware that Sam himself had been rather famous for wittily taunting his opposing team back when he'd been a college baseball star. In a moment of weakness after the emotional chat with her dad the other night on the deck, Violet had comforted herself with her new hobby, which was Googling Sam. She wasn't proud of it. In fact, when she indulged in this shameful activity, she usually kept Sprinkles occupied with a supersturdy, interactive rubber chew toy stuffed with chunky peanut butter so her dog wouldn't see what she was up to. A Dalmatian distraction, as it were.

She told herself she wasn't doing anything untoward. She had a wager to win. Finding out everything she could about Sam was therefore research — including saving the link to that one shirtless picture of him that had appeared in the Chicago Fire Department's charity calendar two years ago.

"Trash talk." Opal pressed her lips together. "If you say so."

"I *do* say so," Violet said, but her elderly friends no longer seemed to be listening.

Mavis cleared her throat in a way that said she meant business. "What we're trying to say is that it seems like you and Sam really come alive whenever you spend time to-gether."

"Come alive?" Violet sputtered, wishing she had a more effective form of denial at the ready, but for some crazy reason, words failed her.

"The tension between you and Sam is palpable," Ethel said, and then she fanned herself in a suggestive manner reminiscent of Blanche Devereaux on *The Golden Girls.*

It was official. Violet's life had become a sitcom. "If there's tension between Sam and me, it's because we despise each other."

That strange electricity that always flickered in the air between them couldn't possibly be romantic tension or, heaven forbid, *sexual* tension. He was her adversary. Her rival. Her sworn enemy. Just the thought of kissing Sam Nash made her stomach turn . . . albeit in a woozy, fluttery, swarming-with-butterflies sort of way.

Oh, no. Violet froze. The truth was suddenly as obvious to her as inky black spots on a Dalmatian. *I want to kiss Sam Nash.*

"Are you okay, dear? You've gone as white as your untorched meringue." Opal wiggled her fingertips in the direction of the tray of cupcakes waiting for a pass of Violet's butane tool.

I am most definitely not *okay.* She pasted

on a smile. "Fine and dandy."

"Good, because Sam just walked in," Ethel said under her breath.

And there it was — that exhilarating and thoroughly annoying crackle in the air. A shiver ran up and down Violet's spine. She absolutely forbade herself from glancing toward the door, but of course she did it anyway. Sam looked as heroic as ever in his fire marshal uniform, all pressed ebony cotton and that shiny silver badge pinned to his impressive chest. How did a man get muscles like that, anyway? It had been years since he played college baseball. Surely it wasn't just from throwing fire hoses around and rescuing kittens from trees. Every firefighter Violet had ever known did those things, and somehow they never ended up shirtless in a charity calendar.

Sam's gaze swept the room and paused the moment it landed on her, causing Violet to tremble like Mavis's Chihuahua.

"I have cupcakes to finish," she said as steadily as she could manage.

Opal nodded. "We should be getting back to the registration table. Barbara said she's expecting a record crowd tonight, thanks to the new overflow seating plan."

Of course she was. Sam Nash saves the day . . . yet again.

Violet turned her attention back to her meringue as Mavis, Opal, and Ethel guided their walkers toward their table. She couldn't believe they'd allowed themselves to be so dazzled by Sam and his Dalmatian that they'd forgotten all the very real reasons why Violet couldn't trust him. It seemed like they would know better. How did the old saying go? Fool me once, shame on you; fool me twice, shame on me.

Exactly. Violet had already been played for a fool, and the entire island had witnessed the fallout. She wasn't in a hurry to do it again.

Anyway, she had a bet to win and a business to run. Sweetness on Wheels was just getting started. Violet would just have to block everything out and finish creating her sugary masterpieces before the last-minute rush that always hit right before bingo got going.

She flicked the button on her culinary torch to the on position and took aim at her next cupcake, but before she could run the blue flame over the perfect swirl of meringue, a familiar low voice growled out a warning.

"I wouldn't do that if I were you." Sam, of course.

What now? Was he going to attempt to

mansplain to her how to make a cupcake?

Sprinkles's tail beat fast against Violet's leg as she and Cinder greeted one another. Violet's greeting for Cinder's master was pointedly less enthusiastic.

"You're not the boss of me," she said.

Ugh, what was she — nine years old? Why did she always behave this way around him?

Sam's lips twitched. "I beg your pardon."

"You heard me." She put down the torch and reached for the little chalkboard she always used to write the name of the special cupcake in brush-style modern calligraphy. Violet had spent four Friday nights last month learning this particular skill via YouTube like the girl boss she was trying so hard to become. "Can I offer you a cupcake? I know how fond of them you are."

Sam narrowed his gaze at her perfectly executed signage. " 'Burn the Fire Department Lemon Meringue?' "

"Tonight's special," she said.

"And I suppose that's what your incendiary device is for?" He pointed an accusatory finger at the butane torch in her hand.

"Incendiary device? Really?" Violet rolled her eyes. "You make it sound like I dragged a stick of dynamite in here. It's a culinary torch."

"It's also illegal." He reached into one of

the pockets of his annoyingly pristine cargo pants and pulled out a familiar pink notepad.

Violet fumed. *Not this again.* "You're not seriously writing me a ticket for another fire code violation."

Sam flipped the pad open and pulled a pen from yet another pocket. Those cargo pants were the fashion equivalent of a clown car. "If you agree to put the torch away, a verbal warning will suffice. But something tells me things aren't going to be that easy."

Violet weighed her options while Sprinkles danced at her feet in an effort to lure Cinder into a game of chase. Thus far, Sam's Dalmatian was as unyielding as the man himself.

Perhaps it was time to take the high road, especially if said high road involved obeying the law. She could afford to lose this one battle, so long as she won the war. Most of the cupcakes had already been torched, anyway.

But just as Violet was about to surrender, Hazel Smith from the Turtle Beach Public Library rushed to Sam's side.

"Oh my gosh, you came!" Hazel clutched Sam's arm like it was a long-overdue library book.

First Barbara, now Hazel. Was Violet going to be forced to watch every eligible woman on the island throw herself at Sam Nash?

"What a nice surprise," Hazel gushed. "I thought you had to work tonight."

Wait. What was happening? Were Sam and Hazel on a *date*?

Violet shook her head as if to rattle the idea completely out of her thoughts. They couldn't possibly be together. Who handed out fire code violations on a date?

No one, except maybe a man who ironed his cargo pants and had a history of shutting down bingo night. Sam was like a firefighter action hero. He probably wasn't capable of going on a proper date without bringing along his pink notepad.

Violet's stomach churned — this time not in a fluttery, swoony sort of way but in a manner that felt distinctly green-eyed-monsterly. She didn't like it. Not one bit.

"Actually, Hazel, I" — Sam cast a fleeting glance at Violet and then seemed to do a double-take. His lips twitched again, like they always seemed to do when he was trying not to laugh.

Clearly he was amused by whatever emotions were written on Violet's face.

"Am I interrupting something?" Hazel said, glancing back and forth between them while her manicured fingertips remained clamped around Sam's bicep.

"I'm afraid so," Sam said.

At the exact same time, Violet flicked her culinary torch back on and said, "Nope."

Forget taking the high road, especially if Sam was going to date the librarian . . . or anyone else in Turtle Beach.

Sam glared at the tiny blue flame. "Give us a minute, please, Hazel."

"Oh," she said flatly. "Sure."

Once she was gone, Sam took a deep breath that reeked of longsuffering. "Violet, I'm going to give you one more chance to put that thing away."

"I don't think so," Violet said and proceeded to run the torch over the top of a cupcake until the meringue turned a perfect golden brown. Then she offered the cupcake to Sam. "This one's on the house."

"I'm going to pass, thanks." He began aggressively scribbling on his pink notepad.

"Are you sure? Your date might want it," Violet said.

Sam's pen stopped moving. "Hazel and I are not on a date. We had a miscommunication."

"Oh." Violet put the cupcake back down on the table, and somewhere in the periphery, she was vaguely aware of a flash of black-and-white spots.

When she glanced down, the cupcake had vanished, as had both Sprinkles and Cinder. Two wagging Dalmatian tails poked out from beneath the polka dot tablecloth.

Violet fully expected Sam to put an immediate stop to their antics, but instead he handed her the citation and regarded her through narrowed eyes. "If Hazel and I *had* been on a date, would it have bothered you?"

The back of Violet's neck went impossibly hot. How dare he ask her that question.

She took the pink slip of paper and crumpled it into a ball. She had half a mind to burn it right there in front of him. "Not in the slightest."

The corners of Sam's eyes crinkled, and he flashed her a knowing smile — too knowing, truth be told. Then he said just one word before he turned to leave.

"Liar."

CHAPTER 10

Violet's jealousy was written all over her face. Sam probably shouldn't have found it as amusing as he did, but he couldn't help it. Watching her pretend not to care if he dated Hazel the librarian was as delicious as any of the fancy cupcakes she was so famous for. Maybe even more so. Sam couldn't be sure because thus far, he'd yet to actually try one of her sugary confections. He'd come close, but something always seemed to get in the way. He looked forward to the day he'd finally get to take a bite.

Alas, today would not be that day. He couldn't exactly give her a citation for wielding a culinary torch — which, make no mistake about it, was indeed a contraband incendiary device according to the Turtle Beach fire code — and then sample the illegal by-product of her crime. So once Sam called Violet on her bluff, he strode away from her heady cloud of zesty lemon and spun sugar feeling achingly dissatisfied.

It wasn't the first time he'd experienced that particular sensation after being in Violet's presence, which was a fact Sam preferred not to dwell on.

At least Cinder had the decency to scramble out from beneath the tablecloth and follow him as he made his way back toward the overflow area on the senior center's front patio. Sam and Griff had already gotten the tables, chairs, and PA system all set up, so technically they could both head home. Sam was reluctant to do so, despite giving Hazel the wrong impression by turning up at bingo. If he left now, Violet would probably fire up her culinary torch again before he and Cinder made it as far as the intersection of Seashell Drive and Pelican Street.

The incendiary device was, indeed, still clutched tight in Violet's grip as she chased after him across the crowded lobby-turned-bingo-parlor and dragged him into the activity director's empty office by his elbow. So much for getting the last word. Was such a thing even possible with Violet March?

She slammed the door behind them, trapping them inside and out of view of the general bingo-playing public. The office was minuscule, with barely enough space for

Barbara Nichols's empty chair and a desk stacked with art supplies, board games, tambourines, and red-and-green-striped maracas. With the sudden addition of two Dalmatians and their overly competitive owners, there was scarcely room to breathe.

"You're calling me a liar? Ha!" Violet tipped her head back and laughed, but somehow didn't sound even a smidge amused. "I couldn't be less interested in your social life."

Or lack thereof.

Sam didn't have a social life, but that was none of Violet's business. Besides, she was kind of cute when she was pretending not to care who he played bingo with — *bingo* being a euphemism, obviously.

Sam knew a jealous woman when he saw one. He bit back a smile.

"Stop that," she said, waving one of her delicate hands in the general direction of his face. Wafts of lemon and marshmallow fluff tickled his nose.

He arched a brow. "Stop what?"

Sprinkles chose that most inopportune moment to spring into a running fit, romping in frantic circles around them. Cinder gave chase and suddenly Sam and Violet were thrust against each other, stuck in the whirling eye of a Dalmatian storm.

Sam's body came to immediate attention. He tried his best not to think about Violet's tumbling mermaid hair and sea-glass eyes and tempting scent — the perfect blend of tart and sweet. But as usual, she was impossible to ignore.

"Stop what?" he said again, swallowing hard.

She peered up at him through her thick fringe of eyelashes.

"Stop looking at me like . . ." Her gaze flitted to his mouth for a telltale second, and her cheeks flared as pink as the giant spinning cupcake that sat atop her food truck. ". . . like you think I want you to . . . to . . ."

Sam couldn't breathe. He didn't dare move, not even to try and stop the Dalmatian excitation going on around them. He had no idea why Cinder seemed to think it was okay to embark on a game of chase when she was on duty. Perhaps Sam's thus-far-unsuccessful attempts at getting her to stop making his bed and turning on the coffee maker had loosened his dog's inhibitions. He couldn't focus on that right now — he couldn't focus on much of *anything,* because every thought in his head was wrapped around the unspoken ending to Violet's sentence.

Like I think you want me to kiss you?

He couldn't say it. Both of them might be thinking it, but saying it aloud would make the nonsensical feelings swirling between them impossible to ignore. The smart thing to do — the *safe* thing — would be to politely excuse himself and return to the harmless world of senior citizens and sponge-tipped bingo daubers.

But for once in his life, Sam didn't feel like being safe.

"Like I think you want me to kiss you?"

There. He'd said it. And he wasn't sorry — on the contrary, the moment the words left his mouth, a surge of satisfaction swelled inside his chest, so potent, so damn delicious that he found himself lowering his mouth . . . closer . . . closer . . . and closer toward Violet's.

Just a taste. Only one, to get it out of our systems.

Violet's lips parted, an invitation.

What's the worst that could happen? Sam thought, only vaguely aware that Cinder and Sprinkles had stopped running in circles to cock their heads and watch the insanity that was about to transpire. It didn't matter. Nothing did. When Violet rose up on tiptoe and brushed her soft lips against his, Sam's eyes drifted closed, but something inside of him seemed to crack wide open. And then he was consumed with warmth, because kissing Violet was like trying to hold concentrated sunlight in his hands — an elusive bundle of joy and heat, as beautiful as it was potentially destructive.

In certain conditions, such energy could smolder and burn, but the old Sam hadn't been afraid of fire. Once upon a time, he'd run toward it while others fled.

Maybe that part of him wasn't so lost after all, because wild Dalmatians couldn't have dragged him away from kissing Violet March.

Violet had hauled Sam into the nearest enclosed space she could find to give him a piece of her mind and emphatically deny the accusation that she could be jealous, so she wasn't quite sure how she'd ended up kissing him instead. But to be honest, she wasn't complaining.

What was it about him that she found so horribly offensive, again? For the life of her, she couldn't remember. From the second the Dalmatians had begun running circles around them, effectively tossing her straight into Sam's broad chest, Violet's brain had turned to mush. She'd forgotten all about convincing him that she didn't care who he played bingo with, probably because she *did* care. Very much.

And then he'd let his gaze linger on her mouth just long enough for her entire body to clench in anticipation. The waiting was the most exquisite form of torture she'd ever experienced. Every cell in her body seemed to hold its breath, her head spun, and all she could think about was how good it would feel to finally let her guard down around this man whom she'd tried oh-so-hard to resist. Honestly, she deserved a medal for holding out as long as she had.

Maybe the Charlie's Angels were right. Maybe Sam wasn't so bad after all — her growing pile of fire code citations notwithstanding. His Dalmatian clearly adored him, so he couldn't be *all* bad.

Violet would just have to see for herself. Just this once. Surely no harm could come from one tiny moment of weakness. She and Sam could go back to hating one another tomorrow . . . or the next day . . . Saturday at the absolute latest, since that's when the next softball game was scheduled to take place.

But for now, Violet took matters into her own hands and claimed her reward — a kiss. Just one tiny never-to-be-repeated kiss.

Wow, though. If she'd thought giving in to

temptation would finally make it easier to breathe again, she'd never been so wrong. The fluttering she always felt in Sam's presence spilled over into a full-on swoon as his arms slid around her waist, pulling her tighter against him until she could feel his heartbeat crashing against hers. Then the kiss grew deeper, more urgent, and Violet heard one of the Dalmatians whimper.

Wait, no. That sound hadn't come out of Sprinkles or Cinder — it had come from Violet's own lips. And she wasn't the slightest bit sorry or embarrassed. Her thoughts screamed only one agonizing syllable. *More.*

"Hot." Sam groaned into her mouth. "So hot."

If Violet hadn't been so weak in the knees, she would have laughed. No man on planet earth had ever told her she was hot, under any circumstances. Cute, yes. Quirky, always. Hot? Not so much. That adjective was reserved for women like Angelina Jolie, Halle Berry, and Scarlett Johansson, none of whom would be caught dead driving a cutesy cupcake truck.

And then she felt it — licks of heat simmering between them, as fierce as hot sand beneath her bare feet on a smoldering summer day. It was exhilarating and terrifying all at once.

What kind of crazy kiss was this?

An explosion of barks made its way through the fog in Violet's head. With great reluctance, she dragged her eyes open. Something was wrong — very, very wrong.

A tiny flame danced along the cuff of Sam's uniform shirt. He stared down at it as if trying to make sense of what it was doing there while Cinder and Sprinkles stood at attention, barking in alarm.

"Sam?" Violet took a backward step and then realized she was still holding onto her culinary torch, the obvious culprit.

Oh goodness, she'd set Sam on literal fire. During that delicious clench of anticipation, she must have accidentally squeezed the ON button.

"Stop, drop, and roll," she blurted.

Amazing. Apparently, she'd actually learned something at Cinder's cute little fire safety demonstration.

"What's going on?" Sam frowned down at his flaming shirt sleeve.

The poor man. Violet had clearly kissed all the common sense right out of him.

"You're on fire," she said, but Cinder and Sprinkles had started barking so loudly that she wasn't sure he could hear her above the commotion.

"Stop, drop, and roll!" she shouted, panic

209

coiling low in her belly.

Cinder immediately dropped to the ground and rolled over. Violet would have rolled her eyes if she hadn't been on the verge of tears.

Then the door to the tiny office swung open, and Griff Martin poked his head inside. "Is everything okay in here?"

So not okay.

But as Violet glanced at Griff filling up the doorframe, she spotted a small fire extinguisher in the corner of Barbara's office. *Yes!*

"What the . . . ?" Griff paused a beat before springing into action and running toward Sam, leaping over the Dalmatians.

Violet beat him to it, though. She dropped the culinary torch and snatched the fire extinguisher from the wall. Hands shaking, she yanked the pin and aimed the nozzle at Sam. She squeezed hard and fine white powder sprayed in all directions, coating pretty much everything in Barbara's office — the desk, the chair, the maracas and tambourines, both uniformed firefighters, and the Dalmatians too, of course. She kept spraying anyway — just to be sure. Plus she wasn't quite sure how to stop. Sam probably needed to add fire extinguisher instructions to his and Cinder's cute demonstration.

Griff planted his hands on his hips. Violet was pretty sure it was Griff, anyway. It was kind of hard to tell, since both men were covered in a thick layer of white. "Release the handle."

Violet relaxed her grip and the fire extinguisher stopped with a sudden hush. Everything was fine, thank goodness. Messy, but fine. The Dalmatians were both sneezing, but Sam was no longer on fire. He was standing right there, completely unharmed, scowling at her like he always did.

Violet had saved the day!

Well, sort of. There was still the teensy problem that she'd been the one who'd started the fire in the first place.

"Um." Violet felt sick to her stomach all of a sudden. The fire extinguisher slipped from her hands and fell to the floor with a clang. She shook her head. "I'm sorry. It was an accident — a terrible, terrible accident. Obviously."

Sam's only reply was stony silence. Cinder pranced at his feet and nudged his hand with her head until he gave her a reassuring pat. *Don't worry,* the gesture seemed to say. *I'm fine. Everything's okay.*

Violet would have given anything to trade

places with the Dalmatian in that moment.

Griff glanced back and forth between Violet and Sam. "What exactly happened in here?"

Sam took a deep breath and then bent to pick something up off the floor — Violet's little culinary torch, which had indeed turned out to be an incendiary device. He held it up and arched an accusatory brow.

A chorus of gasps followed, and only then did Violet notice the crowd of people hovering around the doorway. Senior citizens, sunburned tourists, and any and all manner of bingo enthusiasts gaped at Violet in abject horror. Ethel, Opal, and Mavis were right up front, shaking their heads in dismay.

"Violet, dear," Mavis said, "might you have accidentally set Marshal Nash on fire?"

Violet's throat went thick. Something told her there was definitely another pink citation coming her way.

An hour later — after Sam and Griff had cleaned every last trace of dry powder from the fire extinguisher out of Barbara Nichols' office and after Hazel the librarian had offered to give Sam mouth-to-mouth even though he was fully upright and the only part of him that had been touched by fire had been his shirt sleeve — Sam sat alongside Griff at a worn wooden picnic table at the end of the Salty Dog Pier. A small cooler full of frosted bottles of beer sat between them, along with two brown paper bags containing Turtle Beach's most treasured delicacy: boiled peanuts.

Frankly, damp nuts of any kind hadn't sounded at all appetizing to Sam. But Griff wouldn't take no for an answer. Crazily enough, he'd been right. They were delicious. Maybe there was hope for Sam becoming a true Turtle Beach local after all.

Did he *want* to become an actual islander, though? Sam's determination to start a new life in Turtle Beach was beginning to waver. Something about being set on fire at bingo night had given him serious pause.

"You sure you're all right, bro?" Griff took a long pull from his beer.

"Fine. I told you, I'm not even burned," Sam said.

He would, however, be pitching his uniform shirt in the trash. It was probably still wearable, but he didn't particularly want a scorched reminder of his mortifying lapse of judgment.

What's the worst that could happen?

He'd tempted fate by asking himself that very question. Never in his wildest dreams did he imagine he'd end up in flames.

"You sure? I noticed you keep flexing your fist." Griff waved a peanut shell in the direction of Sam's right hand.

"Writer's cramp," Sam said through gritted teeth.

After the disastrous kiss he'd shared with Violet and the chaos that followed, bingo night had proceeded as usual. As the caller yelled out letter and number combinations, Sam had written out half a dozen additional citations to Violet. Overkill? Perhaps, according to Griff.

Sam disagreed. Vehemently. She'd set him *on fire.* If that wasn't worthy of a stack of pink tickets and a few hefty fines, Sam didn't know what was.

"Writer's cramp." Griff snorted. "That's pretty funny."

Sam wasn't amused in the slightest. He sighed and tossed a peanut to one of the seagulls swooping and diving overhead.

"Don't you think you were a little hard on her, though? I know she's the one who started the fire, but she's also the one who put it out." Griff shot Sam a meaningful look.

He was right, of course — which was the most upsetting part of the entire ridiculous ordeal. Sam had been so caught up in their kiss that he hadn't even noticed what was happening around him. Once he finally did, he'd just stood there. Paralyzed.

What the heck was *wrong* with him?

Maybe he needed to talk to someone, like he had back in Chicago. Maybe moving to a desk job in a small town hadn't been enough — maybe he should have left fire-fighting altogether and pursued something different. Something safe.

But what? Sam wouldn't know what to do with a life that didn't involve firefighting. It *meant* something to him. It always had.

"Yeah, she did," Sam said.

"You know I would have done it, but she got to the fire extinguisher first." Griff shook his head. "Who would have thought?"

Not Sam, that's for sure.

Cinder leaned her warm, spotted form against his leg. Since they were off the clock, Sam offered her a peanut. Her black nose twitched, but she refused to take it.

She's worried about me. Sam swallowed. Even his own dog knew he was in trouble.

"What are the odds everyone in town will forget about what happened and it won't make the gossip rounds tomorrow?" Sam said.

"Zero, my dude." Griff grinned into his beer. "Absolutely zero."

Sam's phone chimed with an incoming

text. Had the rumor mill started already?

He pulled the phone from his pocket and snuck a glance, fully expecting to see a reprimand of some sort from Chief Murray pop up on his screen. The message wasn't from Murray, though. It was from Jameson Dodd, Sam's fire chief back in Chicago.

Don Evans just turned in his notice of retirement.

Interesting. Don Evans was his old department's fire marshal. He had a good five or six years to go before he was eligible for a full pension, so he must have decided to take an early retirement package.

Another text popped up on the screen.

The job is yours if you want it.

Sam went still.

When he'd left Chicago, it had been for good. He'd had no intention of ever going back.

Not that he had any ill will toward Jameson or any of his other former colleagues. Jameson had been like a surrogate father for years, especially after Sam's father had died from a heart attack five years ago. Sam would have laid down his life for anyone at his old station in a heartbeat. He still would . . . especially if it meant he could undo all that had gone wrong in that last fire.

He'd just needed to start over again someplace new — someplace that wasn't steeped in loss and painful memories. Someplace where he could keep to himself. Turtle Beach was supposed to be the beginning of a simple, stress-free life with no emotional attachments.

Of course that had been before Sam realized that the only reason Murray had hired him was because he'd been a college baseball star.

It had also been before he made the mistake of kissing Violet March.

"You know how to stop small-town gossip in its tracks, don't you?" Griff gestured toward Sam's phone with his beer bottle.

Clearly he'd assumed the text had been about the latest bingo night fiasco. Sam opted not to correct the misconception. There was no reason to tell his new friend about a job offer he had no interest in accepting.

"How?" Sam asked.

"You just give everyone something else to talk about. It's as simple as that." Griff shrugged. "Hitting a few home runs at the game on Saturday would definitely do the trick. If there's one thing Turtle Beach loves more than gossip, it's softball."

A few homers.

Sam could definitely arrange that. Maybe he'd go up to Wilmington and hit some balls at the batting cages before Saturday's game. Maybe he'd take a few of the guys from the fire station with him and teach them a thing or two. He *did* have a bet to win.

"This town is nuts," Sam said. "You realize that, don't you?"

"Everyone does," Griff said. He pulled another bottle of beer from the cooler and offered it to Sam. "But it's home."

Is it?

Sam took the beer and twisted the cap off it. There was another gull hovering overhead, angling for a peanut. He tossed one up in the air, and his phone chimed with another incoming text from his old boss in Chicago.

Evans's last day is next month. You've got thirty days to decide.

And then one last message, just as Sam was sliding his phone out of view.

Give it some thought. Maybe it's time for you to come on home, son.

Chapter 11

In the days following the minor fire at bingo night — emphasis on *minor,* because really, Violet had seen votive candles with a bigger flame — Violet did her best to avoid Sam Nash.

He made it annoyingly easy.

They didn't cross paths anywhere — not at the senior center, not at the dog beach, not at any of the local businesses lined up on either side of Seashell Drive. The only thing more irritating than his constant judgmental presence was his sudden absence. Where on earth was he hiding?

Violet didn't have a clue, nor did she care . . . except that she was still waiting for a proper thank you. She had, after all, saved the man's life. There'd been two firefighters in the room — three if you counted Cinder, which seemed legit since she was an official working dog and all — and Violet had been the one who'd extinguished Sam's flaming shirt sleeve.

No one seemed to care about that, though — probably because she'd also been the one who'd set the fire in the first place. But that had been a smooch-related accident, and it would never happen again. *Ever.*

Violet couldn't even think about the kiss without wanting to put a paper bag over her head and hide for the rest of her life. *Hot . . . so hot.* She'd actually thought Sam had been referring to her when he'd said those things when in fact the man had been on fire. How could she have been so foolish?

"No more kissing," she said as she piped frosting onto a tray of cherry vanilla cupcakes.

The second game of the Guns and Hoses softball tournament was set to start in half an hour, and Violet was ready. She'd decorated dozens of cupcakes to look like softballs, complete with tiny red "stitching" she'd meticulously piped with her most delicate pastry tip. She'd also created a completely new blueberry–lemon cake recipe for her Team Blue cupcakes in support of the TBPD. She'd even gone to the blueberry farm just over the bridge yesterday and picked all the berries herself, because that was the sort of thing that serious bakers did.

Violet didn't need a cranky-pants fireman in her life, no matter how great a kisser he was or how much he loved Dalmatians. She was a career woman. A lady boss. Wherever Sam had been and whatever he'd been doing the past four days, ten hours, and thirty-five minutes was none of her concern.

"No. More. Kissing," she said again. It was her new mantra. Violet might never kiss another living soul for as long as she lived.

Except for Sprinkles, obviously. That was a given.

Violet glanced at her Dalmatian, sulking from the confines of her new dog crate at the far end of the cupcake truck. Poor thing. She missed lounging in her window seat, but Violet wasn't taking a chance on her dog making another wild run around the bases. Sprinkles was just going to have to take one for the team, so to speak.

"Don't worry." Violet wiggled her fingers through the bars of the crate. Sprinkles gave them a mournful lick. "This is only temporary, I promise."

"Mercy me, why is Sprinkles in jail?" Mavis's voice drifted through the open window of the cupcake truck as Violet washed her hands.

Violet smoothed down her best frilly apron and headed toward the order counter.

"She's not in jail," Violet countered, although actually, it sort of looked like a doggy jail cell. At least it was pink and therefore totally on-brand for Sweetness on Wheels. "Sprinkles is just taking a little break in her new den until the game is over in case Sam tries to lure her out of the food truck with his magic clicking sounds."

"Magic clicking?" Mavis snorted. "Is that the secret to Sam's popularity?"

Violet wasn't taking the bait, not this time. She was tired of talking about Sam Nash — almost as much as she was tired of thinking about him.

"No more kissing," she muttered under her breath.

Mavis's eyes narrowed. "What was that, dear?"

"Nothing." Violet dusted a fine layer of sugar from her hands. *Nothing at all.* "Where are Opal and Ethel? They're coming to the game, aren't they?"

Violet hoped so. She wanted everyone in town to witness the crushing defeat of the fire department.

"Of course. They wouldn't miss it. They're in the bleachers, snagging seats in the front row." Mavis waved a hand toward the grandstands. From his perch in the basket of Mavis's walker, Nibbles the Chihuahua shivered in agreement. "I was hoping to chat with you in private for a minute."

"Oh." Violet looked up from her buttercream. "What's up?"

She wondered if Mavis wanted advice on the little flirtation she had going with Larry Sims, *Jeopardy!* enthusiast extraordinaire. Then again, why would anyone come to Violet for dating advice?

The memory of Sam's voice rose from her consciousness. *So hot . . .*

A messy blob of frosting came flying from her pastry bag and sailed straight through the pink bars of Sprinkles's prison/crate and landed on the tip of Sprinkles's nose. The Dalmatian's tail beat against the inside of the crate in stunned surprise as she licked it away.

"Oops." *Focus!* Violet set the pastry bag down and tried her best to concentrate on her friend. "What were you saying, again?"

"I started volunteering at the senior center's library," Mavis said. "We're organizing all of the old issues of the *Turtle Beach Gazette* into binders for easy reading, and I came across something I thought you might like to see."

Mavis reached into her handbag, nestled beside Nibbles in her walker basket. She pulled out a neatly folded bundle of newsprint and slid it across the counter of the food truck's order window toward Violet.

The paper was yellowed with age, but otherwise in pristine condition. Violet wasn't surprised. The residents of the senior center had enormous respect for the history of Turtle Beach. In so many ways, they were the glue that held their little oceanside community together.

Violet unfolded the paper, and the first thing she noticed was the date printed in the upper right-hand corner — December 25, 1982. Christmas Day, ten years before Violet had been born. A border of holly leaves surrounded the words *Local News* just below the banner, followed by a headline. *Scenes from Christmas Eve in Turtle Beach.*

Violet scanned the photos, which included a lovely shot of the town Christmas tree in the gazebo by the boardwalk, where it had been placed every year for as long as Violet could remember. There was a cute picture of a group of kids surrounding a "snowman" made from sand on the beach side of the island, topped with a Santa hat, along with a shot of a group of surfers dressed in Santa suits riding a wave. Violet felt herself smile, and then her gaze drifted further and her breath caught in her throat.

"It's my mother." The newspaper shook in Violet's hand. "And Polkadot! I've never seen this picture before."

"I didn't think you had, and I knew you'd like it." Mavis's eyes twinkled. "Polkadot was just a tiny puppy, see?"

The dog's tiny black-and-white spotted form was curled into the crook of Adeline March's elbow — except Violet's parents hadn't gotten married until the following year, 1983, so she'd still been Adeline Sterling back then. She looked so young, smiling up at Violet from the faded newspaper. So happy.

"Look." Violet squinted at the picture. "Polkadot has a big bow around her neck. Do you think she was a Christmas gift?"

Violet had always assumed her mother had adopted Polkadot, the way that Violet had rescued Sprinkles. From what her brothers had told her, Adeline was a big animal lover. She was one of the founding members of the Turtle Beach Sea Turtle Rescue Project and helped babysit turtle nests on autumn nights in order to help turtle hatchlings make it safely from the sand to the water's edge. It had never occurred to her that someone may have given her Polkadot as a present.

"Maybe." Mavis shrugged. Did she seriously not remember, or was she simply reluctant to talk about it, just like Violet's dad? "I should probably go join Ethel and Opal. You keep that, dear. Just don't tell anyone where it came from."

Violet pressed the newspaper to her heart. "Are you sure? Don't you need it for the binders at the senior center library?"

"I don't think that one small section of a single day of the *Gazette* is going to make much of a difference. Besides, something tells me you need it more than the library does." Mavis flashed Violet a wink before steering her walker in the direction of the bleachers.

Violet's chest filled with warmth. Part of her thought she should return the photo to the senior center, but another part — the sweet, sentimental part that was constantly trying to drag more information about Adeline out of her father — was already planning on framing it and hanging it in a place of honor in her wing of the beach house.

She took a closer look at the black-and-white picture. Her mother wore jeans and an oversized fuzzy sweater that draped off one shoulder, the epitome of '80s fashion. The smile on her face was so huge that it stretched from ear to ear. Polkadot couldn't have been more than eight or nine weeks old. The bow tied around the baby Dalmatian's neck looked comically huge in comparison.

The dog *had* to be a Christmas gift. Was it possible her mother had just been given the dog right before the picture was taken?

Violet was dying to know. She was mesmerized by the photo — so mesmerized that when someone greeted her from the other side of the order window in a familiar masculine voice, she jumped.

"Hello." It was Sam, at long last. Cinder stood loyally by his side, as usual.

Violet accidentally smiled at him. *Ugh.* "Good morning. I haven't seen you around much the past few days. I was beginning to think you'd scooted back to Chicago."

A girl could dream, right?

Although the thought of Sam moving away didn't give her the jolt of elation that she might have expected it would. In fact, the prospect made her feel slightly sick to her stomach for some inexplicable reason. The words *no more kissing* swirled in her head, and it took superhuman effort not to stare directly at his mouth.

"No." He shook his head, his expression a perfect blank, as usual. "I've just been busy getting the team in shape for today's game."

Oh. Violet blinked. *Look who suddenly cares about softball.*

Sam's unprecedented enthusiasm for the game was her fault, of course. Nothing like a friendly wager and the prospect of dressing up like a cupcake to light a fire under a man — figuratively speaking of course. (This time.)

"That's . . . great." *No need to worry. The police department will win. They* have *to win.* "Can I get you a cupcake?"

"No, thanks. I was just walking past and you seemed like you might need someone to talk to . . ." His voice drifted off and he cast a glance at the newspaper still clutched tightly in her hands.

Violet practically had to bite her tongue to keep from telling Sam about Mavis's find. She was desperate to share the picture with someone, and Sam had seemed genuinely interested when she'd told him about the other photographs she'd found of Adeline and Polkadot.

But she didn't want to get Mavis in any sort of trouble, and Sam was the absolute last person she should be confiding in. They were adversaries. Competitors. Sworn enemies.

"I'm fine." She slid the newspaper out of sight. "Everything is great."

"Great," Sam echoed. His gaze drifted over her shoulder for a second, and his brow furrowed.

Violet tilted her head. "What?"

"Nothing," Sam said.

"No, really. I can tell you want to say something else." She crossed her arms over her ruffled apron. "Go ahead."

He frowned and said nothing for a prolonged moment before finally shaking his head. "Nope. Never mind. I think it's best if I just drop it."

Aha! So there *was* something he wanted to say. She *knew* it. "Now you have to tell me."

"Violet." He was on the verge of walking away. Violet could tell. Why did he have to be so infuriating all the time?

She held up her hands. "Fine. It's okay. You don't have to say it. We both know what this is about."

"We do?"

"Of course. You're trying to thank me." Violet shrugged. "Like I said, I get it."

Sam's eyes narrowed. "You think I'm trying to thank you? For what, exactly?"

She waved a hand. "For saving your life, silly."

An incredulous laugh burst from Sam's mouth. "Unbelievable. Have you forgotten that you *set me on fire?*"

Violet glanced at Cinder. *A little help here?* But the Dalmatian's expression was as neutral as Switzerland.

She cleared her throat. "If you don't want to thank me, then why are you hesitating to say whatever is on your mind? Has the Dalmatian got your tongue?"

He looked at her like she'd lost her mind. Maybe she had. "That's not an expression."

"You know what I mean."

"I do, which in and of itself is cause for concern." He pressed hard on his temples, as if speaking her language was the worst thing that could possibly happen to him. "For the record, thanking you was the last thing on my mind."

She didn't believe him for a second. "Oh, yeah? Then what was it that you wanted to say?"

He pointed to a spot somewhere behind her, in the depths of the cupcake truck. "You're in violation of the fire code. Again."

Violet felt her mouth drop open.

Seriously? She'd thought he was brimming with unspoken gratitude when in fact he'd once again been looking for reasons to issue more of those annoying citations.

Violet was mortified to her core. The only thing that would have been more humiliating was if Sam Nash, the world's most efficient fire marshal, had forgotten about their kiss.

Had he forgotten about it? By all appearances he had, while Violet had been reliving it every time she closed her eyes.

Hot . . . so hot. She'd give anything to get those aching words out of her head for good.

"It's your extension cords." Sam motioned toward her power strip and the tangle of cords plugged into it. "They're not commercial grade, and you're not supposed to use multiple strings like that. The North Carolina fire code has specific requirements for power cords on food trucks, so technically, you've got two violations."

Of course she did.

Violet wanted nothing more than to offer up a snappy comeback, but she was at a loss. Was Sam's home wallpapered with the Turtle Beach fire code? How did he come up with all these violations off the top of his head? The mind reeled.

"What's the matter, sweetheart?" Sam lifted an eyebrow. "Dalmatian got your tongue?"

Sam was winning — not just the ongoing Dalmatian war with Violet, but also the softball game. The past few nights spent at the batting cages with his colleagues had paid off. Big time. Nearly every chance the TBFD had on deck, a firefighter knocked one out of the park.

The game ended at 6–2, in favor of the fire department. Chief Murray was elated beyond all description. In a rare breach of protocol, he'd accompanied the team to Island Pizza after the game, where the firefighters sat on one side of the restaurant and the police officers sat on the other. Gone was the casual camaraderie of the previous week. The members of the Guns team seemed shell-shocked. *What just happened?* their stunned expressions seemed to say.

Sam happened. That seemed to be Chief Murray's takeaway. In the ultimate power move, he stood on a chair at Island Pizza and named Sam the MVP of the entire tournament even though they potentially still had three more games left to play. When one of the police officers called BS, Murray shrugged it off. After all, the Hoses just needed to win one more game to lock up the championship. If next Saturday looked anything like today, the tournament trophy would soon have a new place of honor in the firehouse.

Sam accepted the praise of his boss and

numerous pats on the backs from Griff and the rest of the team with a certain degree of discomfort. He wasn't sure why he felt so uneasy about the hoopla surrounding their victory.

Liar.

Okay, fine. He had a pretty good idea why the accolades didn't sit well. Throughout the entire pizza party, Violet sat with her usual group of friends from the retirement center, gracious even in defeat. Sam had to give her credit where credit was due. She didn't try and say that the fire department had cheated or blame their victory on a stroke of dumb luck. When Sam had passed her table, she'd shaken his hand and told him he'd played well, but the TBPD would get him next time. That's it. No outlandish trash talk, no name-calling, no setting him on fire.

Sam was — dare he think it — almost disappointed. He'd spotted Sprinkles resting quietly in a fancy pink crate when he'd stopped by the cupcake truck before the game. It was a wise choice, given what happened the previous Saturday. A *responsible* choice. Sam was a big believer in crate-training dogs. Still, the Dalmatian's sad little tail wag had hit him straight in the feels.

What was happening to him? And why did

Violet's grace in the face of defeat remind him so much of Sprinkles's cotton-candy-hued confinement?

He *liked* sparring with Violet, that was why. And God help him, their kiss had been the best thirty seconds of his life, flames and all. Clearly there was something very wrong with him.

Still, he probably should have kept his mouth shut about her extension cords earlier. At minimum, he should have simply given her a verbal warning. But no, he'd whipped out his trusty pad and written her two new citations right there on the spot. Why had he even brought the blasted pad along with him to a softball game, anyway?

You know why.

He was losing it. If he had a lick of sense left, he'd take the fire marshal job in Chicago and leave Turtle Beach and all the accompanying Dalmatian drama in his rearview mirror.

Sam didn't want to move back to Chicago, though. He'd realized as much when he'd come home from the batting cages the past few nights and proceeded to stay up late, unpacking his remaining moving boxes. His clothes were all lined up neatly in his closet. The books on the shelves in the living room were all carefully alphabetized by author.

Sam had even hung a few things on the walls — a framed photograph from Cinder's Medal of Honor ceremony, a picture of Sam's old engine company in front of the firehouse on LaSalle Street, and, in a rare moment of sentimentality, a watercolor painting of Turtle Beach's coastline at sunset.

Sam had picked up the framed piece of art at one of the numerous galleries on the boardwalk while he'd been doing a routine new- business inspection. Something about the painting's delicate hues and soft swirls of color had calmed him. He'd thought hanging it in his new home might make him feel good about the changes he was making in his life.

It wasn't until he'd nailed it to the wall that he'd recognized the location in the watercolor as the dog beach — the exact spot where he'd first encountered Violet March. In fact, if he squinted hard enough, a tiny figure on the horizon definitely looked familiar, as did a spotted dog romping in the waves.

Sam tried not to read too much into it. So he'd accidentally purchased a painting that featured the woman who seemed intent on driving him crazy. It didn't necessarily mean anything.

But the fact that he couldn't stop thinking about her *did* mean something. God, that kiss. Sam had never experienced anything like it. What sort of magic made a man want to keep on kissing a woman while everything around him prepared itself to burn to the ground?

"One more game, eh?" Murray slapped Sam so hard on the back that he nearly choked on a pepperoni. "We can wrap this thing up next weekend. The tournament will be over practically before it started."

All the firefighters around the table whooped in agreement. If there'd been a nearby cooler full of Gatorade, Sam was certain they would have dumped it on his head.

"You're meeting us at the batting cages again this week for practice, right?" Griff said. "Those tips you gave us really helped."

"Sure." Sam nodded. "I think I can do that."

His gaze darted once again to Violet's table. She laughed at something one of her elderly friends said and then took a comically huge bite out of her slice of pizza. Cinder rested her head on Sam's knee with a sigh, and when he glanced down, he realized he wasn't the only one sneaking glances in Violet's direction.

The tournament will be over practically before it started . . .

Victory had never tasted quite so bittersweet.

CHAPTER 12

The following morning, Sam sat at his desk with a renewed sense of purpose. A night of tossing and turning had ended with a revelation as he guzzled coffee in the morning and watched Cinder drag his tangled sheets neatly into place. Violet March was a distraction, plain and simple.

Perhaps that was oversimplifying things, as there was nothing remotely plain nor simple about her. But she was definitely a distraction. Luckily for Sam, years of training Cinder to be the perfect fire dog had taught him plenty about eliminating unwanted diversions.

He just needed to focus. He needed to practice redirecting his attention to other things every time the memory of kissing Violet's perfectly impertinent mouth invaded his thoughts.

Sam could do this. He was *great* at this sort of thing. He'd literally been awarded medals for it. If he'd taught Cinder how to ignore distractions with nothing but a firm tone and a pocket full of bacon treats, surely he could manage to control himself in Violet's presence.

He knew just how to start. Step 1: Become so busy that he didn't have time to think about anything else besides fire prevention. After all, that was why he'd moved to Turtle Beach in the first place.

The fire station on Seashell Drive wasn't exactly a hive of activity, but that didn't matter. Sam wasn't at the mercy of the fire alarm like the rest of the guys were. He could do surprise inspections. He could pop into local businesses and examine their floor plans, their fire extinguishers, and emergency exit plans. He could write citations to people who didn't have perfectly tousled blonde mermaid hair and who didn't wear pink frilly aprons. And he would . . . starting right now.

As luck would have it, just as Sam started crafting a to-do list that was sure to keep him busy for at least a week, Griff popped his head into the office.

"There's a call for you in dispatch," he said, drumming his fingers on the door frame.

"In dispatch? For me?" Calls that came in

on the dispatch line were usually emergencies, and Sam didn't do emergencies. Not anymore.

He gripped the edge of his desk as his heart pounded so hard that his throat grew thick.

Griff shrugged. "It's one of the ladies from the senior center. She asked for you personally — something to do with the sprinkler system."

Sam relaxed ever so slightly. "I've got it, thanks."

"Sure thing," Griff said.

Sam picked up the phone and punched the button with the blinking red light. "Sam Nash."

"Hi, Marshal Nash. This is Ethel Banks. I'm not sure if you remember me, but I'm one of the residents at the senior center."

"I remember," Sam said. If memory served, Ethel was one of Violet's trio of friends . . . not that Sam was thinking about Violet. "Is everything okay down there, Mrs. Banks?"

"Oh, dear. You can call me Ethel. Everyone does," she tittered.

Sam leaned forward and planted his elbows on his desk. "Okay, then, Ethel. What can I do for you this morning?"

"It's the fire sprinklers. They need to be

inspected." Ethel cleared her throat. "Right now."

Sam frowned to himself. She needed an emergency sprinkler inspection? Something didn't sound quite right. "Are the sprinklers going off right now?"

"Yes. I mean, no." She paused for a beat. "I'm not sure exactly. But you should probably get down here immediately. You're coming, aren't you?"

"Yes, ma'am," Sam said. He'd wanted to keep busy, hadn't he? *Be careful what you wish for.* "I'll be right there."

"Perfect. Oh, and Sam?"

"Yes?"

"Make sure you bring that sweet spotted dog of yours," she said. "And hurry!"

Now Sam was really confused. Why would it be necessary for Cinder to accompany him on an emergency sprinkler inspection?

Never mind. He wasn't even going to ask. What difference did it make? He never went anywhere without his dog.

"Will do."

Sam hung up, grimacing at the phone. He'd wanted to keep busy, but this felt strange. No matter, at least it would get him out of the firehouse for a bit.

"Come on, Cinder." He pushed his chair back from his desk and stood. "Let's go see what's really going on down there."

What was going on down at the senior center had little or nothing to do with the fire sprinklers. That was how things looked at first glance, anyway. Sam entered the building to find fifteen or so retirees in wobbly downward dog positions on colorful yoga mats lined up on the lobby floor.

Violet's gentle yoga class was in session. Super.

Sprinkles eyed Sam from a yoga mat situated right beside Violet's. Cinder let out a delighted little snort. The Dalmatians were clearly happy to see each other.

Sam awkwardly shifted his weight from one foot to the other, trying his best not to stare at Violet's willowy form clad in skintight leggings. He looked anywhere and everywhere until his eyes met Ethel Banks's, who was casting him an upside-down grin from her yoga position.

"Cinder," he muttered, "why do I get the feeling we've been lured here for purposes unrelated to sprinklers?"

"Sam. What are you doing here?" Violet shimmied to her feet, and Sam couldn't help but notice that her cute little toenails were painted the same shade of blue as the famous little boxes from the jewelry store in the famous Audrey Hepburn movie. Just like her charming vintage bicycle.

Attraction percolated between them. Sam could feel it from clear across the crowded lobby. All thoughts of avoiding distraction went right out the window.

"Look, everyone! It's Marshal Sam," one of the residents said. "Are you here for yoga?"

Cinder's tail wagged against Sam's leg.

"I'm afraid not." He twirled his pointer finger overhead in the direction of one of the sprinkler heads on the ceiling. "We're responding to a call about the sprinkler system."

A furrow formed in Violet's forehead. "Really?"

She glanced up at the dry-as-a-bone sprinkler head directly above her.

"Really," Sam said.

Ethel remained suspiciously silent.

Violet crossed her arms. "Honestly, Sam. If you and Cinder want to join the class, just say so."

"We're not here for yoga," he said, trying his best to hammer the point home.

"Then what is it?" She gave him a dry smile. "Are my yoga clothes flammable? Are you about to give me another ticket?"

The crowd of retirees tittered behind him.

Sam had a good mind to leave, but his

sense of professional responsibility prevented him from doing so. He was going to have to write a report on this when he got back to the station. Like it or not, he couldn't leave without taking a look at the sprinkler system.

"As I mentioned before, I'm here to inspect the sprinklers. Carry on with your class." He turned to go, and immediately heard an extra set of Dalmatian paws padding behind him. Sprinkles, no doubt.

"Sprinkles, come back here," Violet said.

Sam knew without bothering to look over his shoulder that the Dalmatian was still trotting behind him. Fine. Sprinkles's antics weren't his problem. She'd be enrolled in obedience lessons soon enough anyway.

After checking in with the receptionist, Sam located the control panel for the sprinkler system. He checked the settings and wiring while Sprinkles danced around Cinder, trying to entice her into a game of chase by rolling onto her back and batting her paws in the air. Cinder remained as stoic and professional as ever, but kept shifting her sweet brown gaze to Sam.

Please, she seemed to say.

Cinder wasn't supposed to play while she was on duty, just as she wasn't supposed to have treats. But Sam's efforts to get her to let loose a little at home had been unsuccessful thus far, so he was tempted to cut her some slack. It would be good for her to act like a regular dog. A few minutes couldn't hurt.

"Go ahead," he said. "Take five, and then we're out of here."

Cinder's mouth curved into a huge doggy grin and she darted toward the lobby with Sprinkles in hot pursuit. Sam's heart gave a little twist. *Good dog,* he thought. She deserved to have a little fun. It wasn't as if they were on a legitimate call. Violet's elderly friends had obviously decided to play matchmaker and decided dialing 911 was the most effective way to do it.

He sighed. Ethel probably wasn't going to like what came next.

The yoga class was transitioning into a pose that Violet called *murder victim* when Sam strode toward Ethel's mat. He didn't know much about yoga and *murder victim* didn't sound very Zen, but he knew better than to question it.

No distractions, remember?

He directed all his attention toward Ethel, who seemed to be purposefully avoiding his gaze. "Can we have a word, please?"

"I can't talk right now. I'm supposed to be dead," she whispered and scrunched her eyes closed tight.

What kind of nutty yoga class was this?

"Sorry, Ethel. I'm afraid it can't wait," Sam said.

Out of the corner of his eye, he spotted Cinder and Sprinkles curled up next to each other on Sprinkles's yoga mat. He couldn't help but smile, but then he noticed Violet watching the dogs too. Her blue-green eyes twinkled until her gaze met Sam's. They both promptly looked away.

"Ethel, we need to chat." If she refused to stand up and have this conversation someplace more private, they'd have to do it right there. Sam squatted beside her mat. "Did you call in a false report about the sprinklers?"

Ethel's eyes flew open. "Of course not. They were malfunctioning. Ask Mavis and Opal. They'll tell you the same thing."

I'll bet they will.

He narrowed his gaze at her. "How were they malfunctioning?"

A nearby senior citizen shushed him. Sam felt a headache coming on. Then he was enveloped by the delicious scents of warm vanilla and candied sugar as someone gave his shoulder a sharp poke.

Violet, obviously.

She lifted her chin. "Is there a problem

over here?"

Sam's stomach growled, and he prayed no one heard it. One of these days, he was going to get to eat one of her cupcakes, even if he had to do so in secret. "I've got it under control. Feel free to get back to serial killer pose."

"You mean murder victim pose," she said.

He rolled his eyes. "Of course. What was I thinking? Murder victim pose."

"You haven't answered my question. What's going on over here?" Violet glanced back and forth between Sam and Ethel.

"Are you going to tell her or shall I?" Sam asked Ethel.

"I'm afraid I don't know what you're talking about." Ethel shrugged. "I'm old, remember?"

"Ethel." Violet jammed a hand on her slender hip — not that Sam was looking. "What did you do?"

"I believe she might have called in a false report." Sam cleared his throat. "In an effort to get the two of us together in the same room."

Violet gasped. *"What?"*

Ethel, still flat on her back on the floor, blinked up at them. "That's not true. The sprinklers were acting up. They'll probably start doing it again any minute."

"You know that filing a false report is punishable by a fine, don't you?" Sam said.

"Oh, goody. Another citation." Violet shook her head. "I suppose I should be relieved it's not me this time."

"I have witnesses," Ethel said primly.

"Let me guess — Opal and Mavis?" Violet shifted to face Sam. "Look, I'm sorry. They mean well. They really do. Please don't give Ethel a ticket. I'll talk to —"

Before she could finish, a gush of water exploded from the sprinkler directly overhead. Sam tried to jump backwards, out of its path, but he was too late. Water rained down, spraying both him and Violet from head to toe.

Sam was vaguely aware that they were the only two people being drenched, but he couldn't be certain. He was having trouble tearing his attention away from a very stunned, very wet Violet March. Her strawberry-blonde waves clung to her face, and droplets of water starred her eyelashes. Sam could have drowned right then and there and he wouldn't have cared.

Even so, out of the corner of his eye, he could have sworn he saw Opal Lewinsky and Mavis Hubbard poking a cane at the ceiling. But maybe that was just his imagination playing tricks.

■ ■ ■ ■

"I tried to tell you there was something wrong with the sprinkler system," Ethel said as Violet wiped water from her eyes.

A shiver coursed through Violet. She was freezing . . . and drenched to the bone. What had just happened?

She looked up at a flashing red light above her head. The culprit was situated mere inches away — a sprinkler head that slowed to a soggy drip as soon as Sam hopped onto a chair and somehow wrangled it into submission.

"Mavis. Opal." Sam climbed back down and took a step toward them as water squished from his shoes. He sounded like he was walking around on wet sponges. "Did one or both of you just tamper with the sprinkler head?"

"Don't be ridiculous." Opal snorted, which meant she'd definitely just tampered with the sprinkler. She always snorted when she was telling a fib.

Violet had discovered this little quirk about her friend one night when she and the Charlie's Angels had stayed up late playing poker and drinking frozen margaritas they'd made by spiking drinks from the senior center's slushy machine. Never again. Her hangover the next morning was too much for all the Advil in the world to handle. Those women could drink Violet under the table.

"I didn't see anything," Hoyt Hooper said as he rolled up his yoga mat.

Nearby, another senior yogi shook her head. "Neither did I."

Sam looked around, clearly expecting some sort of corroboration, but all of the assembled retirees seemed to be doing their best to avoid his gaze.

If Sam thought he was going to get one of the residents to tattle on Opal, Mavis, and Ethel, he was fooling himself. As much as everyone in town had fallen for his uber-charming first responder doggy dad routine, they'd never turn on the Charlie's Angels. Opal, Mavis, and Ethel were legends in Turtle Beach. Sam truly didn't know who he was dealing with, did he?

"Never mind," Violet said, teeth chattering. The combination of the senior center's frigid air conditioning and being doused with what had to have been gallons of water wasn't pleasant. "Just write the citations out to me."

What was one more ticket when she had

zero intention of taking any of them seriously?

Sam gave her a look she couldn't quite decipher, but it made her go a little weak in the knees all the same.

Violet wrapped her arms tightly around herself and looked away. "First things first, though. Can anyone get us a blanket? Or at least a towel?"

"Come with me, dears. I've got everything you need in my room." Mavis beckoned them to follow and began guiding her walker toward the hallway just off the lobby.

Sam hesitated.

Violet swished past him and called over her shoulder. "Come on, you know you can't go slogging back to the firehouse like that."

He fell in line behind her with a slosh. *Squish, squish, squish* went his footsteps as they made their way down the hall.

Violet felt her mouth twitch. She pressed her lips together in an effort not to laugh, but she just couldn't help it. She'd seen Sam annoyed on plenty of occasions, but annoyed and wet was a combination she'd yet to witness. It was far more entertaining than she would have imagined.

"Come on in." Mavis pushed the door to her room open and waved them inside.

"There are afghans piled on the sofa. I'll get some towels from the bathroom and put on a kettle of tea."

"I'll put the kettle on. I know where it is," Violet said.

There was zero chance that Mavis was innocent in whatever matchmaking scheme the Charlie's Angels had cooked up, but she was pushing ninety. Violet wasn't about to sit back and let Mavis wait on her and Sam hand and foot.

"I'll get the towels." Sam glanced at Mavis. "If you don't mind showing me where they are?"

Violet smiled to herself as she filled the electric kettle with water. Maybe Sam wasn't entirely terrible, after all. Softball and his over-the-top stance on fire prevention aside, he seemed kind. Chivalrous, even. And yowza, the man could kiss.

But Violet wasn't allowed to think about that. And she certainly wasn't. Not one bit. The riot of goosebumps spreading across her flesh was strictly sprinkler-related.

"Oh, my goodness." Mavis pressed a hand to her chest. Nibbles shivered in her walker basket, eyes going wide. "I forgot something in the lobby."

Sure she did.

Violet and Sam exchanged a glance as he

handed her an enormous fluffy towel.

God bless Mavis and her penchant for fine Turkish cotton. Violet burrowed into the plush terry cloth and felt better at once.

"You two stay here and get warm and dry. I'll be back in a flash." Mavis winked and beat a hasty trail out of the room before either Violet or Sam could object.

Violet took a deep breath. The minute the door closed behind Mavis, the space seemed far too small. Too intimate, which was crazy, considering it was an apartment in a senior living center, filled with hand-knitted granny-square blankets, framed photos of Nibbles the Chihuahua, and a comically large bowl of Werther's Original caramel hard candies. There was nothing whatsoever romantic about the environment . . .

Save for the butterflies that took flight in Violet's abdomen when Sam smiled at her.

"What do you think the odds are that she actually needed to fetch something from the lobby?" he asked.

"Zero." Violet's hand shook a bit as she poured steaming liquid from the kettle into two ceramic mugs from Mavis's cabinet. She added a dash of cream and handed one of the mugs to Sam. "Sorry. I didn't even ask how you take your tea. I'm a little controlling about anything sweet. Just trust me. I defy you to dislike it."

"I wouldn't dare." His mouth hitched into a half grin.

No kissing, remember? Don't even think about it.

Who was she kidding? Her lips went tingly every time she looked at the man. Damn the Charlie's Angels. This was all their fault.

Violet sat down beside Sam on Mavis's small sofa, which she absolutely refused to think of as a love seat. (It was definitely a love seat.) He spread one of the granny square blankets over their laps like they were a pair of octogenarians, and she all but melted. This couldn't be a normal response. Maybe she needed some sort of therapy. Or, good grief, maybe Joe was right. Maybe she really did need to find some friends her own age.

She stared into her cup of tea. "I'm sorry."

Sam's mug paused en route to his mouth. His brow furrowed. "Sorry for what? Nothing about this disaster was your fault."

"I suppose I feel guilty by association." Violet sighed. "They mean well, I promise. They just . . ."

Sam's eyebrows rose. "Care about you an awful lot?"

"I was going to say they tend to meddle, but I like your version better." She sipped her tea. Little by little, she was beginning to feel warm again. "They dote on me. They always have."

"It's because you lost your mother, isn't it?" he said quietly.

Violet's gaze met his. "Yes. Wow, you remember that?"

"Of course I do. I'm not all bad, Violet." He gave her a gentle smile. "I might even let your friends off the hook for today if you can convince them to never pull a stunt like this again."

Violet was tempted to ask him why he was going easy on the Charlie's Angels when he'd been more than happy to give her citation after citation, but she didn't want to spoil the moment — and much to her astonishment, it definitely seemed like a Moment with a capital M. "I'll talk to them."

"Good." He nodded and swallowed a sip from his mug. "This isn't like any tea I've ever tasted before. What is it?"

"Do you like it?"

"Yes, it's fantastic." He took another swallow.

"It's a lemon–lavender blend I bought for Mavis at the farmer's market in Wilmington. I kind of have a thing for culinary lavender. If you like this, you should definitely try my

Earl Grey–lavender cupcakes sometime." Violet had worked on that recipe for months before finally nailing it. It was her favorite on the Sweetness on Wheels menu.

"I'd like that. You realize I've never actually tasted one of your cupcakes?" Sam bumped his thigh playfully against hers.

Violet bumped his right back. "That can't be right."

"It absolutely is." He let out a laugh. "I've come close, but haven't ever bit into one. Something always seems to get in the way. Trust me."

Trust me.

Oh, how Violet wished she could.

"Speaking of my mother . . ." She cleared her throat. What was she doing? She definitely shouldn't be talking to Sam about this. "Do you remember yesterday when you said I looked like I might need someone to talk to?"

"Of course." He nodded and shifted slightly on the tiny love seat. This time, when his thigh came to rest against hers, he left it there.

Violet didn't dare move. Goosebumps pricked her arms again, but she was no longer the slightest bit cold. "Mavis had just given me an old newspaper photograph of my mother with her Dalmatian back when she was just a puppy. I'd never seen it before. I guess it made me sort of melancholy, you know? I love the picture. I've already framed it, but I wish I knew more about the moment it was taken."

Sam studied her. "That's why you were so quiet after the game last night, wasn't it?"

"I suppose so." Violet nodded. "My mind wasn't really much on softball."

Sam gaped at her in mock horror. "Say it isn't so. I thought nothing was more important than softball in Turtle Beach."

She tipped her head back and laughed. "Don't tell anyone. It was just temporary, anyway. I'll be fully prepared to annihilate you on Saturday."

He winked. "Your secret is safe with me."

Their eyes met, and Violet felt so warm and fuzzy that she found herself willfully ignoring the fact that Sam's wet clothes were emblazoned with the Turtle Beach Fire Department's crest. How different would things be if he wasn't a fire marshal, but something else? A pharmacist, a veterinarian, or even a professional baseball player? Anything but her sworn enemy.

"Why did you give up a career in baseball to become a fireman?" she asked.

Sam's smile turned bittersweet. "Joining the Chicago Fire Department was always the plan. My dad was a member of the department, as was my grandfather. I'd wanted to wear that uniform since I was a little kid."

Against her better judgment, Violet let her head drop onto Sam's broad shoulder. Goodness, he smelled amazing — like a beachside bonfire. "Then why did you give it up to move to Turtle Beach?"

It couldn't have been about softball. She might have thought so a week ago, but not now. Now she knew better.

"I just needed a change." Sam's grip on his mug tightened until his knuckles turned white. "That's not the entire truth, actually. We lost a few men in a fire — three of my closest friends. At first, we thought we had it contained. It was a box fire in a mattress factory near Logan Square. The building wasn't up to code, and things went south in a hurry."

Sam's voice sounded rusty, as if he hadn't spoken about the tragedy in a long, long time. If ever. Violet's heart twisted, but she waited for him to continue. There was still so much about Sam that she'd yet to learn, but she knew enough to appreciate the fact that he was opening up to her in a way that wasn't easy for him. It felt like a gift of sorts — beautiful and bittersweet.

He took a deep breath and continued. "Being there just wasn't the same after that. I guess I came here looking for a fresh start."

"I'm so sorry." Violet placed her hand on his knee without even thinking about it.

He covered it with one of his big, warm palms. "Thanks."

"Do you think you've found it?" she asked before she could stop herself.

"Found what?" Sam murmured.

"Your fresh start." Violet tried to smile up at him, but her grin went wobbly. She suddenly couldn't imagine Turtle Beach without Sam and Cinder. In just a few short weeks, they'd become an integral part of the community. As necessary as bingo night or the boardwalk. Saturday softball and dazzling sunsets at the dog beach.

Violet had never seen it coming. She'd been so consumed with one-upping him and denying any possible spark of attraction between them that she'd missed an undeniable truth — Turtle Beach, North Carolina, no longer felt like a one-Dalmatian town. It had changed into something else — something better. Wasn't it funny how adding one more Dalmatian to the mix could change everything?

Which reminded her . . .

Before Sam could answer her question,

Violet flew to her feet, heart pounding. "Where are our dogs?"

CHAPTER 13

The following morning, Sam was a bit worried his most recent lapse in judgment had created a monster. Even so, he had no regrets.

Not many, anyway.

He'd left a large chunk of his heart behind in Mavis Hubbard's room at the senior center. For a few treasured moments, he'd gotten a glimpse of what life in Turtle Beach could be like if there was no nutty feud between the first responders, no Guns and Hoses softball league, and no carefully constructed wall separating himself from the rest of the world. It made no sense, but sitting beside Violet in what felt like his grandmother's old apartment had been the most romantic moment of his life.

Which could only mean one thing: he was falling hard for Violet March.

Sam had even told her about the mattress factory fire, something he'd never talked about with anyone else in Turtle Beach. Not Griff. Not even Chief Murray. As far as everyone on the TBFD was concerned, he'd simply been looking to slow down and move to a department with a slower pace. Murray hadn't asked Sam about the specifics of his time on the Chicago FD during his job interview, and Sam hadn't offered up any unsolicited information. He didn't like talking about the fire — to anyone.

Telling Violet had been different, though. He'd felt a little bit lighter afterward. A little bit freer. He hadn't let his guard down like that in a long, long time.

Letting go had been a mistake, though, as far as the Dalmatians were concerned. When Violet realized the dogs were missing, their brief moment of intimacy had come to an abrupt end. Rightfully so, because Sam hadn't had a clue as to Cinder's whereabouts.

How had he let that happen? Sam had been on duty, for crying out loud. Cinder was his partner, and he should never have let her out of his sight. Not for a second.

Cinder hadn't gotten into any trouble, obviously. Sam and Violet had found the dogs back in the lobby, cuddled up together on the community sofa in front of the senior center's big flat-screen television. It had been tuned to an old black-and-white movie about a dog of dubious heritage who seemed to be some sort of superhero. The Dalmatians had been enthralled, particularly Cinder. Sam still chuckled when he thought about it. Cinder had never taken much interest in television, especially since she'd once been afraid of it. Half an hour in Sprinkles's company had apparently transformed his dog into a couch potato. For a second he'd thought maybe he'd gotten the two lookalike dogs confused, but nope. Sprinkles's trademark cupcake collar was strapped around her spotted neck, as per usual. Even her identification tag was cupcake-shaped.

Sam had only himself to blame for Cinder's newfound love of television. Again, he should never have let Cinder leave his side at the senior center — for the very same reason he hadn't let Violet offer her a treat at bingo night. Cinder was a *working* dog, and they'd supposedly been working yesterday afternoon. Regardless of the veracity of Ethel's call to the station about the fire sprinklers, his visit to the senior center had been official TBFD business. What had he been thinking? Sam may as well have stripped out of his uniform, pulled on a #FreeCinder T-shirt, and called it a day.

"Don't get any ideas," Sam said to his dog as he stumbled toward the coffee maker. Morning light streamed through the windows, bathing the interior of the beach cottage in soft watercolor hues, just like his painting of the dog beach.

Sam paused to take it all in. Beyond the sliding glass doors that led to his deck, the ocean lapped against the shore in gentle, foamy waves. The sea was calm today, and as Sam allowed himself to simply slow down and appreciate the beauty of his surroundings, he realized he felt calm too. There was a stillness in his soul he hadn't felt in months.

Sam didn't want to believe that whatever he might be feeling for Violet March had anything to do with this newfound peace. It just wasn't possible. She was pandemonium personified.

"It's the beach, right?" he said to Cinder. "Everyone feels more at peace at the beach."

Sam glanced down in search of Dalmatian confirmation, but what he found instead was one of his regulation fire department socks dangling from Cinder's mouth.

"What the . . . ?" He blinked. Hard. "Cinder! Drop it."

His Dalmatian spit the sock onto the floor, then let out a squeaky dog yawn.

Sam was stunned. Cinder knew better than to steal socks. She hadn't done such a thing since she was a puppy.

This is your fault, not hers.

Right. Everyone knew the key to training a dog was consistency. Sam had slipped up, and Cinder was taking advantage of his lack of focus. It was a classic rookie mistake.

Never mind the fact that Sam wasn't a rookie.

He drew himself up to his full height and looked at Cinder.

"Yesterday was . . ." *Kind of great, actually.* ". . . a mistake. Everything is back to normal now, got it?"

Cinder cocked her head, which Sam took as a sign of agreement.

He nodded. "Good."

It had been one day. A single call. Surely he hadn't undone years of training in a matter of an hour. Everything was going to be fine.

But when Sam strode back to the kitchen for some much needed caffeine, the coffee maker was stone cold and the pot was empty. He glanced toward his bedroom and sure enough, the bed wasn't made either. Cinder, meanwhile, had stretched out in a sunny spot near the sliding glass door. Her paws were already beginning to twitch as she fell back asleep.

Sam groaned. *Of course.* Cinder's sudden rebellion was all his fault, and not just because he'd left his Dalmatian unattended for a short while yesterday afternoon. For over a week now, he'd been trying to get her to relax at home — no more making the bed, no more turning on the coffee maker. His message had finally sunk in, and now she was confused about Sam's expectations. Now that he'd realized what was going on, it was ridiculously obvious.

Sam had let Violet and her bonkers attempt to start a #FreeCinder movement mess with his head. For the past week and a half, he'd been systematically untraining his Dalmatian.

No more. Sam could make his own coffee and straighten his own bed covers, but when Cinder was on the job, she needed to behave. He couldn't break any more rules, period.

Fortunately, Sam and Cinder had another children's fire safety demonstration scheduled later in the week for a local surf camp. Cinder loved kids, and since their presentation was the new hot ticket on the island, she'd had plenty of practice lately. It should be a piece of cake.

Once he got to the firehouse, Sam busied

himself with paperwork for the first half of the day while Cinder snoozed on her dog bed in the corner . . . mostly. Griff popped in mid-morning to see what time Sam wanted to head out to the batting cages after their shift, and Cinder pawed at his leg until he stopped what he was doing to give her a prolonged head-to-toe scratch.

"Sorry," Sam said. "She's in a mood today."

Cinder rolled onto her back, and Griff rubbed her spotted belly. "Don't apologize. It's good to see her act like an actual dog for a change."

Sam didn't ask Griff what he meant by that comment. He didn't have to — he knew. Sam just hoped his friend didn't have a secret #FreeCinder T-shirt hidden in his locker.

He nearly said so, but before he could get the words out, Violet appeared in the doorway to his office.

A pink bakery box rested in her hands and she wore one of her girly retro dresses that fell around her in a whirl of white cotton, printed all over with ripe red cherries. Sprinkles — dressed in her pink cupcake collar, as usual — stood beside her, wiggling with glee.

"Knock knock." Violet's gaze swiveled

back and forth between Sam and Griff. "I hope I'm not interrupting anything."

Griff waggled his eyebrows. "If you've got cupcakes in that box, you're definitely not interrupting."

"Violet, hi." Sam stood as if he were a flustered teenager greeting his prom date. "Come on in."

Cinder jolted awake and cocked her head. *Yes, I know. I've got no game.*

Once upon a time, Sam could interact with women without a second thought. Of course, that had been before he'd become a self-imposed emotional recluse.

He hadn't been closed off for so long that he'd forgotten how to talk to people, though. And he'd clearly had no trouble whatsoever establishing a rapport with Hazel at the library. No, Sam's social awkwardness was exclusive to Violet-centric interactions. Probably because every time they were together something crazy ensued, and the situation seemed to be getting worse instead of better.

Sam dreaded it almost as much as he looked forward to it.

"We're on our way to the senior center," Violet said, tipping her head toward Sprinkles. The Dalmatian leapt at Sam as if it had been a hundred days since she'd seen

269

Sam instead of a mere eighteen hours. "I made some cupcakes early this morning and thought I'd drop some by."

She set the box down on Sam's desk and tucked a wayward mermaid curl behind her ear. "Earl Grey–lavender."

Was it Sam's imagination, or did Violet seem uncharacteristically nervous too?

He inhaled a ragged breath. She did, and that meant he wasn't the only one experiencing feelings that were strictly off-limits. Something was happening between them — something that went beyond their initial love-hate attraction to one another. Violet felt it too. Sam would have bet money on it.

"Thank you." Sam grinned as he extricated himself from Sprinkles's enthusiastic greeting to lift the lid of the bakery box.

A dozen cupcakes were nestled inside, richly scented with black tea, bergamot, and lavender and topped with a generous swirl of lilac-colored buttercream. A tiny string dangled from each small cake, affixed to a small paper label, giving the effect of teabag immersed in a china teacup. They looked too pretty to eat — painstakingly detailed, edible works of art.

Still, Sam's stomach growled. He was only human. "These are incredible."

Sprinkles dropped into a sit position, so

nearby that her rump landed squarely on Sam's left foot.

"I think someone is developing a little crush on you," Griff said.

"Um . . ." Violet shook her head.

Sam nearly choked. "It's not —"

"Relax, you two. I meant the dog." Griff motioned toward Sprinkles. "That Dalmatian is looking at you like she's the living embodiment of the heart eyes emoji, Sam."

Violet shrugged. "Sprinkles loves everyone. That's why she doesn't need obedience lessons. She's naturally sweet."

Sam and Griff exchanged a glance.

"I'm serious. Sprinkles is a delight. Everyone in town thinks so," Violet said.

Sam wasn't about to disagree, lest she snatch the bakery box away like the last time she'd brought him cupcakes. Although he had to admit, while definitely overstimulated, at least Sprinkles hadn't knocked anything off his desk or tried to ingest a Ping-Pong ball. Yet.

Griff cleared his throat. "Of course they do."

Sam was grateful when his cell phone started to ring, vibrating across the surface of his desk, effectively putting an end to the awkward topic.

"Looks like someone from Chicago FD is

trying to get ahold of you." Griff frowned down at the display on Sam's iPhone. "Hey, isn't that your old department?"

Sam declined the call and shoved his phone in his desk drawer. Jameson Dodd had been texting him every other day about the fire marshal job back in Chicago, and Sam had yet to respond. Apparently, his old chief had now resorted to calling, which meant he was serious about luring Sam back to Illinois. Chief Dodd hated talking on the phone.

"I'm sure it's nothing important." Sam scrubbed at the back of his neck. He was beginning to sweat. His small office wasn't meant for three people and two Dalmatians.

"I won't keep you," Violet said.

Stay. Please. Why couldn't Griff take a hint and make himself scarce?

"Consider the cupcakes a thank you for not dragging Opal, Ethel, and Mavis off to fireman jail."

Sam chuckled. "Fireman jail?"

"Yeah, that's not a thing," Griff said. "Violating the fire code is the same thing as breaking the law. Same fines, same penalties, same jail."

"Oh, wow." Violet's forehead scrunched. "In that case, I should have made you *two* dozen cupcakes."

"This is more than enough." Sam smiled, and warmth filled him like a fiery beach sunrise. He'd have given anything to be back on Mavis's loveseat with Violet's head resting on his shoulder again. "Thank you."

"Wait a minute." Griff pointed to Violet, then to Sam and then back to Violet again. "Aren't you two supposed to be enemies?"

Sam ventured a cautious glance at Violet, and she blinked, seemingly speechless. There was a first time for everything, apparently.

"I —" Sam started to say.

I don't think so.

They'd moved past all that, hadn't they?

Cinder rose from her dog bed and went to stand beside Violet as if to imply that if Sam and Violet were on opposing teams, she fully intended to defect. Great, a Dalmatian desertion.

"Yes." Violet gave a firm nod. "Absolutely."

"That's what I thought." Griff reached for a cupcake.

Sam had the almost irresistible urge to snatch it out of his hand. He crossed his arms instead and nodded.

"Still enemies," he said flatly.

"Totally," Violet said. "Arch-enemies, even."

Okay, then. Maybe they weren't past the

asinine feud after all.

Sam's body went leaden. The thought of eating an Earl Grey cupcake suddenly made him sick to his stomach.

"Right. It was nice to see you, *nemesis.*" Violet lifted her chin. "But I should really be going. I'll see you two on Saturday at the softball diamond. Prepare to be crushed."

She spun on her kitten heels and marched out of the office, but Sprinkles stubbornly stayed put, because of course she did. Cinder looked as if she might follow after Violet until Sam pointed at her.

Don't you dare.

Griff smirked and motioned toward Sprinkles with his half-eaten cupcake. "I told you someone has a crush on you."

Sam had no clue if he was still talking about the Dalmatian or Violet herself — not even when she returned and had to physically drag Sprinkles away.

As wrong as it might be, he wished it were the latter.

Violet would have sprinted out of the firehouse if she hadn't been forced to haul Sprinkles away from Sam's office in a heap of spots and indignation. Honestly, was just an ounce of devotion too much to ask?

"It's okay, Sprinkles." Violet forced a smile

as she huffed to a stop on Seashell Drive. "Everyone loves you, so of course you love everyone back. I forgive you."

Did her dog have to like Sam quite so much, though? Griff was right. It was a full-blown case of Dalmatian fascination.

Violet understood. She wasn't exactly immune to Sam's charms herself, and now, to her utter mortification, Griff had noticed. The last thing Violet needed was for the entire TBFD softball team to think she was swooning over Sam Nash every time he got up to bat . . .

Even though she sort of was.

"Vi?" a pair of familiar twin voices said in unison.

Oh, great. Just who I need to bump into on the sidewalk outside the firehouse. Violet closed her eyes and took a deep breath before turning around to face her brothers. "Hi, Joe. Josh. What are you two doing out here? Shouldn't you be out protecting and serving and all that?"

Josh hitched a thumb in the direction of a police cruiser parked by the curb. "We're about to go park by the bridge with the radar gun. The Fourth of July crowds are already descending, and you know how they get."

Violet nodded. The Fourth was always the

busiest time of year on the island. Beach house rentals filled up months in advance, the town put on a big fireworks show over the water near the boardwalk, and the Guns and Hoses championship game always took place earlier in the day — unless the tournament was a blowout and a championship game wasn't necessary. But that hadn't happened in years.

And it wouldn't happen this summer, either. Not if Violet could help it.

"More important," Joe said, casting a purposeful glare at the fire station, "what are you doing here, Vi?"

Violet shrugged, doing her best to feign nonchalance. "Sprinkles and I are on our way to the senior center to see the Charlie's Angels."

Joe's eyes narrowed. "By way of Sam Nash's place of employment?"

"We heard you carried cupcakes inside the firehouse a little bit ago," Josh said. "Everyone did. This is a small island, remember?"

Too small, obviously.

"We also heard that you *took a shower* with Sam yesterday?" Joe jammed his hands on his hips.

Violet let out an incredulous laugh. "I'll own up to the cupcakes but we absolutely did *not* take a shower together. Where on earth are you two getting your information?"

Josh shook his head. "Never mind that. You've got some explaining to do."

"No, I don't. I'm a grown-up, remember? I don't need your permission to drop off a box of cupcakes, and it's my business who I shower with." Her ears felt impossibly hot all of a sudden, even though a cool, salty breeze had rolled in with the morning tide. The seagrass lining the sidewalk danced and swayed. "Not that we did that. Again, just to be clear, we didn't. Sam and I got doused in a fire sprinkler accident. It was completely innocent."

"Still." Josh frowned. "We don't like it, Vi. Not at all."

Joe heaved out a sigh. "Didn't I tell you to stay away from him?"

Sprinkles — good girl that she was — snorted in apparent derision.

Violet rested her palm on the Dalmatian's sweet head and squared her shoulders. "You've got to stop. I might have been a bit naive in the past, but that was my mistake. *Mine.* You can't keep hovering like this."

"Can't I?" Josh said, casting another death-glare toward the fire station.

Things were getting out of hand. Violet wasn't sure who was behaving more abominably — her brothers or her friends at the senior center. When had she lost complete and total control over her own love life?

The minute you trusted the wrong firefighter.

Joe regarded her until the backs of her knees went as hot as her ears. "Why are you bringing Sam cupcakes, anyway? You're rivals. Or do I need to remind you that there's a bet at stake?"

As if she could forget.

Violet couldn't enroll Sprinkles in obedience school. After the police department's recent loss, she'd done a cursory internet search for nearby dog training programs. *Just in case.* Every single one of them conducted class on the weekends. Who was supposed to man the cupcake truck while she cajoled Sprinkles into doing a series of senseless tricks?

The prospect of losing to Sam was more humiliating than Violet cared to think about. Embarrassment aside, she didn't have time for formal obedience lessons. It simply couldn't happen.

Joe sighed. "Look, we're not trying to tell you what to do."

Really? If Violet had been capable of snorting with her Dalmatian's panache, she would have done so. She opted for a hearty eye roll instead.

"We're just worried about you, that's all," Joe said quietly. "No one wants to see you get hurt."

Again. No one wanted to see her get hurt *again.*

The word hovered between them — unspoken, but very much there. Was the greater population of Turtle Beach ever going to move past Emmett's betrayal?

And then a thought hit her, right out of the blue — if Violet couldn't put her humiliating romantic past behind her, how could she expect anyone else to do it, least of all her own family?

Maybe it was time to forgive and forget, once and for all. Maybe she'd wasted enough time feeling bad about the way Emmett had taken advantage of her. Maybe it was time to give love another chance.

Not with Sam, obviously. That was out of the question.

Wasn't it?

Violet's heart thumped hard in her chest.

"I'm over it," she announced, willing herself to believe it. "I'm not going to let myself get hurt."

She had way too much on the line to take a chance on another relationship. The greater population of Turtle Beach already thought she was a fragile little thing who couldn't think for herself. They'd thought as much since the day she'd been born. Violet couldn't imagine how her hometown would react if she let another firefighter break her heart.

She'd have to walk up and down Seashell Drive with a bag over her head. Or better yet, move to an entirely new city. Maybe even another continent.

Moving away was out of the question, though. Violet loved Turtle Beach, quirks and all. She loved her family too, naturally. She just wished they weren't quite so invested in her personal life.

"Dad knows about your wager with Sam," Josh said. "He thinks your little bet is the reason why the Hoses were so fired up last Saturday."

Ouch.

Violet winced. She hated the thought of disappointing her father. Even after the Emmett fiasco, he hadn't blamed Violet. Ed March had reserved every last drop of his ire for anyone with a Turtle Beach Fire Department logo on their clothing.

This was part of what she needed to leave behind, though. Her dad didn't need to baby her. They should be able to talk about these things like adults, just like Violet should feel comfortable asking questions about her mother. She'd let the March men nurture their overprotective streak for far too long. Enough was enough.

"I'll deal with Dad. And from now on, I'll deal with my own life in my own way." Sprinkles leaned against her leg in solidarity, which reminded Violet that she wasn't completely without fault in the current scenario. "The next time I think someone is kidnapping my Dalmatian, I'll take care of it myself. And from this point forward, I want you both to treat me the same way you treat each other."

Josh and Joe exchanged a dubious look.

"I'm serious," Violet said.

"We heard about bingo night too. You supposedly lit Sam on fire?" Josh's expression dripped with incredulity.

Right. That. "It was a teensy accident. He's fine. I guess you didn't hear about the part where I put out the fire? I saved Sam's life."

Why did everyone completely ignore that important fact?

"So, see? I'm perfectly capable of taking care of myself. I extinguished Sam all on my own, even though there was another firefighter present." Come to think of it, she was still waiting for a thank you from Sam. Ugh.

Violet would deal with that later, after she'd finished putting her brothers in their place.

She gestured at her Dalmatian. "And look how nicely Sprinkles is behaving. We're fine. *I'm* fine."

Violet didn't need a pair of guardian angels dressed in police uniforms any more than Sprinkles needed to go to obedience school.

Josh glanced at Joe, threw his hands up and heaved a weary sigh. "We tried. I give up."

Violet beamed with triumph as she aimed a questioning glance at Joe.

"One last thing," he said.

Violet held up her hand. "No."

"Are you sure? It's really important, Vi." Joe's eyes narrowed.

He was goading her, but Violet wasn't about to fall for it. Not anymore.

"I've never been so sure of anything in my life."

Perhaps it was the run-in with her brothers outside the firehouse, or perhaps she'd decided that a little payback was in order after the sprinkler incident, but when Violet arrived at the senior center, she marched into the building on a mission.

The Charlie's Angels were seated in the living room area of the lobby, half an hour early for the senior center's bi-weekly trivia game. It was an unspoken rule of Turtle Beach's over-seventy crowd that if you arrived right on time for a scheduled event, you were late. Therefore, anything on the senior center's activity calendar that began at ten o'clock was already packed by nine-thirty, sometimes even nine-fifteen.

"Violet?" Ethel called as Violet strode across the lobby's smooth tile floor. Ethel, Mavis, and Opal exchanged worried glances. "I think you have the wrong day again, dear. Yoga class is tomorrow. The only thing on the schedule this morning is trivia."

"I'm well aware of what day it is," Violet said. She'd shown up *one* time for yoga on the wrong day of the week, and she'd yet to live it down. It was like her accidental free dog grooming business all over again.

"So you're here for trivia, then? How nice! We can probably make room." Mavis scooted closer to Ethel on the sofa.

Violet flashed her friends a smile. "No, I'm not here for trivia, either, but keep that space free. I'm inviting a special guest."

She spun around and headed for the hallway that led to the residents' living quarters.

"Where is she going?" Mavis said to Ethel and Opal while Violet was still within earshot. Then, once she'd apparently caught on to Violet's devious plan, Mavis called after her. "Violet! Tell us where you're going right this instant."

Violet kept on moving down the hall, and within minutes the three older women were trailing behind her as if she were the grand marshal in a walker parade.

When she reached the door to Larry Sims's apartment, she crossed her arms and waited for Ethel, Opal, and — most importantly, Mavis — to catch up.

"What are you doing, Violet?" Ethel asked, eyes comically wide behind the lenses of her purple glasses.

"You're not really going to knock, are you?" Opal said.

Mavis didn't say a word, but she was trembling enough to rival Nibbles the Chihuahua, which was really saying something. The tiny dog leapt out of her blanket nest and began pacing back and forth the full length of the walker basket.

Violet raised her hand, poised to knock on the elusive Larry Sims's door. "You all thought it was cute to meddle in my personal life, so maybe it's time I meddle in yours."

"Fine. I lied, okay?" Ethel blurted. "There was nothing wrong with the sprinklers. Go ahead and call Sam and have him throw me in the slammer."

Violet bit back a smile. "No one's going to jail, Ethel. Particularly not you, because I have a feeling I know who the mastermind behind yesterday's stunt was."

She pinned Mavis with a look.

"What?" Mavis's hand fluttered to her chest like a nervous bird. "Surely you don't mean me."

Opal shifted her walker so that she was squared off with Mavis. "Oh, Mavis. Go ahead and tell her the truth. All of it."

Violet only waited a split second to see if Mavis would fess up. It didn't really matter whether or not she did, because Violet had already made up her mind.

She gave the door four knocks in rapid succession.

Opal and Ethel gasped in horror, Nibbles yipped, and Sprinkles dropped into a play bow. Violet half-expected Mavis to flee, but she paused to cast a curious glance at the Dalmatian and by the time she prepared her walker for an emergency retreat, the door swung open.

Larry Sims stood on the threshold in all his cardiganed splendor, gaze swiveling from woman to spotted dog, to woman, to tiny trembling dog, to the other two women, clearly trying to figure out why there was an odd collection of humans and animals gathered outside his room.

"Hi." Violet held up her hand in a wave. "I'm Violet. This is my Dalmatian, Sprinkles, and these are my friends, Mavis, Opal, and Ethel."

"H-hello, there," Larry said. A fluffy gray cat with piercing blue eyes appeared at his feet and began winding its way around his legs. "This is Skippy."

"Skippy is lovely. And wow, she doesn't seem very afraid of dogs." Violet bent to run a hand over the Persian kitty's soft, slender back.

"Oh, Skippy loves dogs. I had a Chihuahua for many years, and they were the best of friends." Larry smiled at Nibbles, and miraculously, the little dog stopped trembling. "Who does this little sweetheart belong to?"

"Me." Mavis lit up like a sparkler on the Fourth of July. "She belongs to me. My name is Mavis."

This was going even more smoothly than Violet had dared to hope. Yes, she'd aimed to teach her friends a lesson about meddling, but she'd also wanted to get Mavis and her secret crush to actually speak to one another. It was the least she could do after Mavis had smuggled the copy of the *Gazette* with Adeline March's picture on the front page out of the library . . . even if Violet still hadn't been able to get her father to tell her where her mother's Dalmatian puppy had come from.

"Mavis was wondering if you might like to join her in the lobby right now for group trivia," Violet said, and with a wink she added, "It's kind of like *Jeopardy!* minus all the Geico commercials."

"That lizard." Mavis rolled her eyes.

"Skippy likes to hiss at that green nuisance," Larry said.

Then he buttoned his cardigan up to the top and fell into step beside Mavis as the seniors hurried back to the lobby. Trivia wasn't set to start for another twenty minutes, so of course Opal, Ethel, and Mavis were warning Larry that they were already late.

Nope, I don't think so. Violet smiled to herself and bent to ruffle Sprinkles's ears. *Something tells me Larry Sims is right on time.*

CHAPTER 14

The next morning proceeded exactly as the previous one had in Sam's quiet, tranquil little cottage on the beach. Except things were no longer so quiet. Or tranquil, for that matter.

Like the day before, Cinder opted not to make the bed. Nor did she paw at the button of the coffee maker to switch it on. This aversion to household chores continued for the remainder of the week. Sam didn't mind either of those omissions from Cinder's morning routine. Of course he didn't. This was, in fact, what he'd wanted all along.

Sam had never intended for his Dalmatian to make his bed. She'd just picked up the behavior on her own after watching Sam straighten his covers every morning. And he could certainly push a button to brew his own coffee. That particular trick had always been more about aesthetics than necessity. Translation: it was cute. Even Sam enjoyed a cute dog trick now and then.

It hadn't seemed so cute after Violet accused him of treating his Dalmatian like the canine version of Cinderella. So, sure, he could live without it.

Teaching a dog to unlearn a behavior was more challenging than most people realized. Old dogs, new tricks and all that. Dogs were creatures of habit. They liked routines and thrived best in environments where they knew exactly what was expected of them. The easiest way to get a dog to stop engaging in a certain behavior — like turning on a coffee maker, for instance — was to replace the action with something else. To trade one behavior for another. That way, the pup would better understand the trainer's expectations.

Sam knew all of this, obviously. He quite literally could have written a book on it after all the time and effort he'd put into training Cinder to be a working fire safety dog. His failure to replace making the bed and turning on the coffee maker with another action had clearly been a mistake.

His motives had been pure, though. He'd wanted Cinder to relax, not perform — which he now realized was about as ridiculous as Violet's assertion that Sprinkles didn't need obedience lessons because she was "naturally sweet." Cinder enjoyed learning new things. Dalmatians, in particular, were very high-energy dogs. A bored Dalmatian could be a disaster. Sam's initial encounter with Sprinkles on the dog beach sprang quickly to mind.

Again, none of this was new information to Sam, which was why he shouldn't have been surprised to find that his very bright, very trainable Dalmatian had apparently decided to choose her own replacement behavior in the absence of specific direction from Sam. But why oh why did the replacement behavior have to involve his socks?

Cinder pranced past him with a sock dangling from her mouth as Sam jammed at the button on the coffee maker. He'd already rescued one sock from her jaws, and within seconds she'd somehow swiped its mate.

Sam needed caffeine. Immediately. Forget making the bed. Rumpled bedsheets were the least of his worries at the moment. He still hadn't responded to his old chief about the job offer, and the texts and voicemails were continuing to pile up. Murray had started showing up at the batting cages for practice in the evenings to remind Sam and the other players how fantastic it would be if they could beat the police department in a sweep. Sam was beginning to wonder if turning down the Chicago job was really such a smart move. What would happen if the TBFD failed to win the tournament? Would Sam even have a job in Turtle Beach anymore?

Surely he didn't need to worry about such a remote possibility. The Hoses were already up 2–0. Odds were definitely in their favor. And it was hard to imagine that he could actually be *fired* for losing an extracurricular ball game. But stranger things had certainly happened in Turtle Beach. In fact, stranger things happened on a daily basis in this wacky town — the sock thing, for instance.

"Cinder, you need to be on your best behavior at work today. We have the fire safety demo for the surf camp kids." Sam wrestled the sock away from her.

The Dalmatian cocked her head as if she were listening, but Sam wasn't entirely convinced.

"Do you hear me? This is serious," he said.

Cinder huffed, and Sam sagged with relief. Then the Dalmatian collapsed on the floor to writhe around and give herself a prolonged back-scratch.

What had happened to his serious, competent dog?

Sam had no idea, and while a small part

him (so small that it would have been invisible to the naked eye) enjoyed seeing his Dalmatian act like a puppy again, he was starting to worry about their presentation.

Sam gulped the majority of his coffee down in one giant swallow. Then he pulled on his damp socks and his carefully pressed uniform, telling himself all the while that he had nothing to worry about. Cinder was the best fire dog he'd ever seen. True, she'd been acting up at home, but at the fire station she'd been business as usual. She'd never embarrass him on the job. Cinder was his partner, and that was an unbreakable bond.

By mid-morning, however, Cinder appeared to be challenging that notion. The setting for the presentation — the beach — seemed to further complicate things.

"Hello, boys and girls. I'm Marshal Sam and this is my dog, Cinder. We're here today to teach you about fire prevention." Sam glanced down at the spot beside him that his Dalmatian typically occupied and saw nothing but a ghost crab scurrying toward its hole.

His audience, comprised of about a dozen children between the ages of nine and ten years old wearing wet bathing suits and long-sleeved rash guards, collapsed into giggles. One of them pointed toward the water's edge, where Cinder was trailing a sandpiper scurrying in and out of the shallows. The bird poked its narrow beak into the sand, and Cinder imitated the sandpiper, doing the same with her muzzle. When she lifted her head, her black heart-shaped nose was covered in sugary sand.

"Cinder," Sam said in what he hoped sounded liked a firm-but-kind voice. "Come."

The Dalmatian swiveled her head in his direction, as if surprised to see him there and then bounded toward him. When she took her place by his side, she sneezed three times in rapid succession, spraying the children with wet sand.

Every black spot on Cinder's body could have fallen off right before Sam's eyes and he would have been less surprised than he was at seeing his beloved Dalmatian behave this way. Astonished didn't begin to cover it.

Was he dreaming? Was this some sort of strange Dalmatian hallucination?

"Gross!" a little girl on the front row wailed as she wiped sandy sludge from the front of her rash guard.

A boy next to her laughed as he smeared the wet sand Cinder had slung at him more fully into his hair.

The camp counselors — a group of young twenty-something surfer types with sun-bleached hair and noses slathered with white zinc oxide — exchanged concerned glances. Sam's gut churned. How awful did you have to be in order to crack the chilled-out composure of a surf instructor?

He took a deep breath. They'd gotten off to a rocky start, that was all. The beach was full of distractions. Sam could save this presentation. They still had half an hour to go.

"Cinder," he said, waiting a beat for the Dalmatian to meet his gaze. "Let's teach the children what phone number they should dial if they smell smoke."

Sam waited for Cinder to bark out 911, like she'd done countless times before.

And waited.

And waited some more.

"Cinder, you know the answer. What number should the kids dial if they smell smoke?" he prompted, taking great care to enunciate in case the Dalmatian was having trouble hearing him over the roar of the Atlantic Ocean.

Could she have an ear infection? That would explain a lot.

Except Sam had given her a thorough

grooming the night before. Nail trim, bath, ear cleaning — the whole nine yards. Sam had noticed nothing amiss.

Cinder let out a woof, and Sam held his breath as he waited for eight more barks.

Woof.

Woof.

Woof.

And then, just as Sam started to relax, the barking stopped. Cinder went completely still for a prolonged moment, and then she tipped her head back to let out a warbling, coyote-style howl.

Sam closed his eyes and prayed for a rogue tidal wave to come carry him away. No such luck.

The kids found the incident hilarious and immediately began echoing Cinder, howling like a pack of surfing werewolves.

"Dude," one of the surf instructors said. "Not cool."

Sam just nodded, acutely aware of just how uncool he was.

"I'm sorry. She seems to be a little distracted," he said. *Understatement of the century.* "We should probably move on to something else."

The presentation proceeded to go from bad to worse. When Sam tried to get Cinder to stop, drop, and roll, she plopped onto her belly, rested her head on her paws and yawned. When he gave her the cue to commando crawl, she rolled over. Every time the Dalmatian made a mistake, the children started howling again.

Sam didn't bother trying to teach the no-playing-with-matches lessons. He just wanted to end this embarrassing episode and hide in his office for the rest of the day. Or week. Or year.

When the presentation ended forty-five long minutes later, Sam cringed as the surf instructors eyed him with pity and shook their heads. He doubted the kids had learned a thing. About halfway through the excruciating ordeal, he'd stopped giving Cinder commands altogether. He'd almost been desperate enough to stop, drop, and roll around in the sand himself. He'd done his best to teach the children the basics of fire prevention, but without a flashy Dalmatian driving the points home, they'd appeared bored out of their minds.

Sam couldn't really blame them. The entire afternoon had been a disaster from start to finish.

As chagrined as he was by Cinder's behavior, Sam wasn't angry at his Dalmatian. His heart still melted every time he looked at her sweet, spotted face, because at the end of the day, Cinder wasn't just his partner. She was his best friend in the world. Before he'd moved to Turtle Beach, he'd often thought she might be his *only* friend.

Sam swung by the dog beach on the way back to the firehouse to let Cinder romp and play in the waves. She bit at the white-caps and chased the back and forth motion of the tide, just a dog enjoying a day at the beach. An ache settled behind Sam's sternum.

This is probably how Violet feels every day of her life with Sprinkles.

He'd deserved what had happened at the surf camp demo. He'd been cocky, arrogant, and judgmental where Violet and her dog were concerned. She'd probably already heard all about his Dalmatian mortification — this was Turtle Beach, after all. And Sam knew without a doubt that she'd have something to say about it.

He shook his head and gazed out over the ocean's shimmering blue depths. Oh, how the tables had turned.

Once the police department had gotten wind of the TBFD's nightly sessions at the batting cages, they'd scheduled evening practices of their own. Every night around seven o'clock, while Violet was baking in the March family beach house's vast kitchen, she saw her father and brothers descending the wooden stairs of the deck in their practice regalia. The men in her life were eating, breathing, and sleeping softball. It was worse this year than ever before.

Josh and Joe seemed to have taken her at her word after their discussion in front of the firehouse, though. She'd been spared any further interrogation about whatever was happening between her and Sam, thank goodness. Although she wasn't sure why she was so relieved to be out of their crosshairs. She had nothing to hide. She and Sam were simply friends. Or enemies, maybe?

Frenemies. That's what they were — frenemies who'd accidentally kissed . . . once.

Which was, of course, one time too many.

Violet was tired of thinking about the kiss, tired of reliving it over and over again in her imagination, tired of secretly wishing it might happen again. And despite all her bravado in front of Josh and Joe, something they'd said was eating at her.

Dad knows about your wager with Sam. He thinks your little bet is the reason why the Hoses were so fired up last Saturday.

Great. So now *both* of the police department's recent losses were her fault?

"The town has gone full-on crazy this

summer, hasn't it, Sprinkles?" Violet pulled a tray of vanilla cupcakes from the oven to cool and removed her oven mitts.

The Dalmatian tiptoed politely to Violet's side at the sound of her name, nose quivering in the direction of the warm vanilla cakes.

Violet bent to hug the dog around her neck. "What are we going to do about it, hmm?"

Sprinkles gave Violet's cheek a gentle lick. It was a puppy kiss, not a scorching hot fireman kiss, but Violet would take what she could get.

"Let's get out of here," she said, reaching for her multi-tiered Tupperware cupcake carrier.

She popped open the plastic lid and started stacking frosted vanilla bean cupcakes inside. Violet stood by everything she'd said to her brothers, but she hated the thought of disappointing her father, particularly when she'd had to hear about it from Josh and Joe. But of course her dad would never tell her to her face that he was upset about the wager or that he blamed her for lighting a fire under the opposing team. (*Fire* in the strictly figurative sense . . . this time.)

He probably thought she was too emotionally fragile to handle that sort of criticism.

Everything between Dad and Violet always had to be rainbows and unicorns — except when he was ordering her not to get involved with a firefighter. He never held back when it came to that.

Rainbows and unicorns may have worked when Violet was a little girl trying to come to terms with the fact that her mother had died bringing her into the world, but she wanted more now. She wanted to really know her dad, and she wanted to know her mother too, beyond secret newspaper clippings or collections of pretty pictures pressed into a book.

"Ready, Sprinkles?"

The Dalmatian's tail beat a happy rhythm against the smooth wood floor.

Violet clipped her leash onto the cupcake collar. "Let's go."

Violet could have taken the Sweetness on Wheels truck down to the softball field, but a cool sea breeze had blown in, stirring the sea grass and shallow tide pools along the crest. It was such a nice night, perfect for a bike ride. So she fastened the cupcake carrier into her bike basket, wound Sprinkles's leash around her hand a few times and took off toward the boardwalk.

Mercifully, Sprinkles trotted politely alongside the bicycle instead of dragging her through downtown Turtle Beach. Violet's front wheel didn't wobble a bit for the entire length of Seashell Drive. Obedience lessons? Ha! She and Sprinkles were perfectly fine. No formal schooling required.

Practice was in full swing when they arrived at the softball field. The players were lined up in groups of three, doing relay toss drills while Violet's dad sat in the dugout, flipping through his playbook. Violet grabbed the cupcakes and kept a firm grip on Sprinkles's leash as she walked toward him, just in case the Dalmatian mistook the situation for an elaborate game of catch.

"Vi?" Her dad stood, removed his baseball cap and ran a hand through his salt-and-pepper hair. At fifty-five, Ed March was quite handsome, in a quiet, understated sort of way. Violet wished he would get out more and try to find someone special. "What are you doing here? Is everything okay?"

"Everything's fine, Dad." Like she'd be bringing cupcakes to the softball field in the event of an emergency? "I just thought I'd bring the guys some treats and keep you company during drills."

"Oh, that's nice. I'd like that." He nodded as a smile replaced his concerned expression, then sat back down and patted the empty space beside him on the bench.

"Have a seat."

Sprinkles planted herself at Dad's feet while Violet set the cupcakes down, tucked her dress beneath her and got situated on the old, worn bench. It had probably been there since Turtle Beach first became inhabited back in the '50s.

The Dalmatian poked her nose at Violet's father, angling for pats. He obliged with a chuckle.

"How's the team looking tonight?" Violet asked.

Ed March nodded. "Good."

She crossed her legs, swinging her foot until her ballerina flat dangled from her toe. A nervous habit. "Good enough to beat the Hoses on Saturday?"

Her dad sighed. "We'll see."

"Dad, I'm sorry if you're upset about my bet with Sam Nash. I certainly didn't think he'd go out and transform the fire department into a semi-professional softball team in the span of a week." Or ever, frankly. The man was a miracle worker.

"I'm not upset," her father said, but he couldn't seem to meet her gaze. Or maybe he was truly invested in the tossing drill. His head moved back and forth, following the movement of the balls, just like Sprinkles's did.

Violet smiled, despite the tiny ache in her heart. They made an adorable pair. "It's okay if you are, you know."

He stretched his legs out in front of him and crossed his feet at the ankles. Sprinkles lay down and rested her chin on the toe of one of his cleats. "I just don't like the idea of you having anything to do with Sam, that's all."

"Even a casual wager?"

But was it really so casual anymore? The past few times she and Sam had been in a room together, things had felt anything but casual.

"He's not good for you. Period." The matter settled, Ed March was quick to change the subject. "I asked Joe to talk to you about something. Did he get around to it?"

Violet's swinging foot went into overdrive. Her dad had been behind the whole "shower" confrontation? Awk-ward. "He and Josh both did. Honestly, though, it's not a big deal, and I told them so."

"But you're taking care of it, yes?"

Violet nodded. "Definitely."

As in she wasn't going to get caught beneath a sprinkler head again with Sam any time soon. She'd given the Charlie's Angels a good talking to about meddling in her love life — non-existent as it was — and they'd sworn to behave from here on out.

"But you know you don't need to have Josh and Joe look out for me like that, right? I can handle things on my own." She swallowed.

Why was it so hard to talk to him like this? At least she was trying, but it still felt like they were tiptoeing around the issue instead of discussing it outright.

"We're just looking out for you, cupcake."

"I know you are, and I love you for it. But I'm stronger than the three of you think I am. I promise." She took a deep breath. "Can I ask you something, Dad?"

"Sure."

"I ran across something the other day — an old picture from the *Turtle Beach Gazette*." Violet hoped he didn't ask her how she'd found it. She didn't want to lie to her father, but she also wanted to keep her word to Mavis. "It's of Mom with Polkadot on Christmas Eve, 1982."

"That's nice," he said, and pulled his baseball cap lower over his eyes.

"Polkadot was just a puppy — so sweet, with little jelly bean toes and a chubby little belly. I was wondering if you remembered it? The picture, I mean." Violet's throat went thick.

There. She'd asked the question. The ball

was in his court now, not to toss a non-softball-related sports metaphor into the mix.

Her dad stood and blew hard into the coaching whistle he always wore on a cord around his neck during practice.

"Tossing drill over. Let's hit a few balls, men," he shouted.

His timing was impeccable . . . and more than a little suspect.

"Dad," Violet said.

"Sorry, Cupcake. We've got a game to win tomorrow. I'll see you later, back at home." He stepped over Sprinkles to head for the opening of the dugout.

All right, then. Violet had swung and missed, so to speak.

"Have a good night, Dad." She stood and gave Sprinkles's leash a gentle tug. Suddenly, she was in no mood whatsoever for softball.

"Vi?" her dad called as she walked away. "Don't forget to get that matter you and Joe discussed taken care of. The sooner the better."

A dash of confusion spiraled through Violet. Had she missed something? This was starting to sound like more than just a warning about keeping her distance from Sam.

"No worries, Dad," she called over her shoulder and waved.

Violet was tired of being on the receiving end of lectures from the March men, especially when she couldn't get an answer to a simple question about her mother. Whatever her dad was referring to, she didn't want to talk about it. So she kept on walking, her sights set someplace else.

Like father, like daughter.

CHAPTER 15

Sam bowed out of batting practice following his and Cinder's dismal performance at the surf camp. He just didn't have it in him — not after all the ribbing he got throughout the course of the afternoon. Word of Cinder's antics had spread far and wide by the time he'd gotten back to the firehouse.

"I guess we don't have to worry about freeing Cinder anymore?" Griff had said, tossing half of a turkey hot dog in the Dalmatian's direction. "Sounds as if she's gone ahead and cut herself loose."

"It was an off day," had been Sam's curt response.

He didn't mind being teased. Anyone who'd survived in a career in firefighting as long as he had could definitely take a joke. Within the first responder community, firefighters worldwide had a reputation for being pranksters that rivaled that of their purported skill at rescuing kittens in trees.

Back in his old station in Chicago, one of the department's leather recliners had a broken seat. Anyone who sat down in it would sink straight through the cushion, practically to the floor. A rookie wasn't considered a true member of the department until he or she had been tricked into sitting in the chair. It cracked Sam up every time — even all those years ago when he'd been the rookie falling through the seat of the recliner.

Of course, it had been a while since Sam had laughed like that at work. The heaviness that had settled deep inside him on the day of the mattress factory fire was still there. He couldn't seem to shake it. Time heals all wounds, everyone said. And time had certainly taken the edge off his grief, but he still hadn't been able to find his way back to being the guy who would coax a rookie into being the butt of a joke. The old recliner wasn't the only thing that was broken.

In truth, though, Sam hadn't even tried to be that guy again. He didn't see the point. And now here he was, the new star of Turtle Beach's hilarious Dalmatian and pony show.

Sam didn't mind being teased, but jokes about his dog rubbed him the wrong way. He was well aware that this made him the worst sort of hypocrite, given his preoccupation with Turtle Beach's original Dalmatian. This unflattering realization made him even less inclined to go out and hit balls. Murray and the guys could live without him for one night.

He kicked back in one of the Adirondack-style chairs on the wraparound deck of his beach house and tried his best to embrace what he'd come to the island for in the first place — relaxation. Deep breaths in, deep breaths out, the roar of the ocean in his head, the damp sea breeze on his face.

No one had gotten hurt today, only his pride. The safety of the islanders was his first, his *only,* responsibility. There hadn't been a single active fire in Turtle Beach since the day he arrived . . .

Unless Violet setting him aflame counted, which it didn't.

Except Sam had written her a few citations for the circumstances surrounding that little mishap, so technically it did.

Crunch, crunch, crunch.

Sam opened his eyes, grateful for whatever distraction was pulling him away from the memory of the stolen kiss at bingo night. No good could come from reliving that dangerously sublime moment, especially since he and Violet were adversaries. Or, as she'd so eloquently told Griff, *arch-enemies, even.*

His gratitude took a hit when he realized the chomping sound he'd heard was Cinder gnawing on one of the legs of the chair he was sitting in.

"You've got to be kidding me," he muttered.

Cinder blinked at him and panted with her tongue lolling out of the side of her mouth and one of her ears folded inside-out. She looked ridiculous. And happy. Delighted with herself, actually.

Sam narrowed his gaze at the dog. "Who are you, and what have you done with my Dalmatian?"

A loaded silence stretched between them until Sam's cell phone buzzed to life, jarring his thoughts away from the impossible.

"Saved by the bell," he told Cinder as he tapped the accept button on his phone. "Hello?"

"Nash. Finally, you pick up the phone," Chief Jameson Dodd said from the other end of the line. "I was beginning to think you were avoiding me."

"Never, sir," Sam said, raking a hand through his hair and fixing his gaze on the smooth surface of the bay. His cottage was situated smack in the center of the narrow island, with views spanning from the bay and the boardwalk on one side, all the way to the ocean on the other. "Just busy, that's all."

"Not busy fighting fires, I hope."

No, busy facilitating bingo night, making ludicrous wagers with impossible women, becoming a de facto softball coach, and myriad other things he hadn't realized he'd signed on for when he'd moved to Turtle Beach.

Like trying not to fall for your nemesis?

"Not at all. Things here are . . ." Crazy pants. ". . . slow. Not what I expected, though. It's just different."

"You know I wish you well, Nash. The last thing I want to do is try and steal you away if you're happy there, but when Don Evans put in his notice of retirement, I had to get in touch. The job is everything you said you wanted back when you said you needed to stop going out on active calls." Chief Dodd chuckled. "Minus building sandcastles and going for long romantic walks on the shore or whatever it is you're keeping busy with in Turtle Beach."

Long romantic walks on the shore. Right.

Violet's beautiful face flashed in Sam's mind — her sea-glass eyes, her tousled mermaid hair, her cherry-red lips. Sugary sweet . . . achingly kissable.

His breath clogged in his throat. "That's not . . ."

"Relax, I was just kidding. Are you interested in the job or not?"

"I'm interested," Sam heard himself say. Until that precise moment, he'd had no clue how he might respond. "Maybe." He swallowed. "Probably."

What was he saying? This wasn't the kind of decision he should be making on a whim — particularly not after the day he'd had.

Cinder pawed at Sam's leg, and she let out a mournful whine.

Sam shook his head. *Not now, Cinder.*

"I'm going to take that as a tentative yes," Chief Dodd said. "I'm not asking for a commitment yet. I just needed to know if I was barking up the entirely wrong tree."

Sam's gaze strayed toward the bay again, and his breath hitched when he saw Violet riding her bicycle along the boardwalk again. Sprinkles ran alongside her, as usual. Sam couldn't take his eyes off the pair of them, cruising along the bay against the backdrop of the setting sun.

Chief Dodd's voice on the other end of the phone barely registered. "Sam? Hello? Are you still there?"

"Barking . . . tree," Sam said absently.

"What was that?" Chief Dodd said.

"Actually, something just came up." Fresh energy filled Sam. If he didn't act now, he'd probably change his mind. "Can we finish talking about this later?"

"Um, sure. Give it some more thought and —"

"Great. Talk soon." Sam ended the call and tucked his phone away.

Violet and Sprinkles were coming more into focus as they drew closer, like a beautiful mirage somehow coming to life.

"What do you think, Cinder? Are you in the mood for a bike ride?"

Ten minutes later, Sam and Cinder were riding toward Violet and Sprinkles on the opposite side of the boardwalk. Violet didn't see him at first, which meant Sam got to witness the moment when her face lit up at the sight of him. Backlit by the deepening sunset, her strawberry-blonde hair looked almost fiery red. The smile she gave him made Sam's heart feel like it was being squeezed in a vise.

Sam lifted his right hand to wave at her, but just as he let go of the handlebars, Cinder launched into warp speed. Her leash, wrapped loosely around Sam's left hand, went taut as she dragged him —

bicycle and all — toward Violet and Sprinkles.

Violet's eyes went wide and she called out for him to be careful, but no sooner had the words left her mouth than Sprinkles took off, barreling toward Cinder.

Sam took his feet off the pedals and tried to slow down by planting his feet on the pavement, but Cinder was moving too fast for him to get any purchase. Before he knew it, the bike bounced off the curb, through a thick patch of seagrass, and into the middle of the street. Cars honked, mopeds swerved, and an ancient VW van with surfboards tied to its roof slammed on its brakes to avoid running over him. Sam sailed past the van just in time to see the pile of surfboards fly off the roof and scatter in the roadway like fallen dominoes.

"Cinderrrrrrrr!" he yelled.

At the same time, he could hear Violet screaming Sprinkles's name, but neither of the dogs was listening. They just kept sprinting at one another in a flurry of spots and happy barks.

"Cinder, stop!"

Sam could barely look. They were barreling straight toward a full-on Dalmatian disaster of epic proportions. When they made it to the other side of the boardwalk,

Cinder dragged him through a group of beachgoers walking out of the ice cream shop. People darted out of the way and ice cream plopped onto the ground with a splat.

Sam jerked his handlebars hard to the left in order to avoid plowing into a patch of grass where a few residents from the senior center had gathered to play bocce ball, and when he did, the two Dalmatians ended up running side-by-side. The dogs slowed down just enough for Sam to try planting his feet on the ground again, but it was too late. They'd reached the end of the boardwalk.

Sam's bicycle slid right into the cool blue water of the bay, followed immediately by Violet's cruiser bike. Their front wheels lodged into the wet sand, stopping the bikes abruptly while Sam and Violet tumbled into the shallows.

Sam scrambled to get to his feet. "Violet? Are you okay?"

"What was *that*? Your perfect dog just lost her mind," she wailed, pushing wet hair from her eyes. Then a tiny silver fish leapt from inside the bodice of Violet's drenched eyelet sundress and flopped into the water.

Sam clamped his mouth shut. *Whatever you do, don't laugh.* She could have gotten seriously hurt. They both could have, plus the dogs. It really wasn't funny.

But when the fish shimmied past him, Sam lost it. He laughed so hard that he nearly doubled over. And when Violet joined in, the sound of her laughter smoothed away his worries of what could have been.

So this was what it was like to live in the moment? It had been so long for Sam that he'd forgotten what it felt like. He wanted to bottle it like one of those messages that people wrote and tossed out to sea.

Violet splashed him, and he splashed her back. Sam's fingertips were beginning to prune.

Meanwhile, their Dalmatians stood in a perfectly matched pair, peering at Sam and Violet from the edge of the boardwalk, heads cocked just so.

Dry as a bone.

"That was *totally* your dog's fault." Violet glared at Cinder, resting in a heap of black-and-white spots with Sprinkles in the living room of Sam's beach cottage, and then back at Sam.

Sam did his best to appear contrite, but it was awfully difficult when Violet March was standing in his home with her damp hair piled on top of her head and her graceful legs sticking out from beneath one of his favorite faded Chicago Fire Department T-shirts.

What kind of gentleman would he have been if he hadn't offered up the use of his washer and dryer for her pretty dress while he changed the tire on her cruiser bike? As she said, the entire ordeal had definitely been his dog's fault. It was the least that Sam could do, even for his sworn enemy.

"Yeah, she's having an off day," he said, as if that could explain away being dragged into the bay.

"I thought Cinder didn't have off days."

So did I. "Your clothes should be dry soon. And your bicycle is good to go."

"Thank you." She glanced down at the fire department crest splashed across the T-shirt she was wearing. "There's no way I could possibly go home like this. People would talk."

"I hate to tell you this, but people are probably already talking." Sam wouldn't be surprised if a picture of them both being dragged down the boardwalk by their unruly Dalmatians made the front page of tomorrow morning's *Gazette.* Accompanied, of course, by an exclusive interview with the fish that had popped out of Violet's dress.

"I can deal with that. But this . . ." She took the edge of the T-shirt between her pointer fingers and thumbs and did a mock curtsy. "Not so much."

Sam laughed, but he wanted to tell her to take the shirt with her, to sleep in it on moonlit summer nights and think of him.

How had his calm, quiet life spun so completely out of control? Nothing was as it should be — not his job, not his dog, not his carefully guarded heart. He needed to reel himself back in before someone got hurt. And make no mistake, if these crazy Dalmatian antics continued, someone would.

"Is that the dog beach?" A smile tipped Violet's lips as she studied the framed watercolor he'd bought in the new gallery on the boardwalk.

"Looks like it." Sam had the sudden urge to throw himself between her and the painting before she discovered her own tiny image delicately rendered on the horizon.

But if she noticed it, she didn't let on. "I like your cottage. It's not at all what I expected. It's very homey."

Sam wondered if she was alluding to his unmade bed but thought it best not to go there. "It's rented."

I haven't put down roots here. I don't even know if I'm staying.

"I see." Her smile dimmed somewhat, and

she wrapped her arms around herself.

"Violet, you can sit down if you like. I'm not going to bite."

"My previous experience with firefighters says otherwise," she said, but she lowered herself onto his sofa and tucked her legs beneath her.

Sam pulled a blanket from a nearby easy chair and handed it to her. "Yeah, I heard a little something about that."

"Of course you did. This is Turtle Beach." Violet rolled her eyes, but beneath her bravado, Sam could see a hint of vulnerability.

Beneath all of her whimsy and charm, Violet was a real person with real feelings. And as he looked at her, curled up on his sofa, a world away from her quirky bingo-playing friends and the food truck topped with its spinning pink cupcake, he realized something.

On the surface, Violet lived a charmed life — the town darling who resided in the biggest house on the island with her doting family and lovable-but-naughty Dalmatian. She believed the best in people, Sprinkles included. Until she'd discovered he'd been a baseball star, she'd even chosen to believe the best in Sam and ventured into enemy territory to bring him apology cupcakes.

Her chosen profession involved frilly aprons, cake, and copious amounts of buttercream.

But all those things weren't evidence of a life without hardships. Quite the contrary. Violet had known loss since the day she'd been born. She'd been hurt and taken advantage of by a man she'd trusted, and every living soul on the island knew about it. And still she'd chosen to embrace the lighter side of life — the good side.

If anyone knew how brave that choice could be, it was Sam. They were the antithesis of one another. When things had gotten tough in his own life, he'd withdrawn. He'd chosen to hide in his darkness while Violet was determined to bloom, leaning as hard as she could into the light.

"Do you want to know what the worst part of it was?" Her eyes were huge pools of endless blue, and Sam wanted to dive right in.

"Tell me." He sat down on the opposite end of the sofa. There couldn't have been more than half a foot between them, but it felt as wide as a canyon.

"I should have seen it coming. It was just so *obvious*. Everyone tried to warn me — my dad, my brothers, my friends. He was the star player for the Hoses, and suddenly he was madly in love with me, right at the start of the season." She sighed. "I knew better. I knew that dating a firefighter would be complicated, but I wanted so badly to believe in a happily ever after that I charged ahead anyway."

"Everyone makes mistakes, Violet," Sam said. "Even Cinder, remember?"

Violet shifted so that they were shoulder to shoulder, as they'd been back at the senior center on Mavis's loveseat. "Well, I'll never make that one again."

"Believe in happy endings?" Sam couldn't see it. Believing in such things seemed built into her DNA. He reached for her hand and his fingertips wound through hers, seemingly of their own volition.

"Date a fireman." Violet turned toward him, and her gaze dropped slowly . . . purposefully . . . to his mouth. "Obviously."

"Obviously," Sam echoed, heart pounding hard in his chest. It took every ounce of self-control he possessed not to cup her face in his hands and kiss her silly.

"I mean, take you and me for instance." She rested a delicate hand on his chest. "It just couldn't happen."

"Nope," he said, as he reached to wind a lock of her hair around his fingertip. He'd been wanting to do that since the day he'd first seen her on the beach, accusations of dognapping notwithstanding.

She inched closer toward him. "I guess it's a good thing we're not attracted to each other, then."

Sam's head dipped lower, until her lips were just a whisper away. "Who says I'm not attracted to you?"

"You can't be attracted to me." Violet's breath was warm against his mouth — warm and impossibly sweet. "And I can't be attracted to you. That's how this whole enemy thing works."

"I'm beginning to think having an archenemy is overrated," Sam groaned.

This was torture. If he didn't kiss her, he thought he might die from longing.

He moved toward her, brushing his lips against hers as slowly and gently as he possibly could. They were playing a dangerous game here, and he didn't want to push her into anything. Not ever.

She smiled against his lips. "Careful, there. The last time we did this one of us burst into flames."

"Worth it," Sam murmured, and just as he prepared to give her a proper, thorough kiss, the dryer buzzed, indicating her clothes were dry.

Sprinkles and Cinder sprang to life, barking in alarm at the sudden noise. Their spotted heads swiveled to and fro, searching for Sam and Violet. Then the dogs wedged their way between them on the sofa, tails wagging, covering their faces with Dalmatian kisses.

Sam was going to have to have a serious chat with Cinder. Being dragged into the bay was one thing, but interrupting a kiss was crossing a line. Even so, this was the best night he'd had in as long as he could remember. He just wished he knew what it meant. Were he and Violet really enemies, or were they something else . . . something more?

So much for living in the moment, he thought as he waited for Violet to change out of his Chicago FD shirt and back into her white eyelet dress.

He didn't know why he was letting himself get carried away like this. His life had never been such a mess. Adding romance into the mix seemed like the worst possible decision he could make, especially if that romance was with the police chief's daughter.

"It's just you and me, Cinder," he whispered, running his thumb over one of his Dalmatian's soft ears. "Right, girl?"

Sam wished the dog could talk. Not only did she have a lot of explaining to do for her recent behavior, but he could have used some advice from someone who knew him inside and out.

The door to the bathroom swung open and Violet stepped out with Sprinkles trailing in her footsteps. Violet had twisted her hair into a messy bun on top of her head, and her dress looked as good as new.

"We should probably get going," she said. "There's a big game tomorrow."

She offered him his T-shirt, folded into a neat square.

He pushed it back toward her. "You keep it. Just don't let anyone catch you wearing it." He winked. "Obviously."

Surprise splashed across her face, but she quickly recovered and echoed him as he'd done just a little while ago. "Obviously."

Violet pressed the shirt to her heart, then bent to clip Sprinkles's leash onto her cupcake collar. Sam held the front door open for them and they stepped out onto the deck.

The moon shone high overhead, and stars filled the sky, shimmering like tiny diamonds on a dark velvet pillow.

Violet smiled up at him. "I'm still waiting for a thank you for saving your life, by the way."

He laughed. "Never going to happen, nemesis."

And then she was gone, pedaling her way back to enemy territory on her cruiser bike with her black-and-white dog trotting alongside her. Sam stood barefoot on the deck and watched them until they disappeared from view. To his right, he could hear the tumbling roar of the ocean, and to his left, moonlight glittered on the quiet surface of the bay. Sam's rented cottage lingered in the space in between.

When he went back inside, he found Cinder sleeping in a tight ball in the center of his perfectly made bed — not a wrinkle or rumpled bedsheet in sight.

Chapter 16

Sam wasn't sure what to make of the made bed. He wanted to take it as a sign that Cinder had come to her senses and everything about their orderly, predictable life was once again intact.

The following morning, though, the Dalmatian jumped off the foot of the bed at first light and headed straight for the deck to bark at passing seagulls. Sam stumbled behind her, pausing to turn on the coffee maker and pull on some clothes so he could take his dog for a quick run on the beach before the softball game.

Nothing about today could be left to chance. It was the fire department's one and only opportunity to take the championship in a shutout. Chief Murray had sent out an email in the wee hours of the morning, announcing that he would spring for a deep sea fishing trip for the entire department if they could beat the TBPD for a third straight time this morning. Griff had responded in a private text to Sam. The message contained no text, just a link to a new fishing pole he intended to buy once they sealed the deal.

Sam definitely should have gone to batting practice the night before. Not that a couple of hours at the cages would have made much of a difference in skill level. In fact, Sam had always been a big believer in rest the night before a big game. But by not showing up, he knew that he'd be the one to take the blame if the Hoses didn't win today. In Murray's eyes, any potential loss would be one hundred percent his fault. There's no "I" in team, etcetera, etcetera.

Fine. Sam would rather Murray be mad at him than at any of the other guys on the team. They'd really stepped up in the past few weeks. Not one of them had struck out in the last game. The pitcher hadn't walked a single player on the police department's roster. For the first time in his life, Griff had hit a home run. The following Monday, he'd put the game ball in a plexiglass display cube on the top shelf of his locker in the firehouse, as proud as if they'd won the World Series.

Sam smiled just thinking about it as he and Cinder picked up their pace, running to the dog beach so he could let her off her lead for a few minutes of free playtime before they had to get back and change for the game. If Guns and Hoses had been just a normal first responder rivalry instead of whatever lunacy it had devolved into in Turtle Beach, Sam might have been forced to admit that he was starting to rediscover his love of the game.

Baseball, or in this case softball, had a lot in common with firefighting, as it turned out. There was the same spirit of camaraderie and friendship on a sports team that came with working alongside a firefighting crew — living, eating, and sleeping under the same roof each and every shift. Playing ball had almost made Sam miss his days fighting fires instead of working a desk job, doing inspections, and issuing fire code violations.

He couldn't go there again, though. Sam had already violated almost every rule he'd made for himself before his move to Turtle Beach. He'd formed friendships when he'd intended to stick to himself, he'd become deeply involved in a community that was only supposed to be a quiet place to lay his head at night, and he'd let his emotions get in the way of his job by issuing citation after citation to Violet.

She'd deserved them, to be sure, and Sam had only been doing his duty as fire marshal. But he'd enjoyed scribbling those tickets out to her time and time again. He couldn't help it. He'd loved every minute of it, just as she'd seemed to enjoy doing everything within her power to get under his skin.

Now she seemed to live there — under his skin. And in the most flagrant of all the violations of his self-imposed rules, Sam had gone and developed feelings for her.

His footsteps slowed to a stop as he and Cinder arrived at the dog beach. He bent to unclip his Dalmatian's leash, and then he pulled a tennis ball from his pocket and threw it into the surf. Cinder leapt over shallow waves and dog-paddled into the whitecaps to clamp the ball in her jaws. Sam shaded the sun from his eyes as she galloped back toward him and dropped the ball at his feet. He picked it up and tossed it again. Wash, rinse, repeat.

"Cinder sure seems to be enjoying herself," someone behind Sam said.

He turned to find Mavis Hubbard, Violet's friend from the senior center, watching his dog with a sparkle in her eyes. Her little Chihuahua pranced in dainty circles around her feet, darting away from the water anytime a wave rushed close.

"Good morning, Mavis." Sam grinned at the tiny animal. "You too, Nibbles."

Nibbles batted at his shins with her impossibly small paws, and he bent to run a hand over her narrow back.

Mavis gave him a curious glance. "I'm surprised to see you here. I thought you'd be busy getting ready for the big game today."

"We're about to head down to the softball field. I just wanted to give Cinder a chance to run off some steam first."

Cinder returned with the tennis ball, dropped it onto the sand, and nudged it toward Nibbles with her nose.

"Ah, yes. I heard that Cinder has been rather excitable lately. Something about a dip in the bay last night?" Mavis's right eyebrow shot up.

Of course she'd heard. The whole island was probably talking about it.

"Cinder is fine," Sam said. "It was nothing."

"Was it, now?" Mavis studied him.

Sam looked away. This conversation was getting a little unnerving. "It was sort of fun, actually. But I'm sure you heard all about that too."

A smile tugged at Mavis's lips. "There's more than a little truth to the old notion about opposites attracting, isn't there? Sometimes the last thing we expected turns out to be the very thing we needed all along."

Sam wasn't dense. There was no way they were still talking about dogs and Cinder's recent Dalmatian insubordination.

"Mavis," Sam warned. "You're not supposed to be playing matchmaker anymore, remember?"

She rolled her eyes. "Please. I wouldn't dream of interfering in your personal life."

A fib if Sam had ever heard one. Oh, if sprinkler heads could talk . . .

"For your information, I was referring to my new boyfriend." A smile danced on Mavis's lips.

Well. This was news.

Sam grinned and tried not to think about the fact that the seventy-plus crowd apparently had a far more active social life than he did. "New boyfriend? Go Mavis."

"Violet introduced us."

Why wasn't Sam the least bit surprised by this detail?

"Don't tell anyone, but he's a —" Mavis glanced around, as if eavesdroppers might be lurking behind a nearby sand dune. Her voice dropped to a whisper. "— *cat person.*"

Sam's eyes widened in mock horror. "Say

it isn't so."

"I know, right?" Mavis scooped her Chihuahua into her arms and kissed the top of her tiny, round head. "But Skippy and Nibbles get along just fine. Like peanut butter and jelly."

"I'm glad you've found someone who makes you happy, Mavis," Sam said, and an unexpected wave of emotion hit him square in his chest. Maybe he wasn't as content to spend the rest of his life alone as he'd thought he would be.

He and Violet weren't meant for each other, though — no matter how tempting the idea. Deep down, Sam knew this. Even if he wasn't a firefighter, and even if the softball feud ceased to exist — which seemed about as impossible as Cinder's spots falling off — he and Violet had nothing whatsoever in common. They were about as opposite as two people could be. Sam sometimes wondered if that was one of the reasons he'd been so attracted to her in the first place. Caring for Violet was safe . . . because nothing real would ever come of it.

Mavis's eyes narrowed, as if she could read his mind. Or maybe Sam's current state of denial was written all over his face. Probably the latter.

"Just remember, Sam. Love is a rare and

precious thing." Mavis winked at Cinder before she deposited Nibbles into her walker basket and prepared to walk away. "And when it's real, it's more than just black-and-white."

Sam attached Cinder's leash to her collar and jogged back to his cottage with Mavis's parting words ringing in his head.

She clearly hadn't given up on her match-making, no matter what sort of promises she'd made to Violet. And she wasn't half bad at it, he'd give her that.

But now wasn't the time to let a meddling grandmother figure convince him he was in love. He had to get his head in the game or else. Today could mean the difference between spending his Saturday afternoons dressed as a cupcake or having the satisfaction of watching Violet's dog learn some basic manners. It was no contest, really. By winning the bet, he'd be doing a service for the community at large.

Sam got Cinder cleaned up and dressed in her TBFD working dog vest, pulled on his softball uniform and cleats, and wasted no time getting to the ball field. The stands were packed when he arrived, without an empty seat in sight, but people were still approaching the softball diamond with lawn chairs tucked under their arms.

"What's going on?" he asked Griff. "This is twice as many spectators as we usually have."

Griff paused from the series of walking lunges he'd been doing — a warmup technique that Sam had taught him. "It's the championship game, man. Guns and Hoses has never been won in a sweep. We've got the chance to make *history* today."

Sam nodded, but when he took another look at the ever-growing collection of lawn chairs, picnic blankets, and foam fingers, his attention snagged on the pink spinning cupcake that rose above the crowd.

"No pressure, though, right?" Griff laughed.

"Right. No pressure," Sam said absently, craning his neck for a glimpse of Violet.

Griff followed Sam's gaze and shook his head. "Nope. No way, man. Now is not the time to be distracted by your alleged enemy. Just look away. Let's toss the ball back and forth or something. You need to focus."

"What do you mean by 'alleged'? We're actual adversaries," Sam said. Good grief, could he sound any more ridiculous?

"Sure you are." Griff tossed a mitt at Sam, but Cinder jumped up and caught it in her jaws before Sam could grab it. "Look, I know all about your little dip in the bay last night. I don't know what's going on between you two, but it can't happen — not until this tournament is over."

"Griff." Sam's jaw clenched. He was growing weary of denying that he and Violet were romantically involved. Perhaps to himself most of all.

"I mean it. This tournament is a big deal. Have you considered that perhaps Violet has orchestrated this entire love–hate flirtation the two of you have going on purely for distraction purposes?" Griff jerked his head toward the cupcake truck.

Sam stared at him, aghast. "Not possible. Violet's not like that."

Of course, if she were looking for payback after Emmett's betrayal last season, messing with the fire department's star player would certainly do the trick.

Griff shrugged. "Whatever you say. No one cares what you and Violet get up to after softball season is over. Heck, you can even ask her to the Fireman's Ball if you want. Just put a pin in things until after the last game. I'm begging you."

"Fireman's Ball?" Sam said. Cinder cocked her head. "I don't even know what that is."

"It's a big formal thing we do every Fourth of July. A tradition." Griff's eyes narrowed. "Wait. You're going to ask her right now, aren't you?"

Griff covered his face with his mitt and groaned.

"No." Sam's gaze darted to the cupcake truck and then back at Griff's beleaguered expression. "Of course not, but I am going to have a little chat with her."

He didn't want to believe she'd been toying with him, especially knowing he'd opened himself up to her in a way that he hadn't with anyone else. He *didn't* believe it . . . except it sounded just crazy enough to be possible, given the hype surrounding Guns and Hoses.

Sam needed to talk to her — *now* — just to be sure. If he didn't, he'd be thinking about it for the entire game. All seven torturous innings.

"Please don't," Griff said.

But it was too late. Sam had already begun stomping toward the spinning pink cupcake with his Dalmatian hot on his heels.

Violet's loyalties were clear — she was rooting for the police department to pull through and prevent the fire department from winning in a sweep. Naturally. She and Sam had a wager, and she fully intended to collect on her bet.

But she was also a businesswoman, so while her heart had most definitely chosen sides, her cupcake offerings on this most important of days catered to both teams. The Sprinkles Special spotty Dalmatian cupcakes had still been her best sellers so far, with the Guns and Hoses team cupcakes she'd created coming in a close second in precisely even quantities. With a quarter of an hour left before the opening pitch, Violet held a Guns cupcake in her left hand and a Hoses cupcake in her right when the line at the window of her food truck parted to make way for Sam, once again marching toward her at a most inopportune moment. Cinder galloped behind him with her cute black-and-white ears flapping in the wind.

Again? What was this — some sort of Dalmatian déjà vu?

Anxiety swirled around Violet, even as her heart did a delighted little flip-flop. The *entire town* was watching, including her dad and Coach Murray, who were both planted on opposite sides of the softball diamond with their hands on their hips.

"Sam." She wanted to reach through the window and squish both cupcakes into his swoonworthy face. "What are you doing?"

"I need to talk to you. Right now." His chest rose and fell with rapid breaths. "And preferably alone."

"I have customers," she said.

"And I have a game to play." He gestured at the chaos surrounding them as — much to Violet's amusement — Cinder collapsed at his feet and began gnawing on his shoelaces. "But this is important."

Violet plunked the cupcakes down on the counter and dusted off her hands. "*Fine.* Meet me at the side door."

She slammed the order window closed and hustled toward the trailer door, but Sam started pounding on it like a Neanderthal before she got there.

"What on earth" — she swung the door open, grabbed the front of his softball jersey and hauled him inside — "could possibly be so urgent?"

Sam practically crashed into her in the tiny space. Before the door closed behind him, Cinder wormed her way inside too. The interior of Sweetness on Wheels felt like it was shrinking by the second.

Violet lifted her chin to meet Sam's gaze and prayed that he couldn't somehow tell that she'd slept in his contraband T-shirt the night before. When their eyes met, his expression slowly changed. Violet watched it morph from irritation to something else — something that made her breath hitch.

"What's the matter?" she managed to say. "Dalmatian got your tongue?"

The corner of his mouth tipped into a reluctant grin. "Still not a thing."

Cinder shimmied on her belly toward Sprinkles's pink crate. Their tails both beat against the floor in perfect unison. Violet almost envied them. No one expected an innocent Dalmatian to choose sides in a softball feud, after all.

As much as she loved Dalmatians, though, Violet didn't want to *be* one. If she were a dog, she probably wouldn't have felt such a lovely warmth flowing through her while Sam gazed down at her, trying to form words for whatever it was that he wanted to say.

"Seriously, Sam. What's this all about?" She tried her best to keep both her head and heart right there in the cupcake truck and not back on the sofa in Sam's cozy beach cottage. She wasn't altogether successful.

"I need to ask you an important question. Are you . . . could you . . ." Sam paused, swallowing before he continued. "Would you go to the Fireman's Ball with me on the Fourth of July?"

Violet felt her eyes go wide.

Sam frowned, and his eyebrows drew

together as if he were confused . . . as if he'd meant to ask her something else altogether.

Was he insane? She couldn't go to the Fireman's Ball with him. The ball was a fancy, elaborate affair. It took place on an enormous yacht floating in the bay and strung with twinkle lights. The firefighters wore dress uniforms with white gloves, and their dates either wore floor-length evening gowns or tuxes. At midnight, glittering fireworks went off over the water.

Violet had never been, obviously. Not even when she'd been dating Emmett, since everything had so spectacularly fallen apart well before the Fourth of July.

"What about Guns and Hoses?" she said. "The tournament could go on for another two weeks. If it does, the championship game would take place . . ."

"On the Fourth." Sam nodded. "I know."

Violet shook her head. "I don't know what to say, Sam."

"Say yes. Forget about Guns and Hoses. Let's agree to do this — you and me, no matter what happens on the softball diamond." Intensity rolled off him. It was almost enough to make Violet believe that was he was saying was possible.

She took a shaky inhale. "No matter what?"

"No matter what." He reached for her hands and squeezed them tight.

This was madness. A million things could happen between now and the Fourth of July, and not one possible scenario ended with both of them winning. The only possible answer to his question was a resounding no.

She opened her mouth to tell him so, but the word that slipped out was quite the opposite.

"Yes," she heard herself say.

Wait, that wasn't right. That's not what she'd meant to tell him at all.

Sam grinned and Violet's knees turned to water. "Yes?"

"Yes," she said again, and this time there was an imaginary exclamation point after her answer. *Yes! Yes, yes, yes.* "No matter what happens."

"No matter what," he murmured, and then he took her face in his hands and kissed her.

And the moment his lips came down on hers, Violet knew this kiss was different from the others. There was an urgency in the way he held her, and a desperation in her grip as she balled his jersey into her fists. She and Sam were no longer playing games. This was happening . . . and it was *real.* No matter what.

"I've got to go win a bet now," he whispered into her hair as he held her tight.

"I'd wish you good luck, but you know it would be a lie," she said.

Would it, though? Did she even care how this tournament turned out anymore? Violet wasn't altogether sure. Somewhere along the way, things had changed between her and Sam. Whatever they were, she liked it a lot more than simply being softball adversaries.

Violet didn't even *like* softball. How had she let herself get so caught up in all of this feud craziness in the first place?

"See you later." Sam gave her another quick kiss — tender and sweet this time — and then he called Cinder to follow him.

He flashed her a wink as the door to the cupcake truck swung shut behind him.

Violet sighed dreamily and sagged against the counter. "Did that really just happen, Sprinkles?"

The Dalmatian yipped and did a little tap dance inside her pink crate.

"Don't you worry. Your days of being imprisoned are numbered." Violet grinned as she slid the order window back open.

The first six innings of the game passed in a blur. Violet did her best to keep up with the action on the softball diamond, but she had a constant stream of customers throughout the morning. She'd never sold so many cupcakes in her life. It was a good thing she'd made extra.

As the game wore on, she noticed that people seemed to be ordering the Dalmatian cupcakes almost exclusively. During a quiet moment in the top of the seventh inning, she planted her elbows on the counter and peered toward the field.

The police department was up by just one hit. The Hoses were up to bat, and Sam waited on the bench, next in line. As usual, Cinder was situated right beside him. But her behavior was strikingly different than it had been during the other games she'd attended. Come to think of it, Violet wasn't sure she'd ever seen Sam's dog so excited.

The Dalmatian paced back and forth in the dugout, rising up to plant her front paws on the chain link fence when the bat made contact with the ball. As Sam's teammate rounded the bases, Cinder jumped up and down on her back legs, as if she were on a pogo stick.

Violet laughed out loud. She looked like a little doggy cheerleader out there.

"Nash!" Chief Murray yelled toward the dugout from his position near third base. "I can't believe I'm having to say this, but you need to get that dog under control."

"Well, well, well," Violet said, grinning at Sprinkles. "Look who's the best-behaved Dalmatian now."

Sprinkles had indeed been extra sweet lately. Not that she wasn't always Violet's favorite dog in the entire world, because she definitely was — no matter how many chewed-up shoes and stolen cupcakes might be sacrificed to Sprinkles's naughty streak.

That naughty streak had been somewhat subdued lately, which only proved Violet's point that a dog would behave just fine as long as you heaped loads of love and affection onto the canine in question. Respect too, obviously.

Finally, Violet thought. At long last, she was getting her life in order. Her Dalmatian was starting to settle down and her cupcake truck business was booming, thanks to her spotted black-and-white culinary creations. Even her love life was looking up. It was almost too good to be true.

"Can I get three of those Dalmatian cupcakes?" A customer slapped nine dollar bills onto the counter. "That fireman's nutty Dalmatian is stealing the show out there."

But what was good for Violet's cupcake business wasn't so great for Sam. Obviously distracted by his dog's antics, he almost struck out when it was his turn on deck. With two strikes down, he hit a bloop single that, fortunately for Sam, landed in no man's land between the infield and outfield. Rattled by the sight of their star player's weak hit, the rest of the Hoses' batting line-up promptly fell like dominoes. Every player up to bat struck out, one right after another. At the end of the inning, the police department was still up by one run. The game was officially over.

"Yes!" Violet screamed from the confines of her cupcake truck.

The Guns team celebrated as if they'd won the World Series. Violet had never seen Island Pizza so packed. Players, locals, and tourists alike jammed inside the pizza parlor to celebrate the continuation of the tournament. The Hoses players didn't seem quite as disappointed as Violet would have imagined they might. She didn't get to talk to Sam, because by the time she closed up the cupcake truck and got the Charlie's Angels — plus Larry Sims, resplendent in a cardigan with red embroidered trim reminiscent of the stitching on a softball — to Island Pizza, there wasn't an empty table in sight.

But Sam's fellow players kept slapping him on the back and vowing to take back the tournament next Saturday, and when Sam's eyes met Violet's across the crowded restaurant, he didn't look at all like a man who'd just lost a championship game.

You win some, you lose some, he mouthed. Turtle Beach was in the throes of softball madness, and no one seemed to want to see the season come to an end.

Violet grinned, warmth spreading through her.

"You seem awfully happy about your team finally winning a game," Ethel said above the din.

"What?" Violet said, tearing her attention away from the fire department's table to glance at her friends. "Oh, right. The game. Yes, I'm thrilled, of course. Go TBPD!"

She snagged Mavis's blue foam finger in the air and waved it around, bopping about half a dozen people on the head in the process.

"Violet, dear, do you mind if we skip pizza this time? It's going to be hours before we're served." Mavis glanced at her watch.

"There's a two-hour wait," a passing server said. "And that's once you get seated."

Larry went pale. *Jeopardy!* started in an

hour and a half. Opal and Ethel were fine leaving early, they said. The chef at the senior center was preparing fresh crab for dinner, an annual summer treat they didn't want to miss. So Violet snuck Sam a flippy wave goodbye, hugged her brothers around their necks, and piled back into the cupcake truck with her friends.

They made it back to the senior center in record time, considering the journey included loading, unloading, and reloading four aluminum walkers and eight obnoxiously huge foam fingers. Violet had just gotten each senior citizen matched with the proper ambulatory assistance device when a police cruiser pulled up beside her sleek silver food truck in the retirement center's parking lot.

"Dad?" Violet peered into the squad car as the driver's side window rolled down, revealing a very weary-looking Ed March. "Is everything okay?"

She'd expected her father to be beside himself with joy in the wake of the TBPD's softball victory. In fact, she was pretty sure she'd seen him being doused with a big orange cooler full of Gatorade near the police department's dugout as she'd sold her last remaining Dalmatian cupcakes.

"I followed you here from Island Pizza,"

he said, as if that made any sense whatsoever.

"Why? Was I speeding?" Violet laughed.
The fastest she'd ever driven her cupcake
truck had been a tame fifty miles per hour,
and that certainly hadn't been on the island.

Violet was a cop's daughter. She *never*
sped, just as she never rode in a car without
her seat belt firmly fastened, never ran red
lights, and never made rolling stops at any
of the stop signs along Turtle Beach's sandy
streets. The rules of the road had been ham-
mered into her before she even knew how
to drive.

Similarly, Violet had never shoplifted a
thing in her life — not even as a child. The
closest she'd ever come to committing a
crime had been joining a group of kids
who'd toilet-papered the house of a baseball
player from a rival high school when she'd
been a teenager. Even then, Violet had been
so guilt-stricken the following day that she'd
shown up on the baseball player's doorstep
to help him clean up the mess.

Violet just wasn't built for a life of crime.
She knew this about herself. It was a rather
convenient truth since she shared a home
with half of the island's police force.

"No, you weren't speeding," Dad said
without a trace of humor in his tone.

"But . . ."

Opal, Ethel, Mavis, and Larry glanced back and forth between Ed and Violet March in obvious concern.

"But what, Dad? Am I in some sort of trouble?" Violet laughed again, but it felt forced this time.

Something was definitely wrong. She could see it in the deep furrow in her father's forehead.

He opened the door to the car and stepped onto the pavement, and that's when Violet realized that he wasn't wearing his softball uniform anymore. He was dressed in his police uniform, which seemed odd. He usually didn't go in to the station on Saturday afternoons.

"Dad?" Violet had a sudden urge to hug her Dalmatian, but she couldn't.

Sprinkles was waiting for her in Mavis's room, like she always did when they went to Island Pizza. She was probably sprawled on the sofa, glued to DOG-TV right this minute, oblivious to Violet's panic.

But why was she panicking? She had nothing to feel remotely guilty about — except yes, she'd accepted Sam's invitation to the Fireman's Ball. Her dad couldn't possibly know about that yet, though. And besides, what was he going to do when he found out? Throw her in jail?

"I'm sorry, Cupcake." Her father's gaze shifted to the gravel parking lot. He suddenly couldn't seem to look her in the eye. "But you're under arrest."

CHAPTER 17

Violet's head spun. Everything around her went fuzzy and she was vaguely aware of Opal, Ethel, Mavis, and Larry gasping in horror as her dad said something about a warrant and fines and started reciting the Miranda warning.

You have the right to remain silent, blah blah blah. Violet knew it by heart. She'd heard Joe and Josh practice it so many times back when they were in the police academy that she could probably recite her rights in her sleep.

Still, it was beyond unnerving to have them read to her by her father while he was standing next to a squad car with that terrible expression on his face.

Was this some sort of horrible joke? What was happening?

"Dad, stop. What is going on?"

She had the right to remain silent. *Ha!* As if.

"Dad! Talk to me, please."

"Violet, get in the car." He opened the door to the back seat. Seriously? She had to get back there, behind the cage thing? "I need to have a word with your friends for a minute. Wait here."

She did as he said, mainly because she was afraid if she balked, he might slap a pair of handcuffs on her. Just the thought of it made a hysterical burst of laughter rise up her throat. The one and only time she'd worn handcuffs was when her dad had come to her middle school classroom for career day. The kids had all taken turns trying them out.

But Violet wasn't in middle school anymore. She was an adult, and apparently she'd gone and gotten herself into adult trouble.

Arrested.

She squeezed her eyes shut tight and tried not to hyperventilate. This was Turtle Beach. The island's jail consisted of a single cell just a few steps away from her father's desk, and it was rarely occupied. Certainly never by Violet.

This cannot be happening.

The driver's side door swung open, and her father slid behind the wheel.

"Where's my dog?" she asked, and she

wasn't sure if the tremble in her voice was caused by fear or fury. Probably a little of both. The only thing she was more concerned about than straightening out her humiliating legal predicament was her Dalmatian's welfare.

"Mavis, Opal, and Ethel assured me they'll take care of Sprinkles. And don't you worry. I just need to take you down to the station and get you to deal with some paperwork. Your friends can come pick you up as soon as that's done. Once the fines are cleared up, you're free to go." He shifted the car into park. "That's how the department handles local code violations. Standard procedure. You're my daughter, but you still have to follow the rule of law. How would it look if I made an exception?"

Local code violations? Was it possible that this whole ordeal *wasn't* a mistake at all?

Dread settled into the pit of Violet's stomach. She stared blankly at the back of her dad's head. He still had a dent in his hair from the ball cap he'd worn to the softball game just a few hours ago.

"Dad, can you please tell me the nature of the fines that I owe?" She glanced at the rearview mirror, where her father's gaze met hers.

"Cupcake, you have unpaid fines from a

number of fire code citations." He sighed and resumed staring straight ahead. "Quite a few actually."

Violet dropped her head into her hands. Sam had showered her with enough pink tickets to wallpaper the entire inside of her cupcake truck. And they'd all been *real*?

Panic flared inside her chest, and she remembered something Griff had said a few days ago when she'd gone to Sam's office to thank him for not throwing her friends in "fireman jail" for their sprinkler stunt.

Yeah, that's not a thing. Violating the fire code is the same thing as breaking the law. Same fines, same penalties, same jail.

Oh, no. No, no, no. She'd balled all those tickets into tiny pink wads of paper in defiance. She'd thought she'd been taking a stand. She'd thought they'd just been part of the silly Dalmatian war she and Sam had been engaged in for the past few weeks. The loser was supposed to have to do something mildly unpleasant, like dress as a cupcake or take their Dalmatian to obedience classes.

Not *go to prison.*

The squad car pulled to a stop in the driveway of the Turtle Beach police station, and Violet tried to tell herself this wasn't a huge deal. It was jail, not prison — more along the lines of *The Andy Griffith Show* than *The Shawshank Redemption.*

Still, her father was the police chief. She should never have allowed herself to get into such a humiliating predicament, no matter how infuriatingly attracted she'd been to the fire marshal who'd been writing her all those citations.

"Dad, can we talk for a second before we go inside?" Violet sniffed. She would *not* cry. No way. She'd gotten herself into this mess, and she was going to handle it like a grown-up.

Oh, the irony! She'd just been patting herself on the back for having her act together and — *boom* — almost instantaneously she'd ended up in the back of a squad car.

"The sooner we get this started, the sooner we can get it over with," her dad said, reaching for the door handle.

"Wait, though. Please." Violet leaned forward, clutching the bars that separated the back seat from the front seat. "I'm sorry, Dad. I should have taken all those citations seriously. I just thought —"

"Cupcake, you and I talked about this just a few days ago. I tried to make sure you knew you had to pay the fines. You assured me you were taking care of things."

What? When had they discussed her fire

code citations? Violet didn't even know her dad knew about them.

"Dad, what are you . . ." Violet's voice drifted off as she realized the conversation he was talking about. They'd been in the dugout at practice. She'd tried to get him to tell her about the newspaper photo of her mom and Polkadot, and all he'd wanted to do was warn her away from Sam — or so she'd thought.

Wow. She and her father *really* needed to work on their communication skills. And they would. Violet would make certain they did, but first she probably needed to get fingerprinted or whatever lovely step came next in this mortifying ordeal.

"Joe tried to tell me. You asked him to talk to me and he tried, but I told him I didn't want to hear whatever it was he had to say," Violet said quietly.

She'd been so mad at him because he and Josh had cornered her about taking Sam cupcakes. Her fault, yet again, because she'd refused to listen. But another common denominator seemed to be popping up with every misstep she'd taken lately.

And that denominator was Sam.

"Come on, Cupcake. Let's get this done." Dad hauled himself out of the car and held her door open for her.

Violet did the walk of shame or perp walk or whatever it was called into the station, where she was officially charged, booked, and taken into custody. Mercifully, the police station was practically a ghost town since everyone in the department was still living it up at Island Pizza. But the reality of Violet's regretful circumstances hit her hard when the door to her tiny cell clanged shut and her dad locked it with a huge skeleton key.

Old-fashioned as it may be, the Turtle Beach jail was still jail. She wasn't sitting in a cute pink wire crate like Sprinkles had to do during the baseball games. This wasn't a field trip to her father's office with her Girl Scout troop. Violet had gone and gotten herself into a major pickle.

"I called Mavis and told her you can get bailed out anytime now. She's on her way," her dad said. He looked as though he'd aged ten years in the past two hours. Again, totally Violet's doing. "I'd do it myself, but it wouldn't be proper. You understand, right?"

"Of course, Dad. I get it." She was actually relieved that her father couldn't be the one to pay her bail. That would only add insult to injury.

After Mavis took her back to her cupcake

truck, Violet would pay her back every last dime from the proceeds of today's cupcake sales. Violet didn't care how broke she might be afterward. She was ready to turn over a new leaf. From here on out, she was going to be the most responsible person on the entire island. No more letting her Dalmatian run amok at the dog beach, no more bringing home random canines to bathe and spritz with her favorite bath products, no more setting firemen ablaze.

And *absolutely* no more kissing the most inappropriate man on the entire Eastern Seaboard. Violet had learned her lesson the hard way.

Her father reappeared, swinging his set of keys as Violet was adding up all her citations, late fees, penalties, and arrest costs in her head. She would need to sell a lot of Dalmatian cupcakes at the next softball game, or Sprinkles might have to start eating generic dog food.

"You're free to go." He frowned as he opened the cell door.

"Thank goodness." Violet threw her arms around her father. "I'm so sorry, Dad. Nothing like this will happen ever again. I promise."

He gave her a cursory pat on the back, and Violet chalked his standoffishness up to the fact that she'd disappointed him in a major way. She vowed to do better. She didn't know how she'd make this up to her dad, but she definitely would.

In the meantime, Violet couldn't wait to see Mavis. She hoped she'd brought Sprinkles with her. Violet couldn't wait to wrap her arms around her beloved Dalmatian and have a good cry into the dog's soft spotted fur.

But when she reached the entrance to the police station, Violet suddenly understood why her father had seemed less than pleased to let her go. Her heart wrenched. Sprinkles was there, waiting for her with a wagging tail, just as Violet had hoped. But Mavis hadn't come to collect her, after all.

The keys to Violet's freedom had been secured by none other than Sam Nash.

"I'm going to kill Mavis." Violet's gaze flashed quickly from Sam to her Dalmatian as she grabbed Sprinkles's leash and walked right past him.

Cinder glanced up at him and let out a mournful whine as the ice cream cone in Sam's grasp began dripping down his hand.

The ice cream had been a bad idea. Clearly. He wasn't picking up a child from summer camp. Violet had been in jail —

because of *him.* But he'd wanted to do something nice for her besides paying every last dime of her bail, her fire code fines, and the accompanying penalties. Ice cream seemed like just the sort of whimsical surprise Violet might like. He'd even had the cone topped with a generous portion of sprinkles in honor of her Dalmatian.

Big mistake, obviously. All of it. Sam had seen the error of his ways in the hard glitter of tears in her eyes the moment she'd spotted him waiting for her in the police station lobby. If looks could have killed him, he'd already have been dead after coming face to face with Ed March and signing Violet's exit paperwork while juggling the ridiculous ice cream cone. But the tearful glare Violet sent his way was far worse. It hit Sam right where it hurt most — the aching center of his soul.

"Come on, Cinder. We're not giving up this easily," he said, pushing through the door of the station and chasing Violet down Seashell Drive.

He sidestepped a couple walking arm-in-arm and nearly crashed into a group of pre-teens headed toward the beach access with flashlights in their hands, chatting excitedly about chasing ghost crabs in the sand. By the time he caught up with Violet, the ice cream was dripping all the way to his elbow.

"Violet, please. Can we talk?" he said to her ramrod-straight back.

Sprinkles cast a longing glance at him over her spotted shoulder and slowed to a stop.

"Sprinkles, no." Violet gave the Dalmatian's leash a gentle tug. "Come on. We are *not* stopping to chat with Marshal Sam right now."

The Dalmatian refused to budge, though. She planted her four paws in place, dipped her head down low, and stayed put.

"Sprinkles, please." Violet's chin quivered, and Sam thought it might be the death of him when her tears spilled over and started streaming down her face.

He took a tentative step toward her. "Violet, love, I'm sorry."

"Don't call me that. My own father just arrested me because of all those tickets you kept giving me. In no way are you a hero in this scenario. You don't get to bail me out of jail, call me sweet names, and bring me ice cream." Her sea-glass eyes darted to the melting mess in his hand. "Are those sprinkles?"

A flicker of hope stirred deep in Sam's chest. "Of course they are."

"Nice try, but no thank you." Violet's eyes met his, she took a ragged breath, and for a second she looked so uncharacteristically defeated that Sam scarcely recognized her. "Sam, why are you here?"

Cinder and Sprinkles touched noses, greeting each other as if an eternity had passed since they'd last seen one another instead of just a few minutes. Sam clung to hope. Their dogs were two sides of the same coin, but that had never mattered. The Dalmatians were crazy about each other. If they could see past their differences and be the best of friends, couldn't that mean that he and Violet could do the same?

Sam didn't want to just be Violet's friend, though. He wanted to be more — much more. He'd lost his heart to Violet from the very start, way back when she'd accused him of being a Cruella de Vil in fireman's clothing. He just hadn't realized it until Mavis had said those fateful words to him as seawater swirled around his feet on the dog beach.

Just remember, Sam. Love is a rare and precious thing. And when it's real, it's more than just black-and-white.

"I didn't mean for this to happen," he said tenderly, and he meant it in so many different ways.

He hadn't meant to get her arrested. He hadn't meant to make the current softball season even more embarrassing for her than the previous one. He hadn't meant to fall in love.

But he had, and now there was no going back. He had no regrets . . . except maybe all those pink citations.

"Well, it did happen. And just because you bailed me out doesn't mean it simply goes away." Violet wrapped her arms around herself, and it looked she was trying her best to keep herself from falling apart. "You do realize that everyone on the island will be talking about this for weeks, right? Just like . . ."

"Just like Emmett," he said. "I know."

The Dalmatians tiptoed at his feet, trying to catch melting drops of ice cream on their pink tongues. Sam pitched the ice cream cone into a nearby trash can. He needed to think. He needed to figure out how to fix things before it was too late.

"This wasn't like that. I had no idea you weren't paying the fines. And I definitely had no idea that you'd end up in jail." Sam's shoulders slumped.

Fire code violations were like traffic tickets. This would never have happened in Chicago. Turtle Beach was a tiny community, though. Unpaid tickets didn't go unnoticed, particularly when the offender was the police chief's daughter.

"We can get past this." Sam nodded to himself, remembering Griff's advice from the night they'd sat on the pier together drinking beer and eating peanuts. "Once everyone in Turtle Beach has something else to talk about, they'll forget all about this."

She crossed her arms. "If you think that something else will be us going to the Fireman's Ball together, you're gravely mistaken."

Ouch.

"And it doesn't matter if everyone else forgets about it, because I won't." She pressed her hand to her heart. "This wasn't just your fault, Sam. It was mine too. I feel like a complete fool. *Again.*"

Violet sighed and began walking down Seashell Drive again. The Dalmatians — who in the absence of the discarded ice cream had stretched out on the ground together side by side — scrambled to their feet and followed, leaving Sam no delusions about whose side they were on.

"Cinder, come back here," he said as her red leash grew taut.

But as Sam well knew, there was no stopping a stubborn Dalmatian. So he chased after his dog, and when he'd gotten a few paces behind Violet, she spun around again.

"And another thing . . ." she said, jabbing her pointer finger at his chest.

Sam stopped as abruptly as he could, but they still crashed into one another. Violet toppled, and he reached out to grab her and keep her from falling.

It felt so good to touch her again — too good. He pressed his forehead against hers and whispered her name. A plea. "Violet."

In a seemingly choreographed effort to keep their owners together, even if just for a short while, the Dalmatians both trotted in circles around Sam and Violet, winding them closer together with the dog leashes.

"Well, this is awkward," Violet said, cheeks blazing Sam's new favorite color — cupcake pink. "You know, Sprinkles has been on her best behavior lately. This is *your* dog's bad influence."

Thank you, Cinder. Sam arched a brow. "You think so?"

He could feel Violet's heart crashing against his own, and he didn't want to move. Not ever.

"Absolutely. Your Dalmatian is the one who tossed us into the bay and your Dalmatian went a little nuts today at the softball game, too." Violet glanced at Sam's mouth and then back toward his eyes. "I'm pretty sure that's why you hit that bloop single."

"How do you know I didn't do that on purpose?" He dipped his head closer, close enough to brush his lips along the soft skin of her cheek. "Maybe I wanted softball season to go on forever."

"You must really want to climb into that cupcake costume." She took a deep breath, and her softness pressed more firmly against Sam's chest. "Which is a good thing, because Sprinkles doesn't need obedience lessons. She's even started making my bed in the mornings. I didn't have to teach her how. She just picked it up on her own. I told you she was naturally sweet."

Violet tipped her face upward until her mouth was just a breath away from Sam's. Every cell in his body was on fire, and there wasn't a culinary torch in sight. He'd never longed for a kiss so badly in his life. But something she'd just said was fighting its way into his consciousness, wrestling for proper attention.

He pulled back a fraction of an inch. "Can you repeat that, please?"

"I said that Sprinkles is naturally sweet. I've been saying that all along." Violet rose up onto her tiptoes, and her arms wound around Sam's neck. "Now kiss me before I change my mind. I'm still quite furious with you."

Just shut up and do as she says, idiot. But he couldn't. A bad feeling had begun to crawl its way up his spine, and he needed to get to the bottom of things. "That's not what I meant. I'm taking about the bed-making thing. When exactly did that start?"

"I tell you I want you to kiss me, and you want to talk about my dog?" Violet tried to take a backward step, but the dog leashes kept her tethered to Sam. She rolled her eyes. "Fine. I don't know . . . a week and half ago or so."

"Right around the time we got drenched by the fire sprinkler at the senior center." Sam shook his head. He couldn't believe this, but it explained so much about Cinder's bonkers behavior lately. "The day we lost sight of the dogs for a while, yes?"

"I guess so, why?" Violet glanced down at her Dalmatian.

"Because that's not Sprinkles you're looking at. That's Cinder." Sam shook his head. Those meddling retirees had gone too far. They'd crossed a line, big time. "Don't you see? We've been tricked into falling for a Dalmatian impersonation. Mavis, Opal, and Ethel switched our dogs' collars when we weren't looking."

CHAPTER 18

In retrospect, Violet really should have seen it. How had she not? Overnight, Sprinkles had gone from being her naughty, mischievous self to practically perfect in every way, à la Mary Poppins.

The bet was to blame, and Violet herself, obviously. She'd been so eager to believe that Sam was wrong about her Dalmatian — that Sprinkles was completely fine and lovable just the way she was and didn't need any formal obedience training — that she'd somehow convinced herself that her sweet, spirited dog had transformed into a model Dalmatian on a dime.

It seemed so obvious, looking back. What she really didn't understand was how Sam had failed to catch on to what was happening. In Cinder's place, Sprinkles had wreaked havoc on his predictable, orderly life. Someone like Sam should have noticed right off the bat that something was wrong.

"I can't believe I fell for this," he said, as if echoing Violet's sentiments. He scrubbed his hands over his face as he paced back and forth in front of Mavis's little sofa.

The moment Sam shared his realization with Violet, they'd untangled themselves from the Dalmatians' intertwined dog leashes and gone straight to the senior center. Something this dire couldn't wait until morning. Now the Charlie's Angels sat in a row on the loveseat in Mavis's room, looking contrite and every bit their age in the fluffy terrycloth bathrobes and matching slippers that Violet had given them for Christmas the previous year.

"Please explain what you were thinking." Violet threw her hands in the air, exhausted on every possible level. Would this awful night ever end? "How could you think that switching our dogs was a good idea?"

Mavis, Opal, and Ethel exchanged guilt-ridden glances.

"It was Mavis's idea," Ethel muttered.

"Oh, please." Mavis rolled her eyes. "You act like I forced you and Opal into it. *You* were the one who called the firehouse and lured Sam here, or have you forgotten?"

Ethel cast a sheepish glance at Sam, who looked as tired as Violet felt. Cinder and Sprinkles, back in their proper collars, sat lumped together, yawning intermittently as if bored stiff by the entire episode.

Opal, sandwiched between Mavis and Ethel, held her hands out. "Stop bickering. All three of us are equally guilty. If one of us is going to get tossed into jail for luring Sam to the scene of the doggy crime, then all three of us are going."

Mavis held out her wrists, ready to be strapped into invisible handcuffs. "Go ahead, Sam. Throw the book at us."

"No one is going to jail, ladies," Sam said.

Violet's annoyance flared. "Excuse me?"

"Right." Sam hung his head. "No one *else* is going to jail."

Violet wouldn't have gone so far as to say that she was grateful for the canine switcheroo, but she was definitely thankful for the timing of the discovery. Had Sam's realization occurred a second or two later, she'd have kissed him right in the middle of Seashell Drive. Would she ever learn?

No, apparently not. Which was why the moment this confrontation was over, she was ceasing any and all interaction with her nemesis. In fact, from here on out, he wouldn't even be her nemesis anymore. She was pulling out of the bet. From this point forward, Violet would have no reason to interact with Sam in any capacity.

She pressed on her breastbone to still the ache in her heart. She could do this. The epiphany she'd had back in her jail cell had been real. New leaf, new life, new priorities.

"You still haven't explained why," she said to her friends.

"It's simple, really." Mavis shrugged. "We just thought if you took care of Cinder that you might develop an appreciation for Sam's positive traits, and vice versa. If Sam got to know Sprinkles, for example, he might . . ."

". . . come to love her sense of whimsy? Realize that life is sweeter with a dash of the unexpected?" Sam said. His gaze slid toward Violet, and his dreamy blue eyes were full of questions.

She looked away. "I suppose you three thought Cinder would make me appreciate the comfort of her heroic sense of honor."

"Something like that," Mavis said quietly.

Sam moved to stand in front of Violet so she had no choice but to meet his gaze.

"Did it work?" He smiled into her eyes.

Yes. Oh my gosh, yes!

Longing whispered through her. The old Violet wanted to throw her arms around Sam and admit how much she wanted him. She didn't care if people talked. She didn't care what her dad and brothers had to say.

She didn't even care about the stupid softball tournament. She just wanted to be with him. For real. No more sneaking stolen kisses, no more pretending that she couldn't stand the sight of him. She'd fallen hard for Sam Nash, and as crazy as the fall had been, Violet never wanted it to end.

But she wasn't that girl anymore. Violet had left that naive, romantic soul back in the jail cell at the Turtle Beach police station. She'd promised her father she'd be more responsible from here on out . . . and as torturous as it was, the here on out started right now.

"Don't be silly," she lied. "Of course it didn't work."

Sam's eyes narrowed, and his gaze bored into her with such intensity that she started trembling from head to toe.

"You sure about that, love?" he said in a voice so soft and tender that it made her want to weep.

There it was again — the endearment that had caught her so off guard the first time he'd said it, Violet had nearly crumbled inside.

She couldn't keep having this conversation. She had to put an end to things once and for all.

"Completely sure." She wrapped her arms

around herself and looked away.

Behind Sam, Mavis, Opal, and Ethel watched her with so much love and concern in their eyes that Violet couldn't help but think that maybe she hadn't missed out on a mother's love as much as she'd always thought she had. Maybe she'd actually experienced it threefold.

She squared her shoulders and forced herself to meet Sam's gaze. "This Dalmatian flirtation, or whatever it was, is over."

"I guess everything can go back to normal now," Sam said, and his tone carried just a hint of the straitlaced man she'd first met back on the dog beach — the one she'd thought had been stealing her dog when in fact he'd come to steal her heart.

"I guess it can," Violet said.

Then she clipped the pink cupcake leash onto the *actual* Sprinkles's collar and left without a backward glance, all the while wondering if perhaps normal wasn't all it was cracked up to be.

Thirteen days later, Sam knocked on the open door of Chief Murray's office at the firehouse. "Chief Murray, can I have a word?"

Murray Jones looked up from his desk and scowled. He'd been doing a lot of that lately

— scowling. Mostly at Sam, both on and off the softball diamond. "Fine. But make it quick. We have practice in less than an hour."

Sam was aware. Murray's dreams of winning the Guns and Hoses softball tournament in a sweep had died, and the following Saturday he'd watched from the sidelines as his star player struck out a record three times. It seemed that when Sam had been reunited with his lost Dalmatian, his mojo went inexplicably missing.

That had been Griff's take. Sam knew better, of course. He wasn't missing his mojo. He missed *Violet.* He missed her *joie de vivre.* He missed her unflappable optimistic attitude. He missed the happy chaos that had taken over his life from the instant he'd fallen in love with her.

Sam still couldn't pinpoint the exact moment it had happened. He just knew that it had. He'd arrived in Turtle Beach a broken man, and somewhere along the way, Violet March and her kooky Dalmatian had put him back together.

He loved his dog, and he was happy to have Cinder back. The trouble wasn't with his Dalmatian — it was with Sam himself. He'd gotten a taste of how it felt to be alive again, and he couldn't go back to be being closed off and isolated. If Violet ever gave him another chance — which was looking increasingly doubtful since she hadn't spoken a word to him since they'd confronted Mavis, Ethel, and Opal at the retirement center — he wanted to be worthy of her this time around. He knew that wanting him to trust her was asking a lot, and he needed to show himself, and Violet, that he was willing to do the same. He was willing to risk everything to build the kind of life he wanted. A life rich with feeling and possibility.

"What is it, Nash?" Chief Murray folded his hands on the surface of his desk as Sam took a seat in the only available chair in the room.

"I've gotten an offer to go back to my old department in Chicago," Sam said.

Murray frowned. "I see."

Sam shifted in his seat. "It's for a fire marshal position, much like what I'm doing here."

"Well, this is a surprise," Murray said. "I'm sure the pay is a lot more than what we can offer here in our small beach town, and I know the softball season hasn't gone quite as well as we'd hoped . . ."

Sam fought back an eyeroll. His boss thought this conversation was about softball.

Wasn't everything in Turtle Beach?

"We can still pull out a win tomorrow, son. It's the championship game, and you're our big champ." Murray nodded, and the crinkles in the corners of his eyes seemed to grow deeper until a rare smile came to his face. "But win or lose, we'd hate to see you go. You're a good fire marshal, Nash, and you're an even better man. You've been an asset to the department. I hope you'll consider staying on here at the TBFD."

The unexpected kindness caught Sam off guard. If he'd been on the fence, it might have even persuaded him to stay. But Sam had already made up his mind. He knew what he wanted. "Actually, I was hoping you'd be willing to transfer me to the regular department."

Murray blinked. "You want to fight fires?"

"Yes, sir. I do," Sam said. "I'll be happy to continue to do inspections and presentations as needed, but I'm ready to get back to what I do best."

He'd been hiding in an office, thinking four flimsy walls could separate him from the rest of his new firefighting family. How stupid could he have been? Above all else, a fire department was a brotherhood. The word was right there on the TBFD crest that Sam wore on his shirt, directly over his heart, every single day.

Fire. Service. Brotherhood.

You couldn't have one without all three. Sam hadn't just fallen in love with Violet. He'd fallen in love with his new home, and he was ready to start a new life here. He still hoped to do so with Violet by his side — somehow, someway — but if that never came to pass, Sam knew he wasn't alone. He had Cinder. He had Griff, Murray, and the rest of the guys at the station. He had those nutty octogenarians at the senior center. And he knew if the time ever came to put his life on the line for any of them, he'd do it in a heartbeat. No questions asked.

Murray stood and offered Sam his hand. "That's the best news I've heard in a long time. Of course we'd love to have you as a firefighter."

"We have a deal, then?" Sam asked.

Murray nodded, pumping Sam's hand up and down as his grin spread from ear to ear. "Welcome to the family."

"Thank goodness this is the last game of the season," Violet said as she piped more spots onto her final batch of Dalmatian cupcakes. The cupcake truck was crammed full. She couldn't fit another baked good inside Sweetness on Wheels if she tried. "I don't even care who wins. I'm just ready for the tournament to be over, for once and for all."

"Yes, you mentioned that already." Opal peered at her through the order window.

Beside her, Ethel nodded. "Several times."

"Well, that's because it's true." Violet put the pastry bag down and wiped her hands on the front of her ruffled apron.

"If you say so," Opal muttered.

"Oh, please." Mavis inched her walker as close to the cupcake truck as she could get it and stared daggers at Violet through the open window. "How long are you going to go on like this?"

"Like what?" Violet said blandly.

Bland was her default mood now. Sometimes it took some effort to rein in her actual personality and do her best to pretend she was an even-keeled, responsible person who thought before she spoke and didn't stand out in a crowd. The good news was that she was getting used to it. The bad news . . .

Well, the bad news was that the reason she'd grown accustomed to being as beige as she could possibly be was because she mostly felt beige inside now. The piercing heartbreak she'd felt when she'd forced herself to walk away from Sam had settled so deep into her bones that she'd been forced to train herself to feel absolutely nothing instead. No joy meant no pain. No happiness meant no sadness. No love meant no loss.

That's what she wanted to believe, anyway. Every time she'd just about convinced herself it was true, Sprinkles would bolt away from her at the dog beach and romp through the waves as if she had springs in her feet. The wonder and sheer delight on her Dalmatian's sweet spotted face as she played in the surf never failed to hit Violet right in the feels. She still had a heart. And no matter how hard she fought, that heart still beat for Sam Nash.

"Like this." Mavis gestured in Violet's general vicinity. "You're like a ghost of your former self. This is no way for you to live, Violet. It's like you're disappearing before our very eyes."

"We know you feel like giving up on love, dear. But it's like you've given up on life," Opal said.

Ethel dabbed at her eyes with the corner of one of her goofy foam fingers. "It's hard to watch, sweetheart. You know this isn't what your father wants for you, either. Or your brothers. They love you just the way you are."

"Were," Mavis corrected. "They love you just the way you *were.* No one knows this new person you're trying to become."

"Even the other residents of the senior center are confused. Yesterday in yoga class, you called murder victim pose something entirely different," Ethel said.

Violet crossed her arms. "I called it *Shavasana.* That's the proper word for it."

Mavis rolled her eyes. "Well, not one person knew what in the world you were talking about."

"Violet, dear, we don't go to yoga because it's proper exercise. We go because you make it fun." Opal shrugged.

Damn these women. They always knew just what to say to crack Violet's increasingly fragile composure.

She nodded. "Fine. Murder victim pose it is. Duly noted."

"Good. Now what are you going to do about Sam?" Mavis backed her walker up a bit, out of cupcake-tossing range.

Violet didn't like to talk about Sam. Ever. And she definitely didn't want to do it here, in front of the entire town. "Mavis, please don't. I can't talk about Sam right now. You know that."

"Very well. We need to get to our seats

anyway, and you have cupcakes to sell." Mavis leaned closer and lowered her voice to a mock whisper. "But just so you know, Hoyt Hooper Sr. heard from Hoyt Hooper Jr., who heard from Griff Martin that Sam has been offered a job back in Chicago. He had a big closed-door meeting with Chief Murray about it yesterday."

All the blood seemed to rush out of Violet's head in a sudden *whoosh*. She swayed on her feet. "Sam's leaving Turtle Beach? When?"

Mavis shrugged. "That's all I know, dear. You know I never pay attention to town gossip."

Violet would have laughed out loud if she hadn't felt like crying. Mavis *lived* for Turtle Beach gossip.

Violet's throat grew thick. Sam was leaving? He couldn't. The island wouldn't be the same without him and Cinder. Turtle Beach was a two-Dalmatian town now. Everyone knew that. What was he thinking?

It's not your business, remember?

She closed her eyes and tried her best to think beige thoughts, but bursts of color kept breaking through the numbness. Luckily, she had a crush of customers to deal with to distract her from her most inconvenient reawakening.

Violet just needed to get through the next few hours, and then everything would be fine. So what if Sam left? Violet's life pre-Sam had been perfectly acceptable. Happy, even. She didn't need a stern-faced fire marshal with a robotic Dalmatian to make her life complete.

Except Cinder had really come out of her shell when the Dalmatians had been switched. Likewise, Sprinkles had learned a thing or two. And Sam hadn't scowled at her in weeks. In fact, she rather liked the way he looked at her — like she was a perfectly frosted cupcake and he'd eaten nothing but bread and water for his entire life.

"Oh, my gosh," Violet said out loud.

Sprinkles sat up in her pink crate and cocked her head.

"Sam and I have switched places, just like you and Cinder." Violet pressed a hand to her stomach. She felt sick all of a sudden. "But I don't have the honor and heroics to go with his comforting predictability. I'm just . . ."

How had Mavis put it?

A ghost of your former self . . . you're disappearing before our very eyes.

Good grief, Mavis was right.

Panic swirled through Violet as she sold

one cupcake after another. She had to do something, but what? The game had already started. The bleachers were packed, and the police department was already up by three runs. Her father and brothers were probably beside themselves. If Violet hadn't called off the bet with Sam, she would have been ecstatic herself.

The game droned on, and with every change of the innings, the sense of doom hanging over Violet's cupcake truck grew thicker. Heavier. What if Sam had stuck around in town just to finish the tournament? It sounded like the honorable sort of thing he would do. For all Violet knew, he was leaving right after the victory party at Island Pizza. If the firefighters lost, he might even scoot out earlier.

There was only one thing Violet could come up with that might convince him to stay — one surefire way to get his attention long enough to tell him how she really felt before it was too late.

She marched over to Sprinkles's pink crate. The Dalmatian sprang to her feet and pawed at the door, as if to say *Put me in, Coach.*

Violet unlatched the crate and then flung the door to the cupcake truck open wide. Sprinkles took off like a shot, sprinted to the middle of the softball diamond, and started running around the bases, barking louder than Violet had ever heard her before.

Everyone in the stands stood and cheered, while the players stopped what they were doing. The umpire blew hard on his whistle.

Coach Murray screamed, "Interference! Interference! They forfeit!"

But no sooner had the words left his mouth than Cinder bolted from the dugout and proceeded to chase Sprinkles around the bases.

"There are two Dalmatians on the field," the umpire yelled. "I repeat — two Dalmatians on the field!"

Chaos reigned, but in the midst of the insanity, Violet spotted Sam walking toward her. They met in the middle, in the emerald-green grass of centerfield.

"Don't go," she blurted.

Sam's brow furrowed. "I'm not going anywhere, love."

Love . . . Violet's heart swelled. She'd never felt less beige in all her life. "Mavis told me you were moving back to Chicago."

Sam's lips curved into the lopsided smile she knew and loved so much. "I thought we learned a long time ago not to believe anything that Mavis, Opal, and Ethel say."

Violet laughed. "Maybe she had the right

idea, just this once."

"Just this once?" Sam shook his head. "I've come to realize those crazy friends of yours were right about a lot of things."

He slid his arms around her and pulled her close, and even though Violet had lived on the same small island for her entire life, she felt like she'd finally come home. "Oh, yeah? Like what?"

"Like the fact that I love you." He pressed a tender, reverent kiss to her lips, and whispered against her mouth, "You saved my life, Violet March."

"Not really. I set you on fire first, remember?"

"I'm not talking about the culinary torch. I mean in general. I was a shell of a man when I got here, and you saved me. You're everything I want to be, Violet. You brought me back to life."

A sob escaped Violet's lips, and she pressed her fingertips to her mouth to keep from breaking down. "You mean you don't think I'm too much? Too . . ."

"Silly woman, I think you're perfect just the way you are." And then he kissed her again, right there in front of everyone, and Violet couldn't have cared less.

When they finally broke apart, Sam dropped to one knee and took her hand in his. "Violet March, will you attend the Fireman's Ball with me tonight as my date?"

"Yes!" She laughed. "Yes, of course."

"Hold up, wait a minute. What's going on over here?" an astonished Coach Murray said as he approached.

Violet's dad marched toward them from the other direction. "Good grief. It's like history repeating itself."

Sam stood back up. "Violet and I are going to the Fireman's Ball together tonight."

"We're in love." Violet pointed back and forth between her dad and the fire chief. "You two are just going to have to deal with it. This has nothing to do with your ridiculous feud."

"Pshhhhh." Her dad scowled at Coach Murray. "The feud was his idea, not mine."

"I beg your pardon. It was not. You started it after . . ." Murray glanced at Violet and went quiet.

Violet searched her dad's gaze. "Dad? What's he talking about? And don't try and wiggle your way out of the conversation this time. Tell me what happened all those years ago."

"Come on, Ed," Murray said. "Maybe it's time."

Her father sighed. "It all started when Murray here gave your mother that rowdy

Dalmatian."

"Polkadot?" Violet gasped. "That's where my mom's Dalmatian came from?"

"I gave her the dog, yes." Murray nodded. "And she loved that pup with her whole heart, but it still wasn't enough to convince her that she was better off with me. She loved your dad even more than she loved that crazy dog."

"That dog never liked me much." Her dad shook his head. "I'm pretty sure Polkadot thought Adeline should have married Murray."

Violet stared at the two men. "You mean to tell me that this insane softball feud started because of an argument the two of you have been having about a Dalmatian for over thirty years?"

Coach Murray shrugged. "Yes."

"No." Violet's dad shook his head.

Sam laughed. "They still can't agree."

"That's not true, son." Murray shot Violet's father a questioning glance. "I think we can both say that you two crazy kids belong together. Pretty much everyone in Turtle Beach saw it coming when Sam here rolled into town with a Dalmatian in tow. What do you say, Ed?"

"If Violet's happy, I'm happy." Ed March gave Violet a tender smile. "Maybe it's time to let bygones be bygones."

"Finally." Violet took Sam's hand, and he squeezed it tight.

"I guess this means no more softball next year?" Sam said.

Murray and Ed both turned toward him in astonished horror.

"Bite your tongue, son," Murray said.

"Guns and Hoses will never end in Turtle Beach." Ed shook his head. "Never."

"At last, something they agree on," Violet said.

And then Sam picked her up and spun her round and round, with Cinder and Sprinkles prancing at their feet until she couldn't tell which Dalmatian was which.

Just the way she liked it.

ACKNOWLEDGMENTS

This book has been a long time coming! It started with the idea to write a rom-com based on one of my favorite Disney films, and I knew I'd found the right publishing home for it when I met Sourcebooks Casablanca's Editorial Director Deb Werksman on a romance writer cruise in Fort Lauderdale, Florida. Deb's enthusiasm for *A Spot of Trouble* meant the world to me, and I'm thrilled to have found my way to Casablanca.

It's probably no surprise that I'm a big dog lover. I've never had a Dalmatian, but some of my fondest memories of my son Cameron's childhood involve seeing the live-action version of *101 Dalmatians* multiple times during the Christmas holidays when he was in kindergarten. McDonald's had 101 different Dalmatian toys in their Happy Meals that December, and I can attest that we ate A LOT of chicken nuggets that month. I love taking classic stories and giving them new, whimsical spins, and writing this story has been a complete joy from start to finish.

Thank you to Deb and the entire team at Sourcebooks Casablanca. And as always, thank you to my wonderful agent Elizabeth Winick Rubinstein and everyone at McIntosh & Otis. I also owe a huge debt of gratitude to my step-dad Lanny Cunningham for giving me the idea for Cinder the fire dog, name and all. Lanny is a retired firefighter for LA County and our family's real-life hero.

This one is for my readers, for anyone who has ever loved a dog, and for every single person who has ever felt like they were too much or too different. You're perfect, just the way you are.

xoxo Teri

ABOUT THE AUTHOR

USA Today bestselling author **Teri Wilson** writes heartwarming contemporary romance with a touch of whimsy. Three of Teri's books have been adapted into Hallmark Channel Original Movies by Crown Media, including *Unleashing Mr. Darcy* (plus its sequel *Marrying Mr. Darcy*), *The Art of Us,* and *Northern Lights of Christmas,* based on her book *Sleigh Bell Sweethearts.* She is also a recipient of the prestigious RITA Award for excellence in romantic fiction for her novel *The Bachelor's Baby Surprise.*

Teri has a major weakness for cute animals, pretty dresses, and Audrey Hepburn films, and she loves following the British royal family.

Feel free to visit and connect with her on social media! You can also add and share her books on BookBub and Goodreads.

CPSIA information can be obtained
at www.ICGtesting.com
Printed in the USA
BVHW030039140122
626201BV00005B/9

9 781432 894931